Originally published in Japanese as *Aoneko kazoku tentenroku* by Shinchosha, Tokyo, 2006
Copyright © 2006 by Naoyuki Ii
Translation copyright © 2011 by Wayne P. Lammers
First edition, 2011

Library of Congress Cataloging-in-Publication Data

Ii, Naoyuki.
[Aoneko kazoku tentenroku. English]
The shadow of a blue cat / by Naoyuki Ii ; translated by Wayne P. Lammers. -- 1st ed.
    p. cm.
ISBN 978-1-56478-641-8 (pbk. : alk. paper)
I. Lammers, Wayne P., 1951- II. Title.
PL853.I2A6613 2011
895.6'35--dc22
                                    2011012938

Partially funded by a grant from the Illinois Arts Council, a state agency, and by the University
of Illinois at Urbana-Champaign

This book has been selected by the Japanese Literature Publishing Project (JLPP), an initiative
of the Agency for Cultural Affairs of Japan

www.dalkeyarchive.com

Cover: design and composition by Danielle Dutton, illustration by Nicholas Motte
Printed on permanent/durable acid-free paper and bound in the United States of America

THE SHADOW OF A BLUE CAT

A NOVEL

NAOYUKI II

TRANSLATED BY WAYNE P. LAMMERS

DALKEY ARCHIVE PRESS
CHAMPAIGN / DUBLIN / LONDON

I imagine I should start with a disclaimer. I'm not some fresh-faced kid of seventeen or twenty, or even an upstart of thirty, which some people actually argue should be considered below the age of majority these days. No, the fact is, I've already slid right on past the big five-oh—a milestone no one thinks is very pretty and few are eager to reach—to become a man of fifty-one.

Now if a reader were to say that it's unsettling to have someone who's passed the half-century mark presenting himself as the narrator of a novel styled after the young writers of a generation ago, I'd have to agree he has a point. But however much I may agree, I expect to press ahead in exactly such a style, for as I struggle to come to terms with my fifty-something self, it has become all too uncomfortably clear to me that a style more suited to a man my age simply doesn't exist.

As I begin writing, I will in my own mind be telling this story to my uncle—my father's younger brother—feeling curious as to how he might react to it. Except, unfortunately, he died some three decades ago. He was a mere thirty-nine at the time, which is to say, still quite young—though to the college student I was then, he represented a decidedly middle-aged figure.

My uncle never married, and he had no children as far as I'm aware. By contrast, his once-much-younger fifty-one-year-old nephew now has a wife of nearly twenty years and two beloved daughters.

Time rushes onward. Lurching awkwardly, but at breakneck speed.

The older of my two girls is seventeen. Having dropped out of high school, she now has her sights set on passing the high school equivalency test so she can apply for college. My younger daughter is still an infant—just two months old, to be exact. She has the blackest little eyes, without the tiniest speck of a cloud in them. They remind me of the plump little tadpoles I used to find in mud puddles every spring when I was a boy. You may well wonder how it came to be that a man of fifty-one is father to a brand-new baby. I'll get to that in due course.

In the meantime, my story begins with a woman named Momo—a long-standing friend of mine. This woman and I may both come across as rather immature for our years. Like so many other things, I could blame it on the times in which we live, but I suppose that would only sound like a lame excuse.

Momo was fuming. I knew how excitable she was, so it didn't particularly surprise me to find her in such a state. I was also well aware how touchy she could become once something had set her off, and this threatened to throw cold water on my own excitement at seeing her again after such a long time.

She sat glaring at the computer screen, the pudgy index finger of a woman in her late forties pressed to her temple.

"I'm furious," she said.

"I'm not all that late, am I?"

Having received her call a little before noon, I'd rearranged my afternoon schedule just for her and headed for the appointed place, a café named Cascade, with all due speed. I didn't think I deserved her disapproval for arriving a little late.

It was just an ordinary coffee shop, not a manga or internet café, but they had a LAN you could log into for Web access and, if you asked, they would even lend you a laptop to use.

"That's not what I'm talking about."

"So what's the problem?"

Normally when you arrange to meet an old friend like this, the initial back-and-forth as you update each other on your current activities is an enjoyable experience. But the look on Momo's face suggested she was seriously put out, so it seemed best to proceed with caution.

She looked up. "This," she said, dropping her eyes back to the screen and reaching for the silver-colored mouse. We were seated across from each other at a table for two, so I couldn't see what she was referring to.

"You mean the computer? Something on the Web?"

Momo cocked her head to one side but said nothing. She merely moved the mouse a little and clicked. Then before I could frame a follow-up question, she said, "I went to this site that offers a love aptitude test. It seemed pretty obvious that over-forties basically weren't welcome, so I decided to say I was twenty-five. Anyway,

I don't mind so much that they claim I'm not a very good candidate for romance, but then they have the gall to say, 'For a twenty-five-year-old, you seem rather immature in your views, especially about love.' I'm so insulted. Immature for a twenty-five-year-old!"

She rotated the laptop for me to see. It showed a percentile score of 45, and declared that under the present circumstances her chances of finding a man and having a happy courtship might not be entirely nil but came pretty darn close to it, so she needed to actively look for opportunities to meet men, as well as make a concerted effort to keep any men she dated from losing interest in her—by going to a beauty spa and working out at a fitness center or by seeing new movies and reading the latest best-sellers everyone was talking about.

We decided I should give the test a try, too. Like Momo, I fudged my age and said I was thirty. Some of the questions really made you think, and if you just started choosing answers at random you soon got yourself in trouble. The test was actually very well thought out that way.

They wanted to know how much importance I placed on the person's looks. I glanced up at Momo as I contemplated my answer. She was busy thumbing the keys on her cell phone.

"Texting someone?"

"Uh-huh," she said, her eyes glued to the phone as if even the briefest glance away might make her mess it up.

I proceeded with the aptitude test.

"All right. That should do it. Send," Momo said. "How'd your test come out?"

I turned the screen toward her so she could see the relatively respectable score of 61 it displayed.

"Huh? No way. What're they talking about?"

"They say I'm not an obvious ladies' man, but I have hidden talents in the ways of love. I know how to carry on a relationship that's satisfying to both myself and my partner. I just answered as honestly as I could, and that's what they told me."

"I don't believe it. I've never heard anything about you being popular with the girls."

"That's why it says hidden. You should consider what you might get if you had an affair with me."

Momo read out the rest of the test-makers' comments about my score. "'. . . But if you let yourself get too smug about it, you could end up letting the person you like most slip from your grasp. Does that perhaps ring some bells? For a man of thirty, your take on women and love seems to include some surprisingly immature views.' Oh. So in the end you're basically the same as me."

We both burst out laughing. The coeds at the next table scowled our way.

Momo leaned over the table and said in a low voice, "My dear ex says he wants to see you. He asked me to tell you. That's actually why I called."

"Are you kidding? Forget it. I have no desire whatsoever to see him."

"I figured you'd say that." She lowered her eyes.

"And I don't like it that he'd use you to contact me either."

The look of indignation had returned. She picked up her phone and began punching at it again. I was about to add that I thought it was rude of him, when Momo raised her head and looked at me.

"Do you use text messaging?"

"Sort of, I guess. But I don't send anything. Mostly I just get junk."

"So you don't know how to write a text."

"I can if I have to."

Momo let out a puffy-cheeked chuckle like an indulgent kindergarten teacher. No doubt she used to have dimples when she was a little girl. But middle-aged Momo was capable of maintaining her indignation even as she laughed. Or, more likely, she was incapable of wiping it away.

I knew I might be asking for trouble, but I couldn't help myself. "You still seem mad about something, Momo. What is it? It's not me, right? At least that's what you said a minute ago."

"Of course not," she cut me off with startling abruptness. "It has nothing to do with you."

"And it's not the love test, either."

"I wonder what it could be," she said as if pondering the question herself.

I peered at her down-turned face looking for a trace of a dimple at the side of her mouth.

Then she let out a long, audible sigh. "I'll e-mail you at your work address later. Promise me you'll read it, okay?"

Her answer left me hanging, but I decided not to press the matter. Somehow it seemed in my own best interest not to pursue it right then and there.

My company's offices were on the seventh floor of a building near the Shibuya exit of the Metropolitan Expressway. The main room looked like it had just one great big desk in the middle, but it was actually two desks pushed together. Through the door on one side was a smaller room with another desk. That was the boss's office and belonged to me, but most of the time you'd find me ensconced at one end of the big desk working elbow-to-elbow with my two salaried and three hourly employees.

Just between you and me, I considered it a minor miracle that my company had managed to keep from going belly-up over the nearly five years since it was incorporated. Needless to say, I had launched the business fully expecting it to succeed. But the early going proved to be rough, and we operated on the verge of bankruptcy for quite some time. That experience drove home just how dependent on the whims of fate the little guy is when he tries to start up a business.

After a long period of walking the tightrope, though, we finally emerged in the clear, and I settled into running the company in a manner that involved taking no big risks. I never bet the store on something going our way. As a result, I don't doubt that I passed up some perfectly good chances to make a bundle, and I may possibly have nipped opportunities for growth in the bud as well.

Of course, I'd always worked very hard to keep the business going—really putting my heart into it, in fact. Still, I couldn't help feeling that the continued survival of my company was due to something more than that—to good fortune that bordered on the miraculous.

It was after ten that evening when I finally read Momo's message. I'd noticed it in my mailbox before five, but I wanted to wait for a good stopping point in what I was doing, as well as for my employees to leave, before looking at it. With work dragging on and everybody sticking around, I'd kept putting it off.

Even at this hour, one of the women was still there, but she was in the midst of negotiations with a customer and seemed oblivious to what I was up to. I pushed her from my mind and opened Momo's e-mail.

Dear Yuki,

Thanks for seeing me today on such short notice.

I did feel a little better afterwards.

But I don't think it actually did any good in the end. I've hardly done a stitch of work since coming back to the office.

I'm upset. And when I realize I'm upset, I get even more upset. And I get mad.

All because of my ex-husband.

A week ago, he called me out of the blue for the first time in nearly a year.

I thought it might have something to do with work, but it didn't.

He said he was in the hospital.

Then he paused a while before finally going on in a shaky voice. I have cancer, he said. Stomach cancer. The aggressive kind. The doctors give me six months if I'm lucky.

As I sat there in shock, my dear ex says, Could you come see me?

He used the wheedling tone he used to use with me back when we were together.

And just like that, all these complicated emotions started popping off inside me. Even now, I still don't know how to describe what I'm feeling.

I kept my cool, though, and said that it was a busy time right now at work, and I didn't know if I'd be able to get away. But I told him to give me the name of the hospital and his room number just in case.

He let out a little sigh and said, You're always cool as a cucumber, aren't you?

In the end, I wound up going to see him the next day.

To tell the truth, I just couldn't sit still. But I acted like I'd only come because I happened to get a break in my work.

And guess what. He greets me with this big wide smile that says I knew you'd come. Pisses me off.

I don't know if it was because of his golfing tan or what, but he looked as good as he always did, not the least bit haggard, and I almost felt like asking if it was all a joke about his having cancer.

Even after he told me they were going to operate on him next week, it still didn't seem real.

He said he knew it wasn't going to do any good, he was only doing it for his mother.

I've never heard him sound so dismal.

After fifteen minutes or so, I got up to leave, and he brought out that wheedling tone again. You don't have to go yet, do you?

I told him I needed to get back to work, but I'd come again. It was then he brought up your name—though we hadn't talked about you before that at all.

I want to see Yajima, he says. Before my operation if possible. You know how to get in touch with him, right? Go ahead and tell him I'm dying of cancer if you want. Just let him know I was asking for him.

If the circumstances were any different, I'd have immediately asked, Why now, after all this time? But somehow . . .

Please go if you can. Having actually seen him in his hospital bed, I feel compelled to add my own request to his. I think he's afraid of the operation going badly and not getting to see you again before he dies.

Ever since he first told me about it over the phone, the palpitations won't stop. Though even that infuriates me.

Sorry for going on so long.

I'll be in touch.

Momo

Letting go of the mouse, I clenched my right hand lightly in a fist and pounded it twice into my left palm.

I heard a giggle from the other side of the desk.

As I looked up from my screen, I saw Ayumi Uchino grinning at me.

"What's so funny?"

"Sorry, boss, but you were sitting there peering at your screen with this big grin on your face. I figured it must be a message from somebody *really* special, if you know what I mean."

She'd caught me unawares, and I was tongue-tied for a moment. I had no idea I'd been smiling.

"Oh, no, it's nothing like that. It just reminded me of something from way back when."

I managed to come up with an explanation, but all my thoughts and feelings had been thrown into a muddle.

Ayumi filled me in on her negotiations with the client.

"Well, don't sweat it too much," I said, taking an easygoing attitude. She was getting ready to leave. "If you're heading home, you want to stop for a bowl of ramen somewhere?"

"Thanks, but that's what I had earlier, so I think I'll pass. See you tomorrow."

She waved her hand in front of her chest like a grade-schooler, then disappeared out the door. My company was a bit short on love.

I got up from my chair to close the blind. The light from the fluorescent fixtures was reflected in the window, and a white billboard saying BOSE seemed to float in fragments beyond.

Ogita was dying. I closed my right fist again. In my mind, I pictured my right arm folding at the elbow and the fist rising to the level of my shoulder. It seemed inappropriate to actually pump my fist at a time like this, so I only allowed myself to imagine it.

I unclenched my fingers and reached for the cord, noting from my reflection in the glass that I was still smiling. But as I started to close the blind, my hand froze.

All of a sudden I felt the touch of my uncle's hand on mine. I'd been reminded of an event that had occurred a long time ago—when I was still in high school.

My uncle and I set out from the farm cottage he was renting near Yokokawa on the old Nakasendo Highway to hike to the railway bridge at Usui Pass.

I had expected the owner's niece, Kanoko, to be coming with us. She was in tenth grade, a year below me, and her parents had sent her to spend the summer with her uncle's family in the main house. Her real name was Kanako, but ever since she'd inadvertently said Kanoko in front of her first-grade classmates, the name had stuck. Nobody called her anything else after that.

My uncle kept up a constant stream of chatter as we walked, identifying various grasses and trees and flowers along the way, pointing out the differences between this and that butterfly, remarking on birdcalls near and far, and anything else he happened to notice. I was only half-listening, so I can't recall a single specific thing he said. What I do remember is the sensation of the path's sharp gravel digging into the rubber soles of my tennis shoes.

I was feeling dejected because I thought Kanoko hadn't come along out of dislike for me. My uncle didn't even seem to notice my low spirits, but I was convinced that the ribbing he and I had given her for her boyish looks the night before had turned her against me. We had presumably gone too far at some point, and I bitterly regretted it.

Kanoko had nothing in common with the conventional image of the delicate highlands girl a guy meets on vacation. The whites of her eyes shone bright against her sun-darkened skin, and her limbs were long and slender yet muscular, which together with her short haircut led me to mistake her for a boy at first glance. But once we started talking she had a gentle, feminine voice and a cute smile, and in less than two days I was completely smitten.

The path that followed a mountain stream was cut with tire ruts the width of a minicar and overgrown with knee-high weeds. We walked with the soles of our shoes angled in the deeply gouged tracks. Inside the forest, it was so dark beneath the canopy that I could hardly see; back out in the open, the sun bore down with stifling intensity. My uncle was continually wiping the sweat from his head and neck with a hand towel.

He had recently returned to the home office of his trading company after a stint in England. The results he produced for the firm while there were impressive, but his health had suffered in the process, so he was taking some time off to convalesce. A friend who frequently rented the farm cottage as a vacation home recommended it as the perfect retreat for such purposes.

Somewhere along the way he had ended his field lecture on flora and fauna and turned to a history of the British rail system.

As soon as the steam engine was invented, a system of rails spread its reach rapidly across England. Extending from one town to the next. Linking mine and factory and farm and port. Connecting the places where goods are produced to the distribution centers, and the distribution centers to the places where the goods are used. Although England was fortunate enough not to be dominated by alpine peaks and canyons, there were nevertheless mountains to cross and valleys to traverse. Since early steam locomotives did not have sufficient power to ascend steep inclines, wherever mountains or valleys stood in the path of the advancing tracks, brick viaducts and tall iron bridges and long tunnels had to be constructed in order to create a rail bed with only the gentlest of slopes for the trains to climb. The massive structures put in place then can still be seen today, and some even remain in use.

"The viaducts were so big, they'd throw your whole sense of perspective out of whack when you stood there looking at them," my uncle said.

"So the brick railroad bridge at the pass here was based on British designs?" I asked, wanting to show that I had been listening.

"The whole idea of bringing the railroad through here originally came from the British. It really is amazing to think that they ran trains over a mountain like this only twenty-five years after the Meiji Restoration."

The going got tougher on the path next to the stream, so for a time we walked along the edge of the highway with cars zipping by. I was now leading the way.

We veered off onto a path through the forest again. My uncle called out from behind, directing my progress. I followed the curve of the path around a large tree stump, pushed a low-hanging branch out of the way as I continued onward, and soon emerged into an open valley with the stream once again in sight. I stopped to wait for my uncle to catch up. As I turned my head to take in the view, I could see a double-arched bridge built of brick spanning the valley some distance away.

I turned back toward my uncle and pointed at the bridge. He mumbled something as he came toward me.

It was obvious that the arched brick span was no longer in use. Farther up the valley, a newer steel-truss bridge crossed parallel to it.

"That's right, it was just about exactly this far away," my uncle said.

I had no idea what he was talking about. When I started to lower the arm I'd raised toward the span, he grabbed hold of my hand and held it in place.

"Don't drop your arm," he said. "Keep your eyes on the bridge."

As instructed, I continued gazing at the bridge. I had no clue what he was trying to do, so I felt a little unnerved.

Moments later, a passenger train appeared on the steel bridge in the distance, beyond the arches of brick, drawn by an electric locomotive. The sound of the train reached us after a slight delay. It was a thin wisp of a sound, like a single delicate thread dangling among the trees in the canyon.

When the train disappeared from sight, my uncle finally released my hand. With his eyes still fixed in the direction of the two bridges, he said, "Could you see the passengers' faces?"

"Are you kidding? Even the windows were barely dots. There's no way I could make out any faces."

"I could," he said. "Not with that train just now, but when I was in England." He lifted his own arm and pointed up the valley. "It was from almost exactly this same distance. I watched a train speeding across a long viaduct, and in one of its windows I saw the face of someone I never would have expected to see there, clear as day. The person—her name was Rieko Kashiwagi—had her elbow propped on the sill and she was gazing out the window with a look of deep melancholy. She seemed to be staring blankly into space, her eyes wide open but not really seeing anything, so I didn't think she could have spotted me. I turned to the staffer I had with me and said, 'See that Japanese woman on the train—toward the back of the middle car?'"

My uncle glanced down at me.

"The guy gave me the same weird look you're giving me right now. He said he couldn't see any faces at all, let alone make one of them out as Japanese. There's no way, he said. But I'm telling you, I saw what I saw. Do you believe me?"

Not quite sure how to respond, I finally said, "Okay, so I'm guessing this Kashiwagi woman was someone you were really aching to see, right? And that's why you thought you saw her. Or maybe you actually did see her?"

"That's pretty much what the other guy said—though your answer goes him one better. He never considered the possibility I might actually have seen her. And in fact I *did* see her. I confirmed it later. She really was on the train."

At that, he fell silent and started walking again. The goal of our hike was to stand on top of the double-arched bridge. With my hand still tingling oddly from the touch of his rougher skin, I fell in step behind him.

After Ayumi had gone, three desktop computers were all that remained on the giant double desk in the main room of the office. My employees were under strict orders to always put everything away in a drawer or storage cabinet before they left for the day. I was surprisingly fussy about such things—"surprisingly" being a word I myself choose to apply. I have no idea whether my employees thought my fussiness was surprising or not.

I was dithering over my response to Momo. The right words refused to come. The trouble was that I couldn't make up my mind about going to see Ogita.

In the end I decided to keep it short:

> I read your message. It's quite a surprise. Can't write any more now.

After sending it off, I took my private cell phone from the desk drawer and dialed my daughter Ryo's number. When I'd called home a little earlier, my wife had said she wasn't back yet. If she was in Shibuya, I thought I'd suggest we take the train home together. But all I got was a recorded message saying she was unavailable.

I had known Ogita since he initiated a conversation with me when we were lined up to practice javelin throws in a fitness class in college. He liked to organize mah-jongg games on weekday nights so he could rake in enough to pay for dates on the weekend. He apparently thought I might make a good mark.

Half of a game was all it took for me to recognize Ogita's skill. Four hours later, I hadn't lost all that much myself, but the other two players had coughed up considerable sums—quite cheerfully, it seemed. I refused his invitations after that.

"What's the problem?" he laughed. "Everybody else is eager to come back—even when they've lost their shirts."

Ogita wasn't just unbeatable at the game, he also knew how to create the right mood. He made the other players feel good even as he cleaned them out.

He and I remained friends for a while. But since he was both a year ahead of me and in a different program, we eventually fell out of touch.

After graduation, I went to work for a mid-sized trading company. My uncle had rarely had anything good to say either about the business in general or about his own company in particular. Even so, I'd always thought he had a cool job. The big-name firm he worked for was in fact my first choice when I sent out applications, but I got a quick brush-off there. This was in the mid-1970s, after the first "oil shock," when recruitment of new college grads was at a low point.

Ogita had joined the same company the year before, and after my initial training period was over, I found myself assigned to the office he was in, handling textile goods. The mostly smooth and uneventful start I got in my new job was thanks in very large part to Ogita, who had the favor of our mutual boss—a man of good business instincts, but with a strong tendency toward favoritism and quite a volatile temper.

The boss handpicked Ogita to go to France on a special assignment. His charge was to work with our office in Paris to cultivate new brands of apparel that looked promising for long-term growth. But not too long after his departure, the boss suddenly had to go into the hospital, and the doctors couldn't say when he might be able to return to work. The person tapped to run the place in his stead was a rival of our out-of-commission boss.

The new man was a chubby fellow with a permanent smile, which gave people the impression he was an affable sort, but he promptly began axing all projects initiated by his predecessor that were not likely to accrue to his own credit. Since he liked to wear polka-dot neckties, he soon earned the nickname of "the Polka-Dot Killer" around the office. Although Ogita had reported back with some promising leads, he brushed them aside as if they were a waste of his time. Ogita was effectively stranded in Paris with the ladder pulled out from under him.

In protest at what we perceived to be a grave injustice, a senior colleague and I continued to offer support to Ogita behind the boss's back. Of course, we had to do this while also keeping up on our own assignments, so it had to be a guerilla action carried out late at night and on weekends. The person who helped us on the clerical side was Momo. She was cute, thoughtful, and attentive to detail, and although every once in a while something would set her off and I'd have to walk on eggshells for a while, I'd invariably discover that she was really only mad at herself—for making a mistake or failing to deliver on something—and that made her all the more endearing to me. In fact, I was very much on the verge of falling in love with her. Unfortunately, it was the exiled Ogita who had caught her fancy.

As Ogita's project began to take concrete shape, we communicated secretly with other departments that needed to be involved, and put in place a framework that could no longer be brushed aside. Then Ogita himself returned to Japan to seek Polka Dot's approval in person.

I'll never forget the scene.

The boss beamed with delight as he shook Ogita's hand. The credit would be his.

Ogita, Momo, and I spent a great deal of time together outside of work as well. The two of them were carrying on a rather ambiguous relationship in which it wasn't always clear whether they were a couple or not, so they apparently found it convenient to have me around. Ogita was in fact playing the field at the time, as he divulged to me once when Momo was not present.

Every so often, Momo would bring another woman along as a fourth member of the group—trying to set me up. But it never worked out. Painful as it is to admit, the woman would often start making eyes at Ogita. Or I would find myself comparing her unfavorably to Momo.

One year during the recruiting season a girl from Momo's alma mater came to sound us out. Ogita happened to be out of the country, so Momo asked if I would talk to her. I sized her up as someone who'd been born with a silver spoon in her mouth.

"You don't want to work here," I advised her. "This place isn't normal. We're not even all that big, but the infighting is like you wouldn't believe. You get caught in the middle and just feel rotten all the time. At first I figured it was probably pretty much the same anywhere you went, but I asked around a bit and found out that's not really true. It's apparently been part of the management culture here since way way back to goad people into competing by going after each other like cats and dogs. Take my advice and look elsewhere. There are plenty more pleasant places to work."

She nodded at me with a vexed look on her face. But in the end she joined the company anyway. I figured she probably wouldn't want to have anything to do with me after what I'd told her in the interview, so I generally kept my distance. But then Momo chose her one day to fill out our group. She told me that the things I'd said had only made her all the more curious about what kind of place it was, and she figured if she really hated it she could always quit . . . To make a long story short, two years later we got married.

Immediately after that, Ogita and Momo rushed to get engaged themselves. I guess he couldn't stand to see me married when he was not. Presumably this was all according to plan for Momo, but to judge from later developments, she did not find the happiness she expected. After getting married, Ogita spent more and more time out of the country on assignments overseas, and we basically lost touch.

One time when Ogita came home for a visit while stationed in the United States, I learned that Momo had gone back to school there. Later, he returned permanently to the home office in Tokyo, but Momo stayed on in America for graduate school. I gathered that their marriage had hit rough waters.

In 1985, the year of the Plaza Accord that became the principal cause of the subsequent economic bubble, Ogita quit the company. I only learned about it after the fact. His new employer was the much larger trading firm my uncle had worked for.

In 1989, the year Emperor Hirohito died, Momo returned to Japan. She found a job in the Tokyo office of a German chemical company. I got together with the Ogitas a number of times during this period. They appeared to have patched up their marriage. Ogita wore expensive designer suits and drove a late-model BMW, the extravagant accessories seeming to fit him to a T.

In 1991, he quit the trading company and moved to a management-consulting firm. This was the year the bubble began to burst—or so analysts concluded with the help of twenty-twenty hindsight many years later; at the time the country was still crawling with people proclaiming that the flush times would last forever. I remember coming across at least two interviews in business magazines where Ogita, too, expressed such views. He quit the consulting firm sometime the following year or the year after that. I'm a little vague on this period because I stopped hearing from either of them.

In 1995, the year of the Kobe earthquake as well as the sarin gas attack on the Tokyo subway, Ogita and Momo got divorced. I learned this from Momo afterwards.

While the Ogitas led their fast-paced lives out on the edge, riding the great undulating waves of the economy and their personal events, I remained with the same employer, spent only a brief period overseas, never even considered divorce, and all in all lived a quiet life. But the months and years piled up equally on both the fast-paced Ogitas and the subdued Yajimas, bearing us all inexorably into middle age.

When I saw Momo again after a six-year interlude, I was forty-five and she was forty-one. Without either of us having to say a word, I could tell we were both thinking how much the other had aged.

But as I noticed the lively sparkle in her eye and listened to her gentle but animated voice, I soon realized she had in fact grown more attractive with the years.

She smiled at me across the table. "You haven't changed a bit, have you?"

"Why? What do you mean?" I asked.

"The way you talk, and the way you seem to drift off when I'm talking, it's all just like before."

"I wasn't drifting off," I replied automatically. I wanted to tell her how much more attractive I thought she'd become. But before I could open my mouth again, her cell phone rang inside her purse.

It was Ogita. I had asked her to contact him for me. She'd told me they still did things together—dinner, concerts, and the like—even after their divorce. They had no children.

"I'd like to see you," I said when Momo handed me the phone. "I need your advice on a business matter."

"Oh, business," he said, sounding deflated. "Here I was, thinking how long it's been since I've seen you, and how excited I was when Momo called. It's pretty pricey to talk to me about business these days, you know."

Ogita still worked in management consulting, though for a different firm than before. It apparently was not the sort of company where he was likely to get interviewed by business magazines.

"So I was hoping you could treat it as a private matter."

"'So I was hoping,' he says blithely. Sheesh." The sound of his voice was exactly as I remembered it. It had the cozy touch of a cashmere blanket on your ear, and just listening to it somehow cheered you up.

This was how I opened the door to my own private hell.

But before I begin detailing the hellish events that followed, I need to attend to a call that came in on the cell phone I'd set down in front of me at the office, which suddenly began vibrating across the surface of the desk. Cell phones are such handy things.

"Hi, Dad. You called?"

It was Ryo. In the background I could hear music that sounded like a cross between hip-hop and R&B.

"Yeah, hi. I was wondering if you happened to be in Shibuya."

"Wha-a-at? If you're asking where I am, I'm in Shibuya."

"Then how about joining me for some dinner?"

"Seriously, Dad, do you have any idea what time it is?"

I looked up at the clock on the wall but it was a blur to me. My eyes have a harder and harder time focusing these days. They're getting old.

"No, what time is it?"

"It's after eleven," she answered.

A high-school girl had no business being out in Shibuya so near midnight. It called for a talking-to.

"Maybe you're working too hard, Dad—if you don't even have time to look at the clock."

This helped mollify me. She was probably just stating the obvious, but to me it came across as genuine concern. The steam I had been building up instantly dissipated.

"So Dad, you have to be almost done for today, right?"

"Uh-huh. I was just getting ready to leave."

"Then could you come get me? We can go home together."

"Going home together sounds good, but what do you mean, come get you?"

"I'm kind of in a fix." Her voice over the phone seemed to stiffen a little. "I'm wearing my school uniform—I mean, because I never intended to stay out so late, you know. I thought I'd be going home right after the movie was over. But then my friend and I got to talking and we lost track of the time, and when we came out of the coffee shop, we saw some juvenile officers on patrol. I think maybe they spotted us, too, so right now we're hiding out in another coffee shop. I guess they don't have anyone else to go after today, 'cause they just keep hanging around. I need you to come rescue me."

Ryo's distress call didn't warm my heart in quite the same way as when she'd said maybe I was working too hard, but at any rate I hurried to the rescue.

Dogenzaka was aglow with artificial lights, and the women who plied the sidewalks to lure customers into the bars along the way were still out in force all up and down the slope. Recognizing me from my daily back-and-forths to work, most of them ignored me, but a few flashed me warm smiles or called out, "Good evening, sir!" Perhaps they were betting on the possibility that if they made sure always to greet me, I might have a sudden impulse someday to drop in. One of them, an intelligent-looking woman who was probably Chinese, could sometimes make my knees wobble with her beautiful smile. A smile so beautiful it was almost scary.

I turned to go up Hyakkendana Lane, and the red and yellow neon of the Dotonbori Theater leaped out at me. Ignoring the heightened pitch of the touts' voices, I mentally clapped my hands twice as if standing before a shrine. The place was like a guardian deity looking down over the "Village of Shibuya" from its perch on the hillside. When it closed its doors in 1995, the entire neighborhood went into a shocking decline—until it reopened in 2001 and the area seemed to bounce back. At the very least, we'd seen a drop in the trash blowing about the sidewalks as well as in the bands of rowdy hooligans who intimidated passersby. I figured it was because the dancers at the Dotonbori Theater offered up their naked bodies to the local spirits each night.

Venido, the coffee shop Ryo had named, was located near an intersection I'd passed through any number of times, but I could not recall ever noticing it before. The clientele appeared to be mainly men and women just off their shifts at nearby drinking places, along with some of the partied-out middle-agers they'd served, but intermingled among them were groups of younger people behaving like they'd barely gotten started. I didn't spot my daughter in the crowd immediately. As I shuffled sideways between two closely spaced tables, I felt a tug on the elbow of my coat.

Ryo was at a table tucked away next to the stairs almost like a hiding place. Her school uniform made her look utterly out of place, but nobody was paying any attention to her. The expression she wore was like none I'd ever seen before. Her eyes showed wariness mixed with relief, her lips seemed braced to say no more than absolutely necessary, and her arms drooped beneath the table like someone spent of all energy after a grueling workout.

When I turned to face her table, I found a boy sitting across from her. He sat with his head bent and a stocking cap pulled down to his eyebrows, so I could not see much of his face. On clear display, though, were the four pierced rings he had in his left ear. His hands, folded together on the table, were pale, with slender fingers.

I sat down in the seat beside my daughter.

"Thanks, Dad," she said.

"So this is the friend you said you lost track of time with after the movie?"

"Uh-huh." She cast the boy a glance.

Without looking up, he made a tiny bob of his head. This was apparently his idea of a greeting.

There's all sorts of blather in magazines and on TV about the moment when a father meets his daughter's boyfriend for the first time. Without any forewarning, I now found myself living that famous moment. And what a fine specimen of youth the fellow was. I'd have found it less dismaying if an octopus-tentacled Martian had shown up. At least in that case amazement would have preceded displeasure.

"Good to meet you. I'm sure you've heard plenty about me. Mind if I ask your name?"

It was hard to tell whether he'd heard me or not, for he did not answer. I saw my daughter urging him with her eyes to speak up.

"Yuta . . . Iwamoto," he finally said. A full five seconds must have elapsed between "Yuta" and "Iwamoto." What was with this kid? He still hadn't looked me in the eye.

"You know, young man," I started in, intending to point out that it surely didn't take all that much more effort to speak in complete

31

sentences, but just then I felt the presence of someone hovering over my shoulder in the aisle.

I turned to see a young waiter gazing down at me in a way that seem to say *I'm wearing this dopey outfit because I need the job, but I actually think this joint sucks.* I didn't imagine the place offered anything decent to eat, but I was hungry.

"Could I see a menu?" I requested.

The waiter gave me a weary look, as if he felt inordinately put upon for being compelled to say what he was about to say. But he did his duty.

"It's the policy of this shop not to allow use of the premises for this kind of thing," he said.

What was he talking about: "this kind of thing"? I saw him move his eyes from me to Ryo and back . . . Oh, so he thinks I'm some middle-aged pervert looking for a date with a teenage girl. I hadn't noticed a type of clientele here that called for blustering about this or that shop policy, but Ryo being in school uniform apparently crossed some kind of line.

"This girl is my daughter, I'll have you know. I work nearby, so I asked her to wait for me here. And this is her friend."

This appeared to have no effect whatsoever on the waiter. It suddenly struck me that maybe that was exactly the story all the perverts gave in this situation. True enough, my salt-and-pepper hair and black turtleneck and half-length black leather coat didn't exactly make me the picture of respectability. If anyone was bringing down the level of the clientele, it might actually have been me.

"Even if she is your daughter, we don't allow customers to have minors with them on these premises so late at night. It's a house rule."

The people at nearby tables were beginning to show some curiosity. They all seemed to be noticing the teenager dressed in her high school uniform for the first time.

"All right," I said. "Come on, Ryo. Let's go."

Yuta's hand moved uncertainly toward the check sitting at the edge of the table. I snatched the slip of paper up just before his fingers reached it.

When I turned around after paying the bill, Ryo had put her coat on and was wrapping a muffler around her neck. Even though it was part of her uniform, the coat made her look very grown up. Her school bag might almost have been an expensive designer bag.

We started back toward Dogenzaka's main drag. Yuta tagged along as if he took it for granted that he should—still not uttering a word. When we reached the point where the bright lights of the main avenue spilled into the lane, Ryo moved around behind me to shield herself from view.

On the corner stood a middle-aged man and woman, looking somehow out of place in these surroundings as they eyed the pedestrians coming and going. I was actually breathing a sigh of relief. On the way there I'd been worried that the real reason Ryo had called for help might be something more serious. If being spotted by juvenile officers was the worst of her concerns, it seemed a pretty good sign that her rebellion hadn't turned into hardcore delinquency.

I hoped we might get by them without incident, but the pair saw us and stepped out to block our path. "Police," the woman said. She had a round, kind face. "Is this your family you're out with at this hour?" The man, who was quite tall, stood a bit to one side, his eyes shifting back and forth between Ryo and Yuta and passing pedestrians.

"We sat down to talk after seeing a movie and the time slipped by," I said. "This is my daughter, and a friend of hers."

"Do you have a business card or something I could see?" the woman said.

I took out one of my cards and turned it in her direction. She reached for it and pulled, but I held on. After a momentary tug-of-war, she relaxed her grip.

The man had remained silent until this, but now, out of the blue, he mentioned the name of Ryo's school and asked, "You're a student there?" What was he—one of those girls' uniform fetishists using his job as cover?

When Ryo said "Yes," he asked to see her ID. The woman leaned in to look at it, too. For some reason, they paid no attention to Yuta.

The woman whispered something to the man, then turned back to me. "Well, it's very late for high school students to be out, so please be getting on home," she said. "Thank you for your cooperation."

We started down the hill in the direction of Shibuya Station. The ladies trying to lure customers seemed a little surprised. The more perceptive ones quickly realized that Ryo was my daughter, but others gave me quizzical looks, as if they were thinking, *He won't stop in here, but he's got a thing for teenage girls.* A few cast suggestive smiles my way, each time prompting a glance up from Ryo. Yuta followed a step behind.

"See?" Ryo said, turning to look at Yuta. "I told you my dad wouldn't take a taxi." Yuta did not answer. "My mom hates them, too, so we almost never use them."

"Aside from being uncomfortable, they always stink of cigarettes," I said.

"Late-night trains are even worse, if you ask me," Ryo said. "They're jammed with men reeking of alcohol, and you have to fend off the gropers."

An aversion to taxis had long been part of our family culture. I'd always assumed that Ryo shared the sentiment, so it caught me by surprise to hear her talking like this.

Still having said nothing more than his name, Yuta veered off toward the entrance to the Inokashira Line. Keeping his reserve, he signaled goodbye only with his eyes.

"Sheesh, what kind of behavior is that?" I muttered, showing my exasperation. The look on Ryo's face turned prickly. She put her nose in the air and offered no reply.

She deliberately stood apart from me on the train. The car was packed with workers headed home, many of them flushed with drink, and a surly mood hung in the air. Neither of us got to sit down before it was time to get off.

On the way from the station to our house was a pretty decent ramen shop, but when I suggested we stop in for a bowl, Ryo said she wasn't hungry. The message *Don't talk to me* seemed to ooze from her every pore. But I thought I had the right to know a few things.

"So is this silent hipster your boyfriend?"

She seemed to hesitate for a moment. "Just a friend," she said brusquely.

"But you've been going out with him, right?"

Ryo was marching ahead of me along the edge of the street. I had to make an effort to keep up.

"Uh-huh."

"Is he always so untalkative?" Her answer had shaken me a little, but I tried to sound unfazed.

"Always . . . ?" She fell silent and I thought she might not say anything more, but finally she went on. "Hardly. He was just nervous from meeting you for the first time is all. At times like that, haven't you ever had it happen where you're so determined to be yourself and not get pushed around that you just clam right up?"

She threw a glance over her shoulder at me, then started walking even faster. I kept pace, feeling as if she'd literally turned her back on me.

When I unlocked the front door, she pushed past me to go inside first. My wife Asako had come into the foyer, but Ryo hurried on up to her room without even the briefest word of greeting.

"What's going on?" my wife asked.

"Well, as you can see, she's in a bit of a mood. Is there anything to eat? I'm starving. I ended up never getting any dinner today."

"Ramen is about all I have on hand. Shall I make you some?"

"That's exactly what I've been wanting all evening," I said.

Ryo had taken the somewhat unusual educational path of going from a mixed public junior high to a private girls' high school. We knew the transition would probably include some rough patches for her, but she insisted it was what she wanted, and Asako supported her decision.

"All right," I told her. "But don't hesitate to come see me if you run into any difficulties . . . Good grief, I'm sounding like a teacher, not a parent."

A wry sort of smile that was hard to read crossed her lips. My wife did not smile at all.

When it came to my daughter's choice of schools, I basically didn't feel I was in a position to argue.

Around the time Ryo was studying hard for the entrance exams to private junior highs in sixth grade, I got myself into some trouble at work that ultimately forced me to resign. To be honest, under the circumstances, the last thing I wanted to think about was taking on the admission fees and tuition payments to a private school. But having been told that Ryo always scored at the top of her class in the exam-prep course she was attending after school, I hated the thought of disappointing her, and put off saying anything.

After a monumental struggle in the aftermath of my resignation, I eventually managed to get myself set up in a new work situation, but even when I felt things were safely on track, I had to admit that sending Ryo to private school simply wasn't in the cards. I broke the news to Asako. To my relief, she took it calmly. But I still couldn't bring myself to tell Ryo. I knew the public junior high school in our district didn't have the best reputation.

"If she gets picked on and things turn nasty for her," I told my wife, "I promise I'll be there to help, even if it means blowing off work."

"Do me a favor," she said with barely contained anger. "I don't ever want to hear any talk about blowing off work again."

In the time since quitting my old job, it had taken quite a while for the new business to get off the ground. I was of course the boss, but it was a constant struggle to pay my hired help, and there were times when I had to give up my own salary in order to meet the payroll. When it reached the point where I had to dip into my personal savings to pay the others, the thought of packing up and skipping town actually crossed my mind.

During this same period, my daughter was apparently getting bullied at the public junior high she'd wound up having to attend. It was a time of tribulation for the whole family. For her part, Ryo kept a stiff upper lip and seemed ultimately to be coping.

She was still in junior high when business finally began to pick up for my company. Once this happened, it didn't take long for the accumulated deficit to disappear, since the initial investment had been low. I even started to think I could end up wealthy if things went on the way they were going—though the growth in sales and profits leveled off around the time I hired my second full-timer.

The improvement at work changed our economic situation at home quite dramatically as well. Putting my only daughter in a private school was easily affordable now. Meanwhile, Ryo was keeping up her grades, maintaining a position near the top of her class.

Even so, I secretly hoped that she would go on to a public high school, where she would get to know a more varied group of peers. I myself had grown up in the country and attended public schools all the way. Perhaps I wanted the validation of having my daughter follow the same track.

But Ryo declared that she wanted to experience a private girls' school.

And there was certainly something to be said for that option. Her mother had attended such schools for both junior high and high school. It no doubt pained her to think of her daughter spending all six of those years in public institutions. Ryo obviously had been swayed by her mother in making up her mind—though it was probably from my own influence that she had spoken in terms of "wanting to experience" something in a context like this.

Happily, Ryo passed the entrance exam to her first-choice school and so earned the right to a private education. On the day of the opening assembly in April, she was noticeably on edge before leaving the house in the morning, but once she arrived at school she seemed confident and relaxed.

Several times that first month, I walked with her to the station in the morning with my chest puffed out. *Just look at this daughter of mine*, I wanted to shout out to all the grim-faced commuters I passed. I was the quintessential proud parent.

But before long, Ryo began to take on that grim-faced look herself. She decided to leave the house a little later, and we never rode the same train anymore.

"It's probably just the May doldrums," she mumbled when asked, almost as if she were talking about someone else.

I was a little concerned, of course, but she never actually stopped going to school. And then . . . well, after that I basically lost track of what was going on in her life. She stopped talking about what happened at school, or about her classmates—at least when I was around. Meanwhile, things got busier than ever for me at the office, so I no longer had time to be worrying about my family.

And the next thing I knew, another year was coming to an end.

On Christmas Eve, I bought presents for my wife and daughter and made a point of getting home early, but Ryo had gone out shortly after noon and didn't come home until nearly ten.

When I questioned her, she answered with annoying nonchalance: "I was at a party with some friends. I told Mom."

"But you only said until evening," her mother pointed out.

"So I'm a little late. Hasn't that ever happened to you?"

"You didn't answer your phone, either," I persisted.

She looked at me like I was utterly clueless. "Everybody turns their phones off at our parties. That's the etiquette. Isn't that what you do?"

I was not entirely blind to the fact that my daughter was unhappy at school. She had complained to her mother—who'd then relayed it to me—that she was being graded more strictly on tests than the other girls, that she got reprimanded for trivial infractions when nobody else did, and that she was having a hard time making friends. I thought it was merely because she was new, and she had to go through an initiation of sorts. But the situation failed to improve even after summer vacation when the second semester got under way.

In her usual manner, she had started out by establishing herself near the top of her class, but now her grades began to slip. She dropped out of the art club and put away her oil painting stuff in favor of drawing manga. She began leaving the house in trendy outfits and makeup, and spending most of her time with a group of friends she'd met on the street instead of at school . . . Which is to say, she was rebelling all of a sudden, and appeared to be starting down the path toward delinquency. That it was a reaction to being ostracized and treated unfairly at school was the only plausible explanation I could think of.

On New Year's Eve, I didn't get home from work until the annual Red and White Singing Contest was wrapping up near midnight.

Asako sat alone in front of the TV, watching members of the Wild Bird Society file on stage to count the audience members' votes with their binoculars. Ryo had apparently gone out to make her first shrine visit of the new year. When I went to bed a little after one, she had not yet returned. It seemed like quite a bit later that I became aware of Asako finally coming to bed. I could tell from the way she was acting that there'd still been no sign of Ryo.

My old company missed its chance to get in on the run-up in real-estate and stock prices that swept Japan in the late '80s. The upper echelons had been caught up in fierce internal feuding, as usual, and their lack of attention to events in the outside world prevented them from responding quickly enough to some very "juicy" (as they were spoken of at the time) investment opportunities. Had senior executives then chosen to accept it as a missed opportunity and just sit tight, we would have been spared any serious damage when the economic bubble ultimately burst, but instead they opted to make some late plays in resort development and overseas real estate, and we got stuck holding the bag.

I slogged away at my career in the department that handled textile goods all the way into the early '90s, so the expanding bubble did not really affect me much, but its collapse generated a massive wave of repercussions that swept me into the maelstrom.

With deepening signs of recession on the horizon in 1994, the company decided to carry out a major restructuring, one component of which was the creation of a "New Ventures Office." The unit was to be staffed primarily by personnel who were in their forties from the Textiles Department, which had once been the backbone of the company but was now operating in the red with scant prospect of recovery, and from the Real Estate Department, which had suffered massive losses when the bubble burst. I was selected to be among them.

We were told that the office would be overseen by one of the directors but otherwise have no hierarchy; each person was expected to find his own work that would generate profits and earn his keep. If our returns did not measure up, we could expect to be "restructured" right out of a job. As it turned out, the man assigned to oversee the office was none other than the Polka-Dot Killer, my supervisor from years before, who had just recently been appointed the newest member of the board of directors. He still favored polka dots, but now he wore a better class of tie that was obviously a lot more expensive.

For the edification of future generations, I will note that the management personnel who carried out this restructuring were the same individuals who had plunged the company into unprofitability and brought it to the brink of ruin, yet not one of them became a target of restructuring.

The employees assigned to the New Ventures Office were not necessarily the most unproductive members of the workforce. The following patterns could be observed in the selection of personnel:

Those associated with the losing side in the internal feud were prime candidates. No one associated with the winning side was chosen.

The least productive were indeed first to go on the list, but having a solid record of achievements did not remove you from consideration.

And finally, anyone who had ever stood up to Polka Dot was sure to be tapped.

Many of the abler workers took reassignment as their cue to find positions elsewhere and left the company. Others impulsively handed in their resignations in fits of indignation or despair. You could say they played right into the company's hands.

Still others were at a complete loss how to proceed with their new directives, yet could not bring themselves to quit and sank into depression or suffered nervous breakdowns.

I chose to stay on. Giving myself regular pep talks to keep from being discouraged, I pursued leads aggressively and produced the desired results. Talk about playing into the company's hands.

As I made the rounds of wholesalers and retailers I'd done business with before, I volunteered my services in the form of unpaid labor or free consultations in the hope of parlaying that into paid work. Sometimes I assisted with sales, other times with making deliveries and taking inventory. Once my foot was in the door, I would begin identifying how that business could be served by my own expertise and the networks I was tapped into.

My company owned the distribution rights to a new American line of apparel targeted at young people that had been unable to gain traction in the marketplace. I was able to finally get sales moving by marketing the label in regional cities. Before that, the department in charge of the brand had been trying to sell it only in the major metropolitan areas. So I talked with a number of distributors and traveled to various regional centers to determine the best places and best timing for introducing the new brand, then pulled together some ideas for a campaign that turned out to be a huge hit.

But as soon as the brand gained a foothold, I was removed from the project. I was told that the regular department would take it from there.

"Good work," they said. "And now that this isn't a new venture anymore, you'll need to move on to something else."

In other words, it was back to square one.

I next turned my attention to the Marianelli brand from Italy, an integrated label with products ranging from leather goods to furniture to ceramics. A company by the name of Handa Enterprises, a wholesale outfit that specialized in placing European apparel in Japanese department stores, held the distribution rights, but with the entire department store sector in a slump, it was feeling the pinch. The products themselves were of excellent quality and design yet not outlandishly expensive, so they had won a devoted following among discerning shoppers. The problem was that brand recognition remained weak.

The business relationship between Handa Enterprises and my company came originally from its young president being one of the regulars at Ogita's mah-jongg games in college. Ogita and Momo had once spent a good bit of time doing things together with the young boss's family. But after Ogita resigned, dealings between the two companies dropped off, especially when Handa Enterprises suffered a downturn in business, and by the time I got involved, we no longer even had a full-time staffer on the account. My previous involvement in dealings with Handa had been very brief, but I'd come away with the sense that the Marianelli line of products offered some promising opportunities. I decided to get in touch with the Marianelli desk at Handa to see if they might be interested in working with us again.

But after extensive negotiations to work out a full-scale business plan for the joint endeavor, when the project rose to the top of the board's agenda I was once again pushed aside with a "Thanks, we'll take it from here." You can easily surmise the rationale they gave. I might note that the project was indeed a success, but it never grew into the huge moneymaker I thought it could be, producing only so-so returns. Fortunately for Handa Enterprises, it shored them up just enough for them to survive the economic rough-and-tumble of the '90s.

And so it went with one project and another. Three full years drifted by like that, and I was wearing myself to the bone. I began to wonder how much longer I could last. One of these days I was going to collapse. It was all too obvious that I had no future at the company so long as Polka Dot had me under his thumb. I thought hard about what I might do.

It was now 1997, the year that a fourteen-year-old boy identifying himself as Seito Sakakibara gruesomely murdered several grade-schoolers in Kobe.

I could try my luck on the job market, but I had neither an impressive title nor visible achievements to show. My heart grew heavy at the thought of having to restart my career somewhere as a bottom-rung sales rep at this stage in my life.

My only real option, I decided, was to use what I'd learned since being reassigned to the New Ventures Office. In the course of my day-to-day work, I had gained an increasingly clear sense of what I had to offer. To put it in business-speak, it was "a total management system for brand marketing built around a core of image creation and control." (Snicker.) In other words, I slapped fancy-sounding phrases on products to get people to buy them. It's scary how even a muddle of words like that comes across sounding like a perfectly normal sentence.

What the industrial giants turned to heavyweight ad agencies and consultants for, I was doing for small businesses all by myself. The English term "brand" had taken solid root in Japan during the '70s, and brand consciousness had been growing ever since. In the new century, brand-driven business models had reached new heights of success. But even though my company was practically crawling with dandies who knew the most desirable brands of this or that product to buy, only a few had any sense at all of how a brand-driven business actually worked.

Among the top brands my company handled was a label that had long produced solid profits but was now experiencing a decline in sales. One of several successful lines that a team led by Ogita had cultivated in the late '70s, it was regarded at the time as fresh and elegant and snappy, but these days the downtown department stores had the merchandise tucked away in a quiet corner of the luxury items floor with only a snooty salesperson or two waiting passively for their well-heeled regulars to show up. The line was still making money, so my company didn't see a problem with it. But if the present trend continued, it would wither on the vine as its existing clientele aged.

Back at home, the manufacturer had shown its concern about current sales and future prospects by hiring young designers and making other moves that indicated change was on the horizon. But the response had been cool here in Japan—which is to say, among those now handling the account at my company. Watching from the sidelines, I was convinced the manufacturer would soon get fed up and start looking for a new importer. That could be a golden opportunity. I simply needed to get on the new importer's team, so to speak. I knew that Ogita had kept in touch with the manufacturer even after leaving my company, so I could get him to help. Once I'd made up my mind to quit, I spent nearly a year laying the groundwork. I gathered the necessary information and conducted extensive surveys and market research. After all, time was one thing I had plenty of.

The various ingredients I needed for my new venture were now in hand. All that was left was to cook them into an appetizing meal—except, as it turned out, I was the one who got cooked.

I had always thought Ryo was artistically talented. From a very young age, she drew strong, clean lines, and had a knack for capturing the essence of a figure. If you gave her crayons, she would choose unusual colors and use them in combinations you would never expect, yet the result was something beautiful rather than weird. At first I wondered if she might just be picking the colors at random, but as I continued to watch her work, I saw that she very deliberately selected the ones she needed beforehand and never picked out an unnecessary color.

When I showed some of her pictures to a neighbor who gave private art classes, he said he thought they were strange. It was also rare for Ryo to win praise for her work in arts and crafts at school. But I figured she was better off doing her own thing at home than being constrained by teachers who had no appreciation of the subject. Give her blank sheets of paper and she would promptly fill them with drawings, one after another. I took her to exhibitions from time to time, and showed her books on artists I liked: Piero della Francesca and Caravaggio, Hiroshige and Hokusai, Cézanne and Picasso, Léonard Foujita and Shiko Munakata. When she found a painting she liked, Ryo would gaze at it on and on, her eyes wide and her lips in a little pout, rooted to the spot as if her shoes had been stitched to the floor.

Upon seeing the first picture Ryo submitted in junior high, her art teacher, Ms. Makita, promptly called us at home to say she wanted to take our daughter under her wing. Ryo then studied sketching techniques and the basics of oil painting with this teacher.

Before long we noticed something curious. Objects in her pictures were always slightly elongated from top to bottom. This was especially evident in the faces she drew: the noses came out looking a bit long. Even when the problem was pointed out to her, she couldn't seem to fix it. She drew portraits of me quite often, but she rarely attempted one of her mother. When she drew the nose in her characteristic manner, the likeness would disappear.

Ms. Makita made no attempt to correct this idiosyncrasy. She regarded the slight distortion as part of what gave Ryo's paintings their appeal. It was like Ingres making an arm too long.

The high school Ryo went on to had a history of sending several graduating seniors each year to top-ranked art schools like Musashino and Tama and Joshi, and occasionally even Tokyo National. Another major factor in making the school her first choice had been the active art club. But she soon told us that she didn't fit in.

"There's lots of girls who're much better than me at sketching," she said one day. "I came in thinking I was pretty good, but I could see right away that I was barely above average here. The thing is, according to Mr. Agata, I'm way lower. He says I'm at the very bottom."

We were at a mall, waiting in a distant corner of the huge parking lot for my wife to emerge from shopping. To pass the time, we'd decided to play a little game, pretending it was still mid-winter and we were warming our hands over a small fire we'd made from a pile of leaves as we talked. I don't recall how we got onto the topic of the art club.

"Because you elongate your shapes?"

"The way he put it was that my proportions aren't natural. He said it shows I'm not looking at things correctly. He also said my lines are good but my overall touch is rough, and I'm too stuck on doing things my own way. I have to admit he has a point. I used to race Ms. Makita a lot at quick sketching. She was big on saying that speed is crucial in any task, but there's no denying that the results look kind of rough."

"I suppose the other kids have been working with Mr. Agata since junior high."

"Uh-huh. I'm the only one who came in new for high school."

"Sounds basically like he's insisting on an academic approach."

"I don't think you can quite say that." Ryo went through the motions of cupping her hands together and breathing on them to warm them. "He says we need to hang on to the freedom we gained 'when art burst the bonds of academicism.' But in order to do that, we first have to master its techniques. Otherwise he says we'll just backslide to the days before academicism came along."

"He throws some pretty complicated stuff at you, doesn't he?"

"But it seems like everybody gets it."

"Do you?"

"Yeah, I think so. Ms. Makita covered some art history with us, too."

"And all this time I thought you were just having fun drawing and painting things."

"We were having fun, too . . . This thing we do where everybody brings their latest paintings and we discuss each other's work—we did that in junior high, too, but now we have a name for it. It's called *critique*."

"Sounds like some kind of cosmetic."

"That's Clinique, Dad. Don't you know any French?"

I knew that much perfectly well, but I let her think that I didn't.

"When you're looking at pictures, you can pretty much tell at a glance which ones are good and which ones aren't, right? Well, the first time I saw my stuff lined up next to everybody else's, I mean, I'm sorry, but I immediately thought we were in completely different leagues. Not that there weren't any good ones at all, but they were all basically just very precise and nothing more. Or they slavishly imitated some popular technique. But even so, my heart was pounding like crazy. I sat there wondering what Mr. Agata and everybody would say, and also thinking maybe it wasn't so cool for the newcomer to be so much better than the old-timers."

"You sound like you were pretty sure of yourself."

Ryo shook her head. "I know there's always something higher to reach for, so I never really feel sure of myself. When we're doing critiques, Mr. Agata goes first, telling us what he thinks about a work, pointing out its strengths and flaws, and it's only after that that he asks us what we think. I was kind of surprised at first because it's so different from in junior high. We had more of a free-for-all then, with everybody saying whatever they wanted and Ms. Makita jumping in now and then to comment on what people had said. What surprised me even more was how everybody stuck pretty much to the same sort of things Mr. Agata said. Like when he praised the use of line, they'd say they liked this or that particular line. They'd all be smiling, but you could tell they were tied up in knots inside, terrified that they might say the wrong thing. Finally, when Mr. Agata got to my painting, he just stood there without saying anything for, like, an entire minute. My heart was in my throat, and I felt like it might come right on up. After I heard what he had to say, I wished it had."

"He came down on you that hard?"

"He basically didn't have anything good to say about it. You can draw with a twisted perspective or use offbeat colors all you want, but if you don't get the fundamentals right, you can't call it original, he said. Drawing long faces isn't going to make you into a Giacometti or Modigliani. When he was done, everybody else piled on, picking up where he left off. Oh so nicely, of course, smiling all the while."

"Wow, that must have hurt," I said. I felt a genuine chill go down my spine, and it had nothing to do with the game we were playing.

"Not really," she said. "Though I admit I was pretty taken aback. What stunned me most was when several of them came up to me afterwards all hush-hush and said they thought my picture was amazing."

"So they actually knew."

"I guess. And here I was consoling myself that only people who had a real appreciation of art could understand my stuff. Turns out they were either being weak or mean. When I realized that, I was really steamed. So I swore I'd make my next painting even better. In the fall, the school has to submit things for an outside exhibition, which means they can't very well pass over stuff that's really good, right?"

It pleased me to see her standing up to such obviously unfair treatment, and being inspired to reach even higher rather than to give up.

Ryo spent her summer vacation working on a new painting that she was convinced outdid anything else she had done. But the painting failed to be selected for the fall show she'd mentioned—a joint exhibition of works by current and former students of all the affiliated schools and colleges. Then later, when a famous alumni artist even I had heard of visited campus and was asked to comment on the students' work, her picture was excluded from consideration. It was a pattern of blackballing you might expect to see in an adolescent girls' manga from decades ago, but it was happening to my very own daughter right here and now.

I got to the office a little after eight and processed my e-mail before anybody else arrived. Once I'd replied to all the work-related items, I wrote a message to Momo. I would visit Ogita, I told her, but I wanted her to come with me. I started to feel uneasy as soon as I'd sent it off.

Ayumi came in looking half asleep. She sat down, switched on her computer, and a look of grim intensity spread across her face. She was apparently picking up where she left off yesterday.

I made some coffee with the Kalita dripper and took her a cup.

"Thank you," she said, breaking into a broad smile. Such a sunny countenance was unusual for her, so I was wondering what might have brought it on, when she pointed at her computer screen. It displayed two bottles of sake in fancy gift wrap. She had persuaded a popular regional brewer to join the online food mall she managed.

We raised our coffee cups in a toast. But within moments she had switched back into work mode, tapping out e-mails and placing phone calls.

The rest of the staff soon arrived. I couldn't be sitting on my hands either. I pushed Ogita, Momo, and my daughter to the back of my mind.

A reply came from Momo in the afternoon. A large group of executives from the main office in Germany would be visiting, she said, so it was unlikely she could find time to visit Ogita with me this week.

After reaching the double-arched bridge and climbing up onto the tracks, my uncle and I sat down in the overgrown grass next to the abandoned line to open our lunch boxes.

"It still baffles me why they would choose a mountain route like this for building a trunk line between Tokyo and western Japan," my uncle said. He was recounting the sequence of events that led to the construction of the Shin'etsu Line, of which this bridge had once been a part.

Various means of getting trains up the steep grades to Usui Pass were considered, including switchbacks and cables, but the engineers finally settled on a rack rail system in which a gear on the train meshes with a toothed third rail running between the two regular ones; they chose a version of the technology called the Abt system, first used in Germany. Unfortunately, having a rack rail segment wound up creating a bottleneck that reduced the transport capacity of the entire line. The single-track line, the extra time and trouble involved in switching the train over to the rack rail system and back, and the lower travel speed over that part of the trip all became limiting factors. As transportation demands grew to levels the system could not meet, the decision was made to build a new track with a gentler grade. Powerful new electric locomotives would be used to pull the trains up and over the pass. The double-arched bridge was shunted aside.

"Some people claim that the military wanted an inland route following the old Nakasendo highway because a coastal route along the Tokaido would be too easy to attack from the sea, but I find that dubious. I'm more persuaded that the inland route was chosen to also allow for improved links to the Sea of Japan side. Still, when you consider how determined they were to avoid the Tokaido, I can't help wondering if there wasn't actually some other less politically acceptable reason they didn't want to reveal publicly. Since they say the Nakasendo was also the chosen route back in the Edo period when the daughter of a nobleman in Kyoto traveled to Edo to marry the shogun, I've speculated that there might be some kind of connection with that. But it's beyond me to try to delve into the question any further."

The heat of the day had ruined his appetite, he said, putting the lid back on his barely half-eaten lunch. Then he got to his feet and walked up the tracks to the tunnel that started a short distance from the end of the bridge. A fence had been placed across the opening to keep people out. As a matter of fact, the bridge and the abandoned tracks were supposed to be off limits, too. My uncle stood in front of the barrier peering into the darkness of the tunnel for a time.

"You seem to be a big eater," he said when he returned.

"Not especially," I said.

"Your parents are worried about you, you know. You skip school, your grades have taken a dive, and now they say you're hanging out with a bunch of new-left radicals."

I felt like I'd been sideswiped. This was about the last thing I'd expected to hear from my uncle here. It had always been a bit vague why he'd invited me to join him in his retreat. My parents had told me he was bored being by himself and wanted my company. He took a lot of flak from other members of the family for being a pleasure seeker (especially of the female-companionship variety) and for his affectations (he'd been spending his spare time since returning to Japan reading mysteries in English), but their real complaint was that he spent so little time with them. Yet for some reason he got along well with my father, who was his next-oldest brother.

"You don't have to look at me like that," my uncle said. "I'm not here to chew your ear off. I played hooky a good bit in my day, too."

Except that, according to my father, no matter how much his younger brother cut out from school to while away the day somewhere else, his grades never fell below the top tier of the class. It aggravated him to no end.

"The thing about the radical group, it's only a friend of a friend who actually belongs. He's trying to get my buddy to join, and he's invited me to go along sometime, too, but I have no intention of getting involved. If anything, I'm putting the brakes on my friend."

"If I'd been invited, I suppose I might have joined. I'm a reckless son-of-a-bitch, and I always liked a good fight."

I didn't smile. In fact, I think I was probably looking pretty peeved. The truth is, I was disappointed. Even though neither of us had ever put it into words, I'd always felt that there was a special bond between him and me. Had my parents actually sent me to see him so he could warn me off the student radicals and lecture me about school? I didn't want to believe it.

"Last year I gave you those books by Oe and Mailer, remember? If they had anything to do with turning you on to the anti-war movement, then I have to consider myself partly responsible."

"Hardly. And besides, remember that book of Tsutsui's sci-fi stories you gave me when I was in junior high? The title story was "The Vietnam Tourist Bureau." When I lent it to a friend recently, he came back fuming about the way it took the war so lightly. I may be against America being in Vietnam, but I still liked that story. That's the way I am, and that's why I don't think I'd ever fit in with those student radicals."

"Come to think of it, I gave you the Marquis de Sade, too, didn't I? I remember your father getting all heated up that I was letting you have such kinky stuff to read."

"I liked that, too. Seems like you have some pretty offbeat tastes in literature. Do all your friends at work read the same kind of stuff?"

"Some do, I guess, but I'd say we're the exceptions. And actually, the only reason I read Oe and Mailer was so I could hold up my end of the conversation with the college girl I was dating at the time. I still like science fiction, though, even now."

My heart grew a little lighter.

He stood up and patted the back of his pants, then started toward the tunnel again.

"Come and have a look," he said.

I stood shoulder to shoulder with him in front of the fence, gazing into the abandoned tunnel. A cool stream of air came out of the blackness and washed over us. I could feel the heavy moisture in the air, like standing by a large pond in the dead of winter. The darkness was deep; the light of day was cut off just inside the entrance, and it was impossible to make out anything beyond.

"I guess there's nothing much to see," I said.

"No, that's not true. If you look real hard, you'll start to see something. Just keep on looking. You'll see a face with big, wide-open eyes staring back at you, not moving a muscle."

"Stop trying to scare me. The other end of the tunnel is blocked off just like this, right?"

"I was up here last week, too. I saw the face then. Today it seems to be hiding for some reason, but I know it's there. I can feel it."

"I don't believe in ghost stories," I said, trying to brush it off as a joke.

He turned to look at me, and gave me the happiest smile I'd seen on his face all day.

He raised his right hand toward the cavernous tunnel. Starting with a fist, he opened his hand, closed it, then opened it again before lowering it to his side.

"Let's go," he said, turning on his heel and striding away without waiting for a response. I hurried after him.

"Did you actually see it?" I asked as soon as I'd caught up.

"No, it doesn't matter," he said dismissively, then went on in a different tone. "Look, Yuki, there's something I want to tell you about. But you might have gotten the wrong idea, so first I need to get one thing straight. I'm the one who originally wanted you to come visit me here. When I called about that, your dad started grousing about the school stuff, so I agreed to mention it once. As far as I'm concerned, what I said a while ago fulfills that promise."

The heaviness I'd been feeling in my chest now lifted completely. I listened eagerly to what followed.

"I have something far more interesting to say, though. It's possible you'll only be annoyed by it, but it's something I need to tell you in any case. You see, I'm the one who brought you into this world . . . You're as much my boy as anybody's—the only son of a confirmed bachelor. I have no intention of ever marrying, and I don't expect to ever father a child. I should warn you, though: there is no moral to the story I'm about to tell."

Before going on, he pinched the top of his left ear between the thumb and forefinger of his left hand.

My uncle was a little surprised when he realized that he wasn't the least bit surprised to run into Rieko Kashiwagi at London's King's Cross Station. They simply began talking as naturally as if they'd met by arrangement in one of Tokyo's own major terminals. For her part, Rieko seemed no more amazed at the chance encounter than he was.

When fate takes you in its grip, he said, the world shrinks to the size of a remote one-room schoolhouse, and you invariably run into the person you're meant to meet. That's just how the world works, apparently.

The woman had in fact come to England to see him. But it had been by pure chance that the two had run into each other at that particular time and place. He had come to the station to see a client off on the train, while she had come to retrieve something from the lost and found.

"I already saw you once," he told her, saying with complete confidence that she'd ridden a train across the famous Glenfinnan Viaduct on the West Highland Line at such-and-such a time on such-and-such a date.

Rieko had a habit of wrinkling her brow and closing her eyes when she stopped to think. My uncle was very fond of the expression that came over her face at times like that. But in this case, he didn't get to see the expression for long, since she almost instantly recognized the date and time my uncle had named as exactly matching her itinerary.

"Your train was crossing the viaduct way off in the distance, but I could see you plain as day, right down to the dismal look on your face. The guy with me insisted I couldn't possibly have made anyone out from so far away. After all, even the windows on the train were only tiny dots. But I was absolutely positive you were on that train, and that's why I wasn't surprised at all to bump into you here today."

"I was depressed, and I came to England for a change of air, hoping it would lift me out of the doldrums, but traveling to Scotland only made it worse. Even the old lady sitting across from me wanted to know if I was all right. But I couldn't very well tell her that I thought her country's scenery was just too gloomy, could I? Even if it was the truth."

Neither the encounter at King's Cross Station, nor his tale of having seen her on the train seemed to faze Rieko in the least. My uncle, on the other hand, was beginning to lose his calm.

If there was one woman in all the world he'd been wishing he could see, it was her. Midway through his thirties, he had fallen totally and passionately in love. For the first time in his life, the thought of marriage began tugging at his mind, and he actually wondered if he might be going mad. But when he stopped to really think, he realized it wasn't that he particularly objected to marriage or didn't like children; it was just that in the course of enjoying himself as a bachelor so much and for so long, he'd fallen into the habit of assuming he simply wasn't meant to marry. With this new perspective, he continued to see her and was preparing to pop the question, when Rieko breathed into his ear one day, "Let's kill ourselves together."

"How long were you in Scotland?" my uncle asked.

"A week. It's a dreadful place."

My uncle was very fond of Scotland. Not for its landscapes so much as its people, with their simple, slightly skewed charm. So he opened his mouth to defend the place to Rieko, but found himself saying something quite different.

"Then why didn't you call me?"

Rieko smiled a wicked smile but said nothing. He felt his blood rising.

The next instant, he had grabbed her hand and begun to walk. Her first instinct was to drag her feet, but before long she had fallen into step. Her hand firmly returned his grip.

"Don't be silly. I was traveling with my husband," she said with amusement. "Didn't your telescopic vision show you that?"

"All I could see was you. I suppose my ability to see is limited what I *want* to see."

"Actually, you're right: on that particular day I was by myself. I mean, our trip was nothing but whiskey distilleries, one after the other—can you believe it? I'd had my fill of that, so I took one day off for myself."

"You said before that you came here to see me. Now you tell me you're traveling with your husband?"

My uncle shook his hand loose from hers. They both stopped short in the middle of the sidewalk.

"That's what I said, and I meant it. My most important reason for coming to England was to see you. And I already had the day scheduled when we would meet. It wasn't the day I was on the train, and it wasn't today."

"It wasn't today? But here we are."

They gazed silently into each other's eyes. The same wicked smile reappeared on her face. The smile reminded him of the moment when they'd parted back in Japan, and he felt as if his heart were being pierced by a thousand needles.

He had not been all that shocked when Rieko said, "Let's kill ourselves together." You'll find people who say things like that in any era—both men and women.

"Let's not," he'd brushed it off lightly.

"If you won't die with me, then at least you have to kill me," she said, a note of urgency creeping into her voice, even as a placid smile continued to hover about her lips. "My husband found out about us. He told me I had to break it off, or else . . ."

She drew her right forefinger across her neck. Then, once she was satisfied by the look of horror she had elicited, she added, "Don't worry, I'm just kidding. My husband wouldn't stoop to murder. He's not that type."

"I didn't even know you were married."

Rieko simply gazed back at him and said nothing. She was still smiling that same smile—a smile that was like a thousand needles stabbing him in the heart. His heart screamed.

She had dropped hints more than once that there might be another man with whom her relationship went beyond mere dating. But he had pretended not to notice, or simply changed the subject. Since his younger days, it had always been his rule to ignore any complications the woman he was with might try to bring up. By now it was a reflex. He assumed Rieko would allow him to carry on in the same way with her. But the moment the word "husband" fell from her lips, he instinctively drew a step back.

He told her about an involvement he'd had with a married woman in the past. In his youthful recklessness, he'd thought such an affair, too, might be exciting, and for that reason alone had forged ahead. The upshot was that he had hurt both the woman and her family in essentially irrecoverable ways. He'd sworn he would never do such a thing again.

His voice grew softer and softer until finally he fell silent. As he gazed at Rieko's smile, the words had simply stopped coming. He could see all the sadness and anger that lay beneath the surface of that smile. He dropped his head.

"I'm sorry," he heard Rieko say.

When he raised his head again, she was already far away. He called after her, but she did not turn. A short time later, he was transferred to London.

Rieko wiped the smile from her lips.

"The stations in England all smell like rusty iron. Don't you find it oppressive?"

My uncle tilted his head and thought for a moment. "I've never really noticed," he said.

He took her hand again and led her toward his Cortina Lotus parked along the curb. This time she didn't drag her feet—though she made no special effort to match his step, either.

As he was fumbling in his coat pocket for his keys, a vehicle pulled to a stop nearby. He looked up to see a silver Jaguar Mark X like the one he used when chauffeuring clients around town, and thought for a moment that the driver had come to pick him up by mistake. Just as he was about to tell the driver he could go on home because he had his own car, he realized the man at the wheel was a stranger.

Rieko walked toward the Jaguar.

"We're not done talking," he called after her.

Without turning around, Rieko simply raised her right arm and waggled her fingers.

"When exactly is it that we're supposed to meet?"

With the precise, efficient movements characteristic of all British chauffeurs, the heavy-set driver got out and hurried around the car to open the door.

"This coming Friday evening," she said, turning to look at him before getting in. "You're off on Saturday, right?"

"I'd have to look at my calendar."

"We're staying with a friend in Hampstead, and I want you to come there. The friend and my husband will be gone on Friday and Saturday, so I'll be alone."

He said nothing.

"I was thinking I'd call you at the office. Is that all right?" she said, sounding much less sure of herself.

My uncle let out his breath before saying, "I can't think why not."

When Ryo got home at half past seven on New Year's morning, I was still sound asleep. There was a bit of a flare-up between her and her mother at the front door, however, and the sound of their jagged-edged voices penetrated deep enough into my consciousness to pull me from the depths of my slumber. But I apparently decided not to let them wake me all the way: since I was not in full command of my mental faculties at the moment anyway, I would surely be spared charges of nonfeasance.

But when I finally did get out of bed a little after nine and emerged into the dining room laid with the red lacquer tableware reserved for New Year's, I felt pangs of guilt. I knew my wife had prepared the traditional holiday delicacies all by herself, starting several days before, and she obviously wouldn't have had any help getting things set out that morning either. In the past, Ryo had always lent a hand. She routinely balked at being asked to pitch in around the house the rest of the year, but at New Year's she had always helped her mother without a peep.

"So Ryo didn't get back till this morning?"

"Right," Asako answered curtly. I sensed that she was angry not only with our daughter, but with my own failure to rouse myself earlier as well.

She reported that Ryo had come in shivering and coughing and breezily announced, "We wound up doing karaoke all night. Sorry." It did constitute an apology of sorts, but the girl's casual manner had rubbed her the wrong way and made her snap at her.

My wife placed our three-tiered lacquerware box containing the traditional foods in the middle of the table and asked me to go wake our daughter.

I knocked on her door and said, "Time to get up, Ryo." There was no answer.

Hanging from the knob was a "Do not disturb" sign she had picked up somewhere. Even though the door had no lock, I was reluctant to open it uninvited.

Despite failing to respond to my knock, Ryo came downstairs before all the final items were in place. With her hair mussed up and rubbing sleep from her eyes, she asked if there was anything she could do.

"Go fix your hair," was her mother's reply.

Ryo did as she was told. I went to the bathroom to shave. As I slipped past her in the hallway when she came back down from her room, I said, "Let's talk later," but she again gave no response.

The three of us sat down together in our usual places. After formally wishing each other a Happy New Year, we sipped our spiced sake and dipped into our celebratory rice-cake soup. Eating our first meal like this was the only family ritual we had for bringing in the new year. We had no custom of going to a shrine together, or making calls on anyone, or receiving any visitors in our home. Ryo's grandparents on both sides had died before the new millennium, so neither my wife nor I had parental homes to visit anymore. This was our family's "parental home" now.

"Mom's New Year's cooking is really good, isn't it?" Ryo said, taking a kelp roll from one of the tiered boxes and placing it on the small plate in front of her. "Though her usual cooking is good, too."

"Yeah," I agreed. "It's a shame we're the only three who get to enjoy it."

"Remember when I was little and we went to Grandma's for New Year's and Auntie and Uncle and my cousins came? Did you do the cooking those times, too?"

"I wonder which of your grandmothers you mean," Asako said. "If it was my mother, then I did help cook."

Ryo cocked her head as she tried to remember. The family tradition of getting together for New Year's had lasted until about ten years ago, but her memories of it had apparently grown faint. After all, ten years for her was two-thirds of a lifetime.

"You can butter me up all you want, but we're still not done talking about last night," her mother said. I suspected this was intended more as a reminder to me than to our daughter.

"I didn't mean it that way," Ryo said, pursing her lips in a pointy pout. Her lips actually stuck out past the tip of her nose. She was a good-looking girl, if I say so myself, but she had a rather flat nose—a trait both she and my wife blamed on me.

"I'd rather not speak ill of my mother after she's gone, but I don't think I ever thought the foods she filled her lacquer boxes with were particularly good," I said. "Her rice-cake soup is the only thing I remember looking forward to."

"Oh, but they were all very good," Asako disagreed. "Though her recipes were totally different from my family's."

"But even apart from how they tasted, everything just looked so drab, you know. So the lid would come off and all you'd feel is gloomy. Our boxes look much more festive, and I like that."

"But I think originally the things people made for New Year's were probably more like your mother's. They weren't supposed to be fancy. They were an offering to the god of the new year, and the main consideration was that they keep for several days without spoiling."

It was just the three of us, but the conversation continued to be livelier than usual around the table. Feeling in a good mood, I got out a bottle of expensive sake I'd received as a year-end gift and started drinking.

All too soon, I looked up to find my wife washing dishes in the kitchen and my daughter gone from the table.

Tonk tonk tonk . . . I heard quick, rhythmical footsteps on the stairs, then caught a glimpse of Ryo with a white down jacket in her arms shuffling past the crack in the dining room door toward the front foyer.

"Going somewhere?" I called after her without getting up.

"I'm supposed to meet a friend."

The front door closed with a bang.

My wife emerged from the kitchen and gave me a look.

"I told her I wanted to talk to her, but it looks like she got away," I said. "I guess I let down my guard."

"She's so irresponsible. Doesn't it make you mad?" she said.

"More disappointed than mad."

"You're too easy on her."

"Not really," I said.

"Way too easy," she told me emphatically.

I sat in the living room flipping through the New Year's cards we'd received, but I was mostly thinking about my daughter. Asako was reading New Year's cards, too.

Where had Ryo been all night? On the street in Shibuya? In a corner of some dark nightclub with blaring music? In a friend's apartment, or worse, a room in some crowded love hotel? . . . Wherever it had been, it was somewhere beyond my reach.

Where oh where have you gone, dear Ryo?

I don't have the first idea. But wherever it may be, Ryo, I assume it's a place with no grown-ups in it. Kids your age live in a world that pits one generation against the other. In this corner, all of us grown-ups; in the other, all of you not-yet-grown-ups. It's a world where grown-up rules don't apply. Maybe what you're really looking for is somewhere with no rules at all. But even your separate world cut off from grown-ups can't exist without rules. No matter how far you run, you can't get away from them. *That's the problem with grown-ups*, I can hear you scoffing. *Always so negative.* Unfortunately, we older people have no idea what your rules are. After all, we can't even see this separate place you've gone running off to. That's one thing you can set your mind at ease about. But just because we can't see it, doesn't mean we don't realize it exists . . .

"It seems like we get more cards every year," my wife said, interrupting my thoughts.

"Mmm," I grunted, unable to shift gears quickly.

She gave me a quizzical look.

"I was thinking about what I need to say to Ryo," I explained, even though she hadn't asked.

"So what've you decided?"

"Like I said, I'm still thinking about it."

She said nothing for a moment, then returned to the previous subject. "Why do you suppose we keep getting more and more cards?"

"Probably because business is good. Back when I quit my old job, we got a whole lot less all of a sudden. People are basically mercenary."

"I'm sure there's that," she said as if I'd missed the point, "but your business is on the Web. They talk about how people are switching to electronic greetings and not sending so many regular cards anymore, but we're actually getting more."

"That's true. But I guess for people in my line of work, e-mail is something you use all the time, day in and day out, so it doesn't seem quite proper for New Year's greetings. Actually, my money's on the world at large switching back to regular cards, too. Not that my prognostications count for anything."

I realized I hadn't checked my e-mail yet in the new year. I went to my room and opened my laptop to find a dozen or so e-greetings waiting for me, most of them no more substantial than a traditional card. I glanced through them, composing replies where necessary, and when I pushed the button to send them all off, a new message arrived. It had been sent from a cell phone and displayed no sender's name or subject:

> I'm not avoiding you. I honestly had to meet someone. Tell Mom, too.

Hmph. So I'm just a messenger between her and Mom? I tapped out a curt reply:

> Where are you?

The moment I hit the SEND button, all the things I needed to say to her began swirling through my mind. I wished I could talk to her right then and there.

I went back to the living room, where my wife had the morning paper spread in front of her.

"Can we talk a minute?" I said. She looked up from her paper. "I got a message from Ryo. She asked me to tell you she's not avoiding us. And I think I've figured out what I'm going to say to her."

My uncle pulled his Cortina Lotus up to the curb in Hampstead and gently revved the engine before turning off the ignition. It had been misfiring quite a bit more lately, so he made a mental note to adjust the carburetor on Sunday. As he took in the stately home surrounded by a thick wall and neck-wrenchingly tall trees, he wondered if he would reemerge from the place unscathed. He had a premonition that he was entering the house at his own peril—a premonition that was in fact borne out by events—but he'd come this far and he had no intention of turning back, no matter what the consequences.

It being summer, the sky was still light at eight o'clock. He pressed the bell on the gate thinking about all the times he'd been deceived by Rieko. Perhaps "deceived" was too strong a word. He hadn't known she was over thirty or married because she hadn't looked it, on either count, but since he was the one who had jumped to conclusions, he could hardly pin the blame on her. Of course, to the extent that she knew he was getting the wrong impression and chose not to correct it, she clearly wasn't being straight with him, so she wasn't entirely innocent either. The funny thing was, the more he learned about the differences between the way she appeared on the outside and the woman she was on the inside, the more deeply he fell under her spell.

To his surprise, Rieko herself emerged from the house to open the gate. Even if it was true that her husband was away, he had expected to be greeted by a butler.

"Welcome," she said with a rather formal-looking smile. She didn't meet his eyes again.

My uncle was expecting dinner—a reasonable assumption, given the hour for which he'd been invited. And even if this was some kind of trap in which her husband was set to return home unexpectedly, surely that would come only after a certain interval had passed, with sufficient time to eat a meal first. But there was to be no such delay.

The lights abruptly went out, and the entire house fell dark.

"Where are you?" my uncle called out to her in the blackness.

She failed to reply.

After a brief time, his eyes began to adjust. It was not a total darkness. A small amount of outside light filtered through the blinds covering the windows high on the wall in the entrance hall. He could now make out Rieko's silhouette. She stood ramrod straight and motionless, as if every joint in her body had been bolted tightly in place.

"What's going on? Is it a power outage?"

She still said nothing.

A single tiny light came on some distance away. It was at the apex of a long, narrow triangle with the line between my uncle and Rieko as its base. They both stepped toward it as if under its spell.

From my uncle's perspective, it appeared to be shining at the far end of a corridor. But when they had traversed about half the distance to it, his shoulder bumped into what felt like a doorjamb. While he was regaining his bearings, Rieko moved on through the doorway. He followed her into the room, and suddenly a bright light came on behind him.

He spun around in surprise, but at the same instant the door swung shut. He heard something heavy fall into place with a *thud* on the other side.

As if to escape the darkness that closed in on him again, he pivoted back to face the tiny beacon that had drawn them into the room. Rieko was now standing beside the light. He saw that it was at the head of a large bed covered in white sheets.

"My husband wants to play a little game," she said. The bulb was positioned too low for him to see her face.

"A game?"

"He didn't tell me what the game would involve. This is as far as I know—that you and I were to be locked into this room together. It's built to keep any light from getting in and any sound from getting out. Which I guess makes it perfect either for watching movies or for unlawful detention."

"So you're telling me you agreed not only to lure me here under false pretenses, but to let yourself be locked up with me too? I don't get it. I'm sure you're aware that holding a person against his will is a crime. If I press charges . . . Or am I maybe never going to see the light of day again?"

He circled the room in the darkness, pounding on the doors and walls. Needless to say, the door through which they had entered would not budge, and neither would any of the windows. The one door that opened led into a bathroom. There was another small lightbulb in there.

"I don't think it'll be never. But I don't think you'll file charges, either. I'm a full partner in the crime."

A phone rang. It was not far from the light at the head of the bed, but it sat in darkness. Rieko picked it up. She stood listening to the caller, saying nothing of her own. The yellow circle of light reached halfway up her cheek. My uncle had never seen her look so solemn.

"Your turn," said Rieko, holding the handset out to him.

It seemed he was now about to make the acquaintance of the woman's husband. Calling in secret instructions over the phone was a device straight out of low-budget spy films. Whatever cockamamie scheme the man had in mind, he was apparently also someone of distinctly lowbrow taste and imagination.

He let out a deep breath before taking the phone.

"Hello?"

This was answered immediately by an odd *ka-chunk* sound, followed by a voice saying, "Welcome. So you really came."

It was a recording. The *ka-chunk* had been the sound of a reel-to-reel tape recorder being set in motion. The voice was not a young one. A man in his fifties or sixties, perhaps . . . ?

"You're quite a remarkable fellow. You made my wife fall head over heels in love with you. But lest your head swell up too much, let me hasten to add that Rieko is also in love with me. Why else would she agree to go to such lengths for me? I'm the one who asked her to bring you here."

The speaker on the tape paused to clear his throat with a little cough.

"I have no intention of keeping you confined here forever. Simply satisfy my conditions, and you'll be able to leave as early as tomorrow. I don't think you'll find those conditions too onerous. Basically, I want you to make love with Rieko three times in this room. Heh heh. Not a bad deal, eh? The penalty for sleeping with another man's wife is to sleep with her some more. Seems too good to be true, doesn't it? . . . So I decided to add a rider to this requirement. Here's what it is. Just making love to her isn't going to be enough; you have to truly satisfy her three times. As I'm sure you are well aware, Rieko is quite a connoisseur of lovemaking. Run-of-the-mill isn't going to do it for her. I expect you to bring her to such heights of pleasure that she thinks she's going to slip away, body and soul, from this earth. The judge of your success will be yours truly. The room is wired with microphones so that I can hear every sound, every cry of rapture. It is also equipped with a small peephole.

"Once you've earned three approvals, I will allow you to leave. But you can never see my wife again after that. If you do, the consequences for both of you will be far worse than this. At any rate, for the time being, Rieko will remain with you until you've brought her to the peak of ecstasy three times. As you can see, I'm a generous man. I have arranged for the two of you to enjoy a final lovers' tryst."

The voice fell silent for a few moments, but he could still hear the reels spooling on the tape recorder. There was another little cough, and then the voice resumed.

"Should you fail to transport her to these heights, I will still release you after, well, let's say two weeks. Though by that time I imagine your standing at work will have suffered from being absent so long without notice. You might even get fired. If you wish to ensure against that, then I suggest you begin pleasuring her without delay.

"For my part, I don't exactly have an unlimited amount of time to be keeping tabs on the two of you. With that in mind, though I regret that it has to be this way, the only provisions I've placed in the room are a single box of McVitie's Biscuits and three bottles of mineral water. Your supply of these items will not be replenished. Except for the toilet itself, the water to the bathroom has been shut off. I'm being a terrible host, I know, but in my own way I mean it kindly, as an incentive for you to complete your assignment quickly, before hunger overcomes you. I hope you understand."

The phone went dead.

"This is insane!" my uncle yelled at the top of his lungs. "What do you think you're trying to do? I'm not some common slob with time on his hands to play stupid games like this! I know you can hear me. If you don't let me out of here right now—"

"Stop it!" Rieko cut him off. "Screaming and shouting won't do you any good."

She was perched on the edge of the bed looking at him. He walked over and sat down beside her.

"There's no way I'm going along with anything like this. This isn't funny."

The room was too dark to be able to really see her face, even at close range. But he could hear her calm and rhythmical breathing.

"So you don't care no matter what your husband does to you, or makes you do?"

"I wouldn't say I don't care. But I can accept it."

"The man's obviously touched in the head."

"And so am I," she said. "Almost as much."

He put his arm around her and pulled her to him.

"Have I ever made you feel like you were slipping completely away before?" he whispered in her ear.

She shifted her head and kissed him on the lips. "You really don't remember?" she asked, looking him in the eye.

Instead of answering, he pressed his lips to hers. He thought he heard a light cough somewhere in the distance.

The chocolate cake was supposed to be for when all three of us were present, but Asako cut two pieces and brought them to the living room along with two cups of tea.

"So, here's how—"

"Wait!" she said. "Give me just one second, will you?"

I waited for her to settle into her easy chair before opening my mouth again.

"Here's how I plan to begin. As we're growing up, we all have to learn a lot of different rules."

My wife picked up her fork and broke off the tip of the cake before responding. "You say that as if you're talking about people in general, not just Ryo or yourself. Sounds pretty heavy, right off the bat."

"Yeah, maybe. In the course of growing up, we all have all sorts of rules drilled into us—though in Ryo's case, you and I were on the side doing the drilling. Use the potty when you have to pee or poop, take a bath, put on your socks, listen to your mom and dad, don't go anywhere with strangers, go to school, don't be late . . . and so on and so forth. But by the time we've actually internalized most of the basic rules, we generally also realize that we don't have to follow all of them all of the time. We can spend our money on candy if Mom and Dad aren't around, and we can share homework so long as the teacher's not looking. But that doesn't make the rules meaningless. Because by then we also understand that some rules are bigger and more important than all the routine little stuff. And we realize we can't just casually break those bigger rules the way we can the smaller ones—nor would we ever want to."

"Are you talking about crimes? Like no one should kill another person?"

"That's part of it, yes, but what I'm really trying to get at here is rules about rules. Which is not to say I'm going to bring up God, or philosophy, or launch into a discourse on ethics. Dealing with stuff like that is way over my head. I figure I'll limit myself to the context of school.

"School's a pretty complicated place. You've got the teachers who are there to teach and the students who are there to learn, all thrown together in this big group, of course, and needing to get along, yet also competing with each other; and the individual faces may change from year to year but the school remains the same school. It has lots and lots of rules, stretching like spiderwebs over the entire place. The students do their best to avoid being trapped in those webs, sometimes following the rules, sometimes breaking them, relying on their wits to get them safely through the school day. And it's actually pretty much the same for the teachers—except that they're also supposed to be providing guidance to the kids in their charge. Needless to say, since the teachers are the ones who dictate the rules, the students expect them to hold to a higher standard. But by the time they get to junior high, most of them have lost the illusion that their teachers always obey the rules. A teacher grousing before the starting bell that he got caught in a speed trap for going twenty kilometers over the limit is just something to laugh about. But if he lies to them, or shows blatant favoritism, or is himself lax in following the strict standards he's laid down for them, then they feel betrayed, they get angry, maybe even feel like giving up. Because then the teacher isn't just breaking an ordinary rule; he's breaking one of the rules that allow the other rules to function.

"So let's look at what happened to Ryo. I think it's clear that her teacher violated the basic principle of fair and impartial treatment for all."

I popped two bites of cake into my mouth, and followed them with three sips of tea.

"Fair? . . . Impartial? . . ." My wife looked skeptical about the direction this was taking.

"I suppose bringing up terms like that makes me sound like some by-the-book class president or something. But this is actually very crucial. I think probably for the at-risk kids, too. If all the smaller rules at school are going to work, they have to be backed up by a meta-rule that all rules will be applied fairly and impartially. I mean, if some teacher insists everybody else has to be in their seats by eight-thirty but tells you he thinks you're cute so you don't have to come in till noon, well, it would soon lead to chaos, right? Arbitrarily bending a rule violates everybody's sense of fair play, and giving special treatment to a student you like violates the principle of impartiality.

"Fairness and impartiality aren't objective measures you can enforce from the outside, like rules about being on time. They're abstractions that you have to have a personal commitment to, and that you hope others will have a commitment to, too, because they're universal, I think. That's probably what makes violations of rules about rules seem worse than breaking ordinary rules.

"So, back to Ryo. I've been thinking a lot about that art teacher, Mr. Agata. Fairness and impartiality in evaluating paintings isn't as straightforward as judging who's late for school. We don't have an objective or absolute standard for measuring the quality of a painting the way we can measure punctuality by looking at a clock. That doesn't mean there are no standards at all. No one would say Da Vinci's *Mona Lisa* and some kindergartner's drawing of her mother are equal—at least not in the world we live in now. So anyway, when there are no absolute standards to go by, it makes it extremely difficult to render fair and impartial judgments. But if you ask me, that only makes what Agata did all the more reprehensible—he ran Ryo's paintings down knowing he could get away with it because there are no absolute standards. And I have to say, I'm pretty damn angry about it. But let's not get into my personal feelings for the moment; let's consider his reasons for treating Ryo so unfairly."

"Reasons? Don't you think he just didn't like the fact that a girl who'd been trained by someone else did better work? Why should you have to go into all this convoluted rules-about-rules stuff?"

"Sure, that's got to be part of it. But I want to dig a bit deeper. I mean, this is a man who violated a rule about rules, right? He doesn't seem to have much respect for the principles of fairness and impartiality. So, does that make him a bad apple, a law unto himself? I'm actually not inclined to think so. He's worked year after year at a girls' school with tight discipline, and in each of those years a number of his graduating seniors have been accepted into leading art institutions, so I have to believe that he's in fact a pretty competent teacher. I imagine he's well regarded by the school's administration, too.

"The first reason for his behavior that comes to mind is self-preservation. If the work produced by a student who came in at the high school level—and from the public system at that—is superior to that of the pupils he's had under him since seventh grade, it calls into question the effectiveness of his teaching. But do I think he callously threw fairness and impartiality out the window and hurt Ryo purely to protect himself? Whatever role that may have played, I'm not convinced it's the whole story.

"Most people don't like to think of themselves as acting entirely out of self-interest. If you knowingly hurt someone else in order to benefit yourself, you're a bastard. But it's actually not all that easy to be a real bastard. I imagine it's just about as hard as keeping to the straight and narrow through life's never-ending storms—though obviously I'm only guessing, since I've never had to do anything so bad that I'd deserve a label like that. Maybe it's easier and more fun than I realize. At any rate, let's posit for the moment that Agata is not an out-and-out bastard. We then have to assume he must have found a reason that, at least to his mind, justified his ignoring the principles of fairness and impartiality. That's what I've been trying to ferret out.

"And after puzzling over what could have motivated him to hurt Ryo the way he did without a second thought, the only thing I've been able to come up with is . . . love. Needless to say, I'm not talking about love for Ryo."

"Love? . . . What could you possibly mean?"

Rieko and my uncle took off their clothes and folded them, then placed them under the bed. My uncle still had his watch on; it was a habit of his never to remove it except when taking a bath. He took Rieko's hand and drew her to him.

In the darkness, all too aware of the faceless man listening in, he lay in a naked embrace with the woman of his longings. But it could hardly have felt less like a dream come true. It did not feel real at all. The thought that Rieko might somehow actually be dead took hold of him, and he began to wonder if perhaps he, too, without being aware of it, had joined the ranks of the deceased. He pressed his ear to her chest.

He heard her heart beating.

As they gently moved their hands over each other's bodies, a light flush of perspiration rose on Rieko's skin and softened it beneath his touch. It was as if an invisible barrier separating them until that moment had melted away. Their senses became heightened, bringing them new pleasures with every movement they made. The proof was in each lingering touch of his finger or tongue to her warm, moist parts. Her gentle moans grew louder. She was breathing with every muscle in her body. He entered her first from behind, then, as he neared the brink, reentered her from in front. The mattress on the bed was apparently quite old and bounced like a choppy sea; the frame creaked like the timbers of an old sailing ship tossing in a storm. He hesitated. Should he simply push on to his climax now? But before he had time to decide either way, he felt himself being drawn up into an immense swell of pleasure. As if sucked uncontrollably into a dark, distant place, he began to ejaculate. The ejaculation and the thrill of climax seemed to extend on and on, beyond anything he had ever imagined, refusing to let him go.

The phone rang.

Rieko's body quivered at the startling sound, and she slowly pulled away. He felt another surge of pleasure pulse through him.

"Yes?" she answered, her voice husky. She turned to pass the phone to him, her hand trembling. It took him another moment to catch his breath.

"Very good." The man's voice sounded dark and sunken. "Rieko seems to have been utterly delighted. So I approve. You've cleared the first hurdle."

My uncle realized that he was silently congratulating himself over the man's assessment and felt a twinge of shame. But any relief he felt was immediately blown away by the man's next words.

"I must say, though, that it was all thoroughly conventional. Your technique lacked any originality or highlights. It was an acceptable first effort, but I'll certainly be expecting more the next time. You need to take it to another level."

The phone went dead before my uncle could open his mouth to reply.

Rieko lay uncovered on her stomach, her shoulders still gently heaving. He reached over to stroke her hair.

"He called it good. But he also said I didn't show any originality, and he won't be so easy on me next time. I actually thought it was pretty darn amazing myself."

"Oh, dear," Rieko said with a heavy sigh.

My uncle slowly slid his right forefinger along the line of bumps formed by her spine. When his finger reached her waist, a shudder ran up her back. He felt ready to tackle the next round right away.

"Let me catch my breath a bit," she said, heading him off before he could get too aroused again.

He opened one of the bottles of water and took a swig, then passed it to her. Feeling suddenly hungry, he downed two McVitie's biscuits. They weren't the sort of thing he wanted to keep eating one after the other. When he offered the box to Rieko, she said she didn't need any yet. They both drifted off to sleep for a time.

When he awoke, he found himself still in the same darkened room lit only by a single tiny light. As soon as he began stirring, Rieko opened her eyes, too. He reached out with his left hand to touch her cheek.

"Take your watch off," she said.

"Huh?" He had forgotten he even had it on.

"It digs into my skin and hurts."

After removing the timepiece from his wrist, he wound it up, then swung his arm over his head to lay it on the shelf at the top of the bed. But when he let go, it fell into the space between the shelf and the headboard instead.

Rolling over on top of Rieko's back, he began making love to her a second time. He decided he would give special attention to the erogenous zones he had discovered—or rediscovered—the first time around. He took his time, and she guided him with suggestions as well, but for some reason they failed to reach the same pinnacles of excitement.

The phone rang.

"I'm afraid not. That didn't cut it at all," her husband said. Then he began playing back a tape of their efforts, accompanying it with a commentary on all the ways in which they had come up short, like a teacher correcting a student's paper.

My uncle ate another McVitie's. Rieko took a drink of the bottled water.

"What can I do?" she asked.

"No, this is my responsibility." My responsibility? Listen to me! Good grief!

They made love two more times in relatively quick succession, but failed to gain a favorable verdict in either case. The man offered his critique of what my uncle was doing wrong each time—in minute detail. Concentrating on technique was not bringing them to a climax that surpassed the first. My uncle's self-esteem was taking a beating.

As he began yet another attempt, he found at first that his heart wasn't really in it. But then to his surprise, as he continued to kiss her and caress her body, his fingers began to pick up a different kind of response, stronger than before. Soon he had abandoned himself to instinct, and let himself melt into the flow of whatever heightened their mutual pleasure. As she drew him onto her and he began gently thrusting his hips, he felt himself being ushered in deeper and deeper with every movement she made, until he rose to a climax that seemed to lift him body and soul into the air. She let out a cry. A wordless cry of ecstasy. And in that moment, it was as if every last barrier that stood between them had vanished.

The phone remained silent. Not wanting to let each other go, the lovers remained in each other's arms and drifted off to sleep. They began making love again in their dreams.

Finally the phone rang. Rieko didn't move, so my uncle picked it up.

"I nodded off, so I've been listening to the tape." There was a note of fatigue in the man's voice. "It does sound like you made a new breakthrough. So okay, you have your second thumbs-up. Though once again, I'll be expecting you to go even farther next time."

Ka-chunk. The tape began playing. It had captured not only Rieko's cries, but his own voice too, racked in paroxysms of pleasure.

"This part here, this is really very good," the man said with another little cough.

"You're telling me, that the reason Mr. Agata treated Ryo the way he did, had something to do with love?" Like someone treading very carefully on uneven ground, my wife haltingly restated what I had said. "He dished out undeserved criticism, and deeply wounded our daughter, out of love?"

"I've been turning it over and over in my mind, and that's the only answer I can find."

She cocked her head dubiously.

"The problem is, it's a biased love. It's directed at the students he's been teaching from before, and at the art club as a group, and by further extension, at the school as a whole. Being a new transfer student, Ryo was an outsider, beyond the compass of his love. But the man must be a hardened bigot, since even after summer vacation, when the second term started, he still wouldn't treat her as part of the family . . . So it's a narrow-minded and even cruel love that we're talking about here. I think it's probably the kind that's called eros. You learned in high school that there are two kinds of love, right? In ethics class or something?"

She nodded. "There's eros, and there's agape, which is God's love. I think at my school we got that in Bible class."

"It's a pretty odd way of thinking, don't you think—dividing love in two? One's an individual kind of love, deriving from physical desire: eros. Its polar opposite is God's love, which is universal: agape. Making this distinction seems to reflect a view that us mere mortals living here on earth are incapable of universal love. At any rate, agape isn't considered a human attribute. Which implies that human love can't be an all-encompassing thing; it's always directed at a specific other."

"What you're saying reminds me," my wife interrupted, "I read somewhere that love has a negative connotation in Buddhism. I think they see it as becoming too attached."

"I suppose that means they're talking about something closer to eros," I speculated. "But you know, I don't think you can say that's necessarily so bad. For example, suppose Ryo had a lover—it's not really something we want to contemplate yet, but just suppose— then if the guy suddenly said he loved some other girl or girls just as much, you can bet she wouldn't feel very good about it, right? What you want from a lover is eros, not agape. You want exclusive love. A narrow-minded love. It's the eros kind of love that creates a bond between one person and another. And that's what all of human society is built on. Without eros, we'd have no children—or at least it'd be a lot harder to have them.

"Eros is required for people to come together. But there's a major contradiction at play here, because this kind of love creates both a bond and an exclusionary wall. A couple of lovers might not even notice the contradiction, but when it comes to groups, you can have a serious problem. I'm talking about where love for one's group of friends, or club, or school, or community is involved. The largest collective a person can love would seem to be his country. It's probably not just a joke when they say that if we want global love, we'll have to get some extraterrestrials to attack us.

"Saying outright that the collective is created by its enemies would be going too far, but there's an element of truth to it. Groups are defined by a sense of *us* versus *them*. In that context, love is what gives shape to the sense of *us*. But as shown by its bi-asedness, love is divorced from reason. Love alone can't sustain a group. That's because human love can only be directed at a particular other. And these narrow-minded loves inevitably come into conflict. Jealousy and hatred and all the other 'bad' emotions we're so familiar with are probably born out of such contradictions and collisions of love.

"Which means the collective has to find a way to control the jumble of self-interested, haphazard inclinations that arise within the group. It needs traffic laws to regulate the flow of selfish love. You see where I'm going with this?"

My wife thought about it for a few moments.

"You mean what you were talking about before—fairness and impartiality?"

I nodded.

"Love makes the group possible. But if that's all you have, the group will decay and fall apart. In order to endure, it must also be governed by principles of fairness and impartiality. To put it a bit pompously, love is the principle of existence, while fairness and impartiality are the principles of action. In other words, at the most elemental level, the group requires two contradictory forces to coexist within it. A group ungoverned by rules will disintegrate. But a group without love can't survive either."

A foul smell assaulted him when he went into the bathroom, and he immediately recognized it as coming from his own body. My uncle sniffed his armpits. The stink was like a sweaty judo jacket unwashed in six months mixed with the gamey smell of a zoo and the odor of aroused female genitalia.

He sank onto the toilet seat and sat staring blankly into space, forgetting even to urinate. Since winning his second approval by simply letting go, no amount of trying had produced a third success. He was afraid his virility was nearly exhausted, as he found it all but impossible to rise to the next occasion. He had even begun experiencing genuine pain in his penis.

Each time he woke up, he found the same oppressive darkness weighing on him. Knowing he was confined in that darkness with another person made it all the more unpleasant. Perhaps it would have been even worse to be all alone, but when you had company, the other person became a source of repugnance, too. He could tell that Rieko felt the same. He'd noticed how she shrank from his touch, in spite of herself. If their hands brushed against each other as they dozed, they would both reflexively jerk them away.

There was a knock on the bathroom door. He jumped like a child caught red-handed in some mischief.

"I'll be right out," he said.

He expelled his breath before opening the door so he could sniff Rieko as they slipped past each other. Her odor was virtually indistinguishable from his own—utterly disgusting. But it doesn't take long to become inured to a smell. On the other hand, it was nearly impossible to block out the sticky, scuzzy sensation that now occupied every corner of his skin. With no way to even sponge themselves down, there was nothing they could do about the accumulating layers of sweat and grime. He wondered how many days had gone by since they'd entered the room. His sense of time had deserted him. Would he next lose his sense of self?

He heard the toilet flush, and a moment later Rieko opened the door.

"I have an irresistible urge to drink from the toilet," she said.

"We still have some bottled water left."

"I'm tired of getting nothing but little sips. I want to sink my head in the bowl and lap it up in great big gulps."

After emptying the second of their three bottles, they had set tighter limits on how much water they could drink each time, but even so the last bottle was now half gone. They were down to only a few biscuits as well.

"Let's ask your husband for more. Even after what he said, he surely can't like the thought of you drinking from the toilet."

"If we go begging to him, he'll like it all the more. Otherwise, he'd never even be doing something like this."

My uncle fell silent. She had put a cruel reality into words. He knew that he was himself nearing the end of his tether in their present predicament. But it seemed clear to him that Rieko was in an even shakier psychological state. He guessed that it came from some old, deep wound (though he knew scarcely anything about her past), and that that trauma was now being made worse.

She lay down on her side, stretching her body as straight as a rod along the edge of the bed. He picked up the last bottle and held it out to her.

"Go ahead," he said. "Drink as much as you want."

"No thanks," she snapped. "I want to drink from the toilet. And I want to drink your pee."

"There's no need for that yet. If it comes to that later on, you can do it then."

"Will you drink my pee, too?"

"Sure."

He held the bottle out to her again. This time she took it and brought it to her mouth. That's better, he thought, and turned away, but then he heard splashing.

She was pouring the remaining water over her naked body.

"That's such a waste," my uncle said. "Let me lick it up."

Rieko smiled with her eyes like slits—he'd grown so used to the dark by now that he could make out her expression—and slowly rolled over on her back.

She seemed to be extremely ticklish, squirming and squealing beneath the stroke of his tongue. He soon became aroused and quite naturally began moving into foreplay.

But she pushed him away. "Stop it," she said. "I can't stand this anymore. I'm absolutely sick of making love."

"But . . ."

"But what?"

"I don't think we have a choice."

"Don't think we have a choice? Why not? Why should we have to make love? He said he'd let us go anyway, eventually. All we have to do is wait him out. At least we have water, so we're not going to die."

"But this perpetual darkness is really starting to get to me. And besides, even under these circumstances, you still turn me on. It's been great."

"Two grubby bodies grinding against each other endlessly is great? You're just saying that. You just want to get it over with so you can go back to work. You're quaking in your boots that you might be fired—that's what I think. I knew it all along. You weren't thinking about me for a minute. But I tried my best to help you out anyway. I was doing it partly for my husband. Him and his disgusting games. They're the worst. But I play along because he's my husband. And I was doing it partly for you. Because I love you. I milked it for all I was worth. I put on a real good show, all for your sake."

"It was more than just a show," he promptly said.

"Don't be so full of yourself. Men are so delusional. Don't you know we can make it look any way we want. Absolutely any way at all. This body happens to be all mine, I'll have you know."

My uncle listened in silence, but not without feeling a bit wounded.

She rolled over on her side, facing out over the edge of the bed, with her back turned his way. But this didn't mean she was finished talking.

"We get one more trip to heaven, and then it's all over for us, remember? After that, we can never see each other again. Is that what you want?"

He was caught short by the abrupt reversal in her words. But he knew what he had to say.

"Sure we can. Whatever it takes, I don't intend to let this be the end. No way."

"Don't be so naïve. It's simply not possible. This is the end for us, and there's nothing we can do about it."

"I really don't see why not. Unless he means to kill us."

"I don't think he'd do that. But there are worse things, you know. That's why I wanted to die with you before."

"I'm not about to listen to that sort of thing."

"But you should have."

There was silence in the room. He stared at Rieko's back, which she now refused to let him touch: the beautiful, pale-skinned back that soon he might never see again.

He closed his eyes, but he didn't feel the least bit sleepy. Rieko, too, remained wide awake.

"Could you come closer?" she said. "I feel scared."

He slid across the bed until he was all but touching her naked back.

"Scared of what?" he asked.

"Of the darkness. Little by little, day by day—though I have no idea how many days it's actually been—the unbroken darkness gets scarier and scarier."

"I know exactly how you feel. We're both pretty close to the breaking point."

He had a sudden idea and brought his lips up close to Rieko's ear. She twisted her body, trying to pull away. "Stop. That tickles."

"Let's talk," he breathed into her ear. "Let's talk so quietly your husband can't hear."

She stopped trying to squirm away. Instead, she rolled over to face him, and brought her mouth almost near enough to touch his before speaking.

"What about?"

My wife finished her cake and folded her arms across her chest. But I didn't get the sense that she was losing patience with my argument, so I went on.

"The central figure in a thriving group is typically someone who has a surplus of love in him. An erotic personality, you could say, or maybe more aptly, a lech. Any group normally has to put on a good face to the world at large, so at least on a superficial level, even someone like that will treat others properly, both within the group and without. But that's not his true nature; he's merely behaving that way because he knows he has to. The truth is he won't think twice about throwing fairness and impartiality out the window if it's for the sake of love. In fact, that's actually the very source of his appeal.

"People join the group because they're drawn to his loving personality and hope that his love will be directed their way. So any unfair behavior he displays toward someone outside the group raises no objections from insiders. They may even welcome the behavior. Because excluding other people amounts to an expression of love for the group. But soon he shows unfairness within the group as well. To a person who has faith in his own erotic appeal, prevailing standards of right and wrong are easily overridden.

"When his abuse comes to light, he may be criticized by the true believers who take the noble front put up by the group at face value. But this will usually be limited to a small minority. The majority will go along with the excuses he offers, or even willingly aid and abet his offense. Because they don't want to be cast out of the group that embodies his love. Even if it's been sullied. Or precisely because it's been sullied.

"In any group, there's a constant battle between these two conflicting forces: the principle of love on the one hand and the need for fairness and impartiality on the other. But most of us aren't generally aware of this. It's because the clash is between things that normally stay beneath the surface—between something that provides the hidden underpinnings for the specific rules the group follows, and something that constitutes the basic foundation for the group's existence.

"What we see on the surface are violations of rules, self-interest and self-preservation, favoritism, feelings of jealousy and hatred, and so on. But if you drill down below, you discover deeper layers that terms like favoritism and self-preservation don't convey."

I took a sip of tea and tossed the last bite of cake into my mouth.

"To return to Ryo again, when I said her art teacher had treated her badly 'because of love,' I meant it in the sense I've just been describing. So we have Mr. Agata as the central figure in the art club, and we think we know his motivation for treating Ryo unfairly. We then have to ask: Is that sufficient reason to forgive him? Or is it at least a mitigating factor that we need to make allowances for? What do you think?"

Asako took her time thinking about it. I drank the rest of my tea.

"From what you've been saying, I suppose the answer ought to be yes. Though maybe just for making allowances rather than forgiving him entirely. But I can see from your face that you don't even like the idea of making allowances. You look like you're not willing to forgive him in any way, shape, or form."

I nodded. "Not that withholding forgiveness will actually accomplish anything, of course."

"Is your reluctance a purely emotional thing? Or have you worked out a rational justification?"

"I've actually thought it through. It has to do with the responsibility he has as a teacher."

"Responsibility? I don't think that word's come up before."

"This may actually be a bit of a weak link in my argument. Every member of a group bears a responsibility for ensuring that the group persists. But the responsibility of the leaders and those entrusted with training the young is a lot greater. People like that are supposed to be bound by a strong obligation to regulate themselves. That's why I'm unwilling to admit any mitigating circumstances in Agata's case. For now, I'll leave it at that."

"Seems like things get a bit dicey when you start talking about supposed-tos." A hint of a smile softened her face. "If people started throwing supposed-tos at you based on conventional expectations, I bet there are things *you'd* feel you hadn't lived up to either, don't you think?"

"Oh, I don't know . . . How about you?"

"No, I asked you."

I imagine the smile on my face at that moment would have to be described as strained.

"Well, okay, so I'm invoking conventional expectations. But don't you think they're important?" I pressed on. "If people our age can't raise issues like fairness or responsibility, then who's going to do it? Most of the noise you hear kids making about justice is nothing more than a teething fever that flares up in their growing process. Woe be the day when the only people shouting about fairness and impartiality are our iron-skinned politicians and religious hypocrites . . . Wow, listen to me, I can hardly believe I'm hearing such fancy phrases coming from my own mouth.

"There are people in this world who are rotten to the core, and there are others, also a source of trouble, who have no guiding principle besides their biased love. Agata isn't an evil man; he's just one of the people who're motivated only by love. The kind so easily influenced by connections and gifts. If the world becomes a place where honest people never bring up conventional expectations, while scumbags who'll stop at nothing and people who know how to milk their connections to get ahead carry the day, then I think ordinary folk like us are going to wind up having a real hard time of it. Only the strong and the smooth operators will be able to make decent lives for themselves."

"You're probably right . . . But there's a question that's been nagging at me as I listen to you. All this is supposedly what you intend to say to Ryo, but do you really think she'll get it? I don't mean will she be able to follow; she's not stupid, so I imagine she'll see what you're saying just fine. But do you think you'll be able to get through to her heart? Because I really don't think what she's struggling with right now is a semantic or intellectual thing; it's an emotional thing."

"But even to get through to her heart, you still have to use words, right?"

"Well, yeah, maybe so, but not so much words that explain as words that can touch her directly, deep down inside." She stopped short and shook her head. "Don't get me wrong. I'm not saying the argument you've been making is meaningless, or that I don't find it interesting. I'd never stopped to consider any of this the way you have. You've obviously been thinking about it deep and hard, and I'm really glad that you shared your thoughts with me like this. It's just that I don't know if it's the right approach for getting through to Ryo right now. In fact, I'm sorry, but to be perfectly honest, I don't think it is."

"What makes you say that?"

"Because I get the feeling your argument's actually directed more at yourself than at me or Ryo. You're trying your best to figure out exactly what the problem is and to understand it for yourself. That's how it sounds to me."

"That cuts pretty deep, but if that's the way it comes across, that's just how it'll have to be. I think it's important for Ryo to hear it once, even if she can't fully appreciate it right away.

For a moment Asako looked as if she was about to say something more, then she pursed her lips.

I went to my room and checked my e-mail again. I had no new messages.

"Anything. It doesn't matter," my uncle answered, not having thought far enough ahead to have a particular topic in mind. "The important thing is to talk. Like, say, about your husband's worst eccentricity, or—"

"No thanks. How about instead you tell me more about that married woman whose life you ruined?"

"I don't think so," he said, brushing the suggestion aside.

But before long they were having a good time carrying on a nose-to-nose conversation in barely audible whispers. Rieko talked about her trip to Scotland, while my uncle offered assorted observations he'd made about the people and companies he'd dealt with during his stay in the UK.

When their bodies happened to touch by accident from time to time, Rieko no longer recoiled. But the moment he made any deliberate move, she slapped his hand away.

"Hey," he said as a question popped into his mind. "I can't believe I've never asked you this till now. What was your name before you got married? Kashiwagi's your husband's name, right?"

"You really want to know?"

"That's why I asked."

"I'm not going to tell you."

He nibbled lightly on her ear. She bit into his upper arm hard enough to leave tooth marks.

"My maiden name was Okamoto. Sounds common, doesn't it."

He tried it out. "Rieko Okamoto. It makes you seem like a whole different person. But actually, I think I like Okamoto better than Kashiwagi."

"Now it's your turn."

"My name's always been Yajima, as you well know."

"I wasn't asking that. You have to tell me some big secret, too, like me telling you my maiden name. Something really juicy."

"But you actually don't know anything at all about me, right? Because we never talked about our private lives before. For you, I'm nothing but secrets from top to bottom. I have no idea where to begin."

He saw the faint white spots that were her eyes disappear. She had lowered her eyelids in denial of what he'd said.

"I know a lot more than you think. My husband hired some private investigators to ferret out everything there was to know about you. Of course, they didn't dig into the older stuff, or every tiny little detail. Like your fling with that married woman. But I know all the basic facts of your life, and I'm up to date on your recent activities. The name of the last prostitute you slept with here in London, for example, as well as how much you paid her, and what you asked her to do."

"Well, well, I can't imagine he learned anything particularly exciting. After going to all that trouble."

Without warning, he reached for Rieko's ear with his thumb and forefinger and pinched the spot he'd bitten before.

"What was that for?"

"I'm going to tell you a secret. Something I'm sure the PIs missed."

"Ooh, what could it be?"

"I have a kid," he said. "A boy. Bet you didn't know that."

"You're right, I didn't. None of the reports said anything like that. You've never been married. You never recorded any births on your family register, and nothing turned up to suggest that you might have a love child somewhere."

Her voice had risen slightly above a whisper. My uncle released his grip on her ear and pressed his index finger to her lips.

"It's the truth. I'll tell you all about it. My boy's name is Yuki."

"I'm sure it's a shock to hear your own name come up at this point," my uncle said. Most of the ice had melted in his whiskey and water, and he now downed about half the glass in a single go as if quenching a massive thirst, his large Adam's apple sliding up and down with each big gulp. "I was actually pretty startled myself when you suddenly popped into my mind just then."

The time it took us to hike back to the cottage had been insufficient for my uncle to finish his story, so we'd both taken turns in the bath and finished dinner before he picked up where he'd left off earlier. Even though the language he used was restrained, the effect on my over-eager adolescent sex organ was predictable. As I listened, I experienced an embarrassing bulge inside my jeans from time to time. Under the circumstances, I did not find my arousal pleasurable. One's own uncle is not the person from whom one would normally wish to hear an erotic story. I felt awkward. But he seemed completely oblivious to my potential discomfort.

"There I was, feeling totally grungy and lying on a bed that reeked from all our coupling, and for some reason I found myself thinking of you—the boy I'd sometimes claimed in jest was my own son. I remembered you the way you were soon after you were born—a tiny little bundle of innocence wrapped in the softest, warmest baby skin. I could feel the sensation of your silky smooth ear crushed between my thumb and forefinger as if you were actually there. For a moment, the darkness in which Rieko and I were confined became like a tunnel that connected me to anywhere and everywhere on the entire planet. And I affirmed without a shadow of a doubt in my mind that I had a son, who was even then living and breathing halfway around the world on the extreme eastern fringe of Asia."

"Yuki is officially my brother's son on the family register," my uncle said.

"So you had an affair with your brother's wife," Rieko gleefully breathed into his ear. "And you got her pregnant and broke up the family. You naughty little rascal. You're the lowest of the low. Tee hee."

"No, my brother really is Yuki's biological father."

"Huh? So are you saying you adopted your nephew? That's no fun."

"Hear me out," he said, closing his hand over the hair at the back of her head to stop her from moving away. Then he wrapped his whole arm around her neck and whispered, "I want to tell you the story. The story of how my nephew became my son.

"I was in college when my brother and his wife had their first child and named him Yuki. He was a strangely passive baby from the day he was born—not crying much, not moving much, not wanting to nurse much—and I remember people remarking that he was acting like he hadn't even been born yet.

"I went to see him for the first time when he was about two weeks old. I asked if I could hold him. I'd never held a baby before, so I was sort of nervous, but I tried not to let it show. Well, talk about bad timing: at that exact moment, there was an earthquake. A pretty big one, in fact. I started to drop the baby—or more accurately, I *thought* I was dropping the baby—and in an attempt to keep him from tumbling to the floor, I grabbed his left ear."

"But he didn't fall, right?"

"Of course not. It turned out I was holding him securely in my two arms the whole time, so there really wasn't any reason for me to grab his ear. And you can't stop a baby from falling by grabbing his ear anyway."

Rieko gave a barely audible giggle.

"When his ear was crushed between my fingers, Yuki began screaming at the top of his lungs, and suddenly my brother and his wife and everyone else in the room were jumping up and down for joy. You see, this was the first time the baby had let out a really full-throated cry, so they all felt as if he'd finally actually been born. And in fact, from that moment on, Yuki acted like any normal baby, crying all the time. So in a way, I'm the one who brought him into this world. And because of that, I've always loved him as if he were my own son. Though I've never had a son of my own to know what that's actually like. And to this day, Yuki still has a little dent in his left ear. Proof positive that he's my boy."

He pinched the upper part of his own ear with his right thumb and forefinger and urged Rieko to do the same.

"But don't you think it's a little strange?"

"What is?"

"Pinching your ear doesn't hurt. So long as it's not your earlobe."

"You're right. I can pinch pretty hard and barely feel a thing."

"Exactly. But in that case, why did it hurt Yuki so much? To judge from the way he started screaming, I mean."

"Maybe it hurts more for babies. They say the younger you are the more intensely you feel pain."

"Uh-huh."

"But anyway," Rieko said, gently sliding the pad of a finger along his arm, "if you loved Yuki so much, didn't you ever think you might like to have a real child of your own? You must have had plenty of opportunities if you'd wanted—or for that matter, it could easily have happened even by accident."

"I never once thought I wanted a kid, nor did I ever get anybody pregnant. I'm pretty sure."

"So sex for you is all about the pleasure and has nothing to do with procreation."

"Except I don't think you can say it's purely for pleasure. Okay, I admit that sometimes it's been for sheer lust, but it's just as true that sometimes it's been an act of love. Like with you. Actually, though, if we keep this up, I really could get you pregnant, couldn't I? We've been going at it like a couple of animals."

"That may be exactly what my husband wants."

"For you to get pregnant?"

"Uh-huh. He's been impotent since before we got married."

"I can't say that surprises me, considering how he seems to get his jollies. But whatever he may be thinking, if we made a kid together, it'd be all the more reason for not letting this be the end for us."

"Trust me, that's not going to happen."

"No really," he started to say, but Rieko rolled over on top of him and pressed her mouth to his left ear.

"I'm going to tell you my deepest, most personal secret." Her breath on his ear felt wetter than before. "I can't have children.

Because of a uterine problem I had when I was still a teen. My husband doesn't know about it. So he gets his kicks putting me through all this, and figures it'll be two birds with one stone if I get pregnant. Serves him right, as far as I'm concerned."

"I thought you loved your husband and wanted to make him happy. You were even willing to do this for him."

"Of course. He's my husband, so I love him—and I hate him, too."

"I only *love* you," my uncle said, tipping his head to kiss her.

She tried to turn away, but he forced his lips firmly on hers. As if to even the score, Rieko grabbed his penis hard, intending it to hurt. He thought she was being provocative, but when he started to respond, she resisted his caresses. Then as soon as he withdrew his hands, she seemed to encourage him again. They went on with this push-and-pull for quite some time—entangling their limbs, being pushed away, then moving in again . . . Beneath it all lay a shared but unspoken wish that they could simply go on like this forever.

For him, a rush to intercourse would be a betrayal of her trust. For her, to lead him on endlessly without ever yielding would at some point become a form of torture. They both knew they were playing a hellish game in which there could be no happy resolution.

Drinking from the toilet wouldn't bother him in the least, and he'd long since ceased to care what might happen with his job. But slowly, ever so slowly, the urge to join their bodies began to build within them. They both knew that consummation would lead directly to a final separation. If only they could hold that moment forever in suspense. But at some point this desire gave way to their need for completion, and they found themselves locked deeply together. The unchanging darkness wrapped them in its embrace. Now if only they could sustain this bliss forever. Forever and ever . . .

The telephone was ringing. Neither of them made any move to answer it.

I suggested we go for a walk, but Asako begged off on account of a headache, so I went alone. The headache came from the spiced sake. She couldn't tolerate even the smallest amounts of alcohol. Possibly it came partly from the situation with Ryo as well.

The trees lining the outer edge of the sidewalk stood bare of leaves. Their growing root systems had lifted the paving slabs at uneven angles, so you invariably scraped the bottom of your shoes if you didn't watch your step. I knew this perfectly well, but nevertheless found myself repeating the same mistake over and over. My mind was on Asako's reaction to what I'd said and her doubts about my getting through to Ryo with a speech like that . . .

In an attempt to distract myself from such thoughts, I began observing the other people who were out and about on this New Year's Day.

New Year's used to be a time when you could feel a snap-to-attention crispness in the air. For one thing, the temperature itself seemed colder back when I was a kid. But that wasn't the only difference. There was a shared sense that New Year's is a truly special occasion. That's what gave the air its distinct feeling.

By the time I was in my mid-teens, the extra-special treatment New Year's got began to seem old-fashioned to me. I passed the holidays in my ordinary clothes. When the extended family gathered at Grandpa and Grandma's to celebrate, I stuck around no longer than absolutely necessary to collect my New Year's money. It was funny to see my elders turned out in their New Year's finery, exchanging ridiculously stiff greetings with people they were on the most familiar of terms with the rest of the year.

Maybe twenty years later, I began to notice that even the older generation wasn't dressing up for New Year's anymore—going about in colorless jackets and dark half-coats in spite of the occasion. The same went without saying for the younger set. The whole city actually looked drabber. The festive season had become completely casual, demoted to the level of any other holiday.

I had a pretty good idea when this transformation had taken place: with the change of reign. Although I couldn't sympathize with the lavish praise heaped on Emperor Hirohito after his demise, there was no denying that something had changed with the end of his era.

This bedroom community was quite new, built only a short time before the emperor died, and almost no one who lived here ever got decked out in flowery kimonos or formal New Year's attire. Amid this pervasive casualness, the occasional elderly man I passed on the sidewalk dressed in coat and tie was a reassuring sight. It seemed that somewhere deep inside, I actually missed that crisp atmosphere of New Year's past. And yet, today, I myself had come out in my everyday jeans, turtleneck, and black leather half-coat.

When I reached the park, two little boys who looked like brothers were playing catch with a yellow plastic ball. A toddler holding her young parents' hands was calling out to the ducks swimming about the pond. A group of kids were riding around on their bicycles. A boy watching his father fly a kite craned his neck at the sky. Several pigeons rocked their heads smugly back and forth as they toddled about. On a bench to one side sat a girl all by herself. She was staring at the ground with her hands buried in the pockets of her white down jacket. I realized it was Ryo. Even with the changes that had come over the holiday in recent times, the sight of a teenage girl sitting alone in the park on New Year's Day seemed unsettling. Had she already finished with her friend? Or had she actually been here all along?

"And that's pretty much the end of the story."

The hands of the clock showed nearly midnight.

My uncle was still refilling his glass with whiskey from time to time but no longer bothering with water or ice. He didn't appear the least bit drunk.

"The next thing I knew, I woke up behind the wheel of my Cortina Lotus on the street in front of my apartment, fully dressed in pants, shirt, and jacket. Except my watch was missing. And it was an Omega, too. There was a peculiar smell in the car, like nothing I'd ever smelled before. It reminded me of a cologne I'd encountered on someone somewhere or other before, yet it wasn't quite the same. Then I realized it was the smell of sex working its way out from beneath my shirt, mixed in with whatever the cologne was. In a sudden rush, the events of the preceding days came back to me—moment by moment, sharp as can be. The smell told me instantly that the events had been real. And I knew then that I'd been torn away once and for all, against my will, from the woman who completed me . . . without even a chance to say good-bye."

"Did you really never see her again?" I asked.

"Never. I couldn't find the faintest trace of her. The house I'd been confined in was still there—*is* still there. But it was occupied by an elderly Russian who couldn't speak English. Nothing I said or did would induce him to let me inside. I even offered to buy the place, but to no avail. Rieko and the man she called her husband covered their tracks so completely they might as well have vanished off the face of the Earth. I have no way of knowing whether she's even alive anymore."

"What about your job? You're still working for the same company, right?"

"As it turned out, it was only Monday afternoon when I came to in my car. I figure what I felt then must have been something like what the guys in old fairy tales felt after being bewitched by a fox. Considering we were in that darkened room long enough to go half mad, I would have sworn we'd been shut up in there for at least a week or ten days, but it had actually been less than three. I don't know if I went through a time warp, or got carried off into a parallel universe, or what.

"I went inside and fell asleep. I didn't feel like calling the office. I was just completely fed up with everything. But that evening, when one of the guys from work came by to check up on me, I couldn't feign absence. So I invented a story. I told him I'd been out tying one on and had only just gotten home. My colleague stood there looking kind of uncomfortable. I guess it was the smell. I hadn't taken a bath yet. I didn't have the energy. In some ways, I still don't. My life basically came to an end during those three days."

"I wish you wouldn't say things like that."

"Okay, starting tomorrow, I promise I'll never bring it up again. But I hope you'll bear with me just a little more for now . . . I had put Rieko's husband down as a common fool, but I couldn't have been more wrong. I may only have met the bastard as a voice over the phone, but I can tell you he was an absolute genius at knowing exactly what would make a person suffer most—*and* being able to carry it out. The damage I sustained in that darkened room penetrated right through my heart down to the very bottom of my soul. The more time passes, the more I feel it. It was a truly awful experience. Worse than being killed. And yet I live on, in spite of it all. Not simply live on, mind you. Live on *in spite of it all.*"

"The only thing that matters to me as your son is that you live on. I don't care whether it's *simply* or *in spite of.*"

"But just living on isn't good enough." I could smell the alcohol on his breath as he let out a sigh. "In the days after the old geezer turned me loose, I developed a persistent cough. A cough just like his. I became sickly, and kept coming down with fevers. I forced myself to keep up my usual schedule at work, but it was difficult for me even to walk, and I couldn't go much of anywhere on my days off anymore. Sometimes I wondered if maybe the bastard had swapped bodies with me, turning me into an old man my-self. Though I really tried hard to tough it out, I finally decided I needed to take a break to recover my strength. Once I'd decided that, the cough finally went away."

"You seem fine now. You've managed to hike up to the tunnel at Usui Pass and back twice."

"To be honest, it still took a lot out of me. But I've been thinking it's about time I get back to work."

He smiled. What caught my attention more than the placid smile were the deep wrinkles that formed at the corners of his mouth and eyes.

The rumble of a motorcycle engine approached, then came to a halt on the road nearby.

"There he is." My uncle's voice returned to a more normal tone, its wistfulness gone.

"Who?"

"Haven't you noticed? It's Kanoko's boyfriend coming to pick her up. Her parents sent her to stay with her uncle precisely to keep them apart, but the guy's apparently followed her here. Listen a minute and you'll hear footsteps coming from the main house."

Sure enough, I soon heard the sound of someone sneaking out toward the road. The engine roared to life again with a single kick.

"They'll be back around dawn. Well, what can you do? Promise me you won't say anything."

I nodded. I knew right away I wouldn't be able to sleep that night.

The story my uncle had told me was a bit too heavy for the seventeen-year-old boy I was at the time to fully grasp. Events had been extremely unkind to him. In some small measure, maybe my presence had helped him get safely through the immediate crisis. This made me happy. But I doubted there was anything I could do to soothe the wounds that continued to fester deep inside him. In fact, there was probably no one in the world who could help him (though I don't think he was asking for help; it was simply important to him to tell me his story). As a seventeen-year-old, hearing his tale was like having a dark fog descend abruptly over me. Then with devastating force came the revelation of Kanoko's midnight assignations, dealing a crushing blow to my one-sided infatuation. That's why I didn't think I'd be able to sleep, but in fact, I don't recall hearing the sound of the motorcycle at dawn.

Ryo looked up and our eyes met. She neither got up to flee nor showed the slightest sign of surprise.

"Okay if I sit down?" I asked.

She nodded.

"You already saw your friend?"

"Uh-huh."

"Then you should have come on home. Aren't you cold?"

"Not really." She opened her mouth wide and let out her breath. It didn't turn white.

"You seem like you knew I'd come and were waiting for me."

"I texted you a while ago that I'd be here. Replying to your e-mail."

"I didn't see that."

"I figured you'd come anyway. Unless we're somewhere on a trip, we always come here together on New Year's, right? You and Mom and me? About this time in the afternoon."

"Do we?"

"If you're gonna give me a sermon, can we get it over with now?"

The way she put it made me bristle.

"I have no intention of lecturing you."

"That's a relief. Then what is it?"

My blood rose some more.

"I've been trying to figure out why you seem to be turning into a teen rebel all of a sudden."

"I am not." She flatly denied the whole reason for my argument.

"Isn't that what it's called when kids start hanging out in places like Shibuya until all hours of the night?"

"I'm not in junior high anymore, you know. Everybody does stuff like that. You and Mom are just out of touch is all."

Suddenly I found myself doubting whether I'd be able to get through to her.

"But I'm sorry if I've made you worry," she added.

I felt like she'd given me an opening.

"Mom tells me you quit the art club."

"Uh-huh."

"And you've quit doing oils?"

"Not really quit. But I can't get into painting right now."

"You mean because of Mr. Agata? I understand you've had some differences with him."

To my surprise, she shook her head.

"No, it's not that. After the 9/11 attacks last year, or I guess it's the year before last now, I was, like, in total shock, and I felt like something had changed even when I was painting. I'm not quite sure how to put it, but it was like oils were just too slow."

To hear my daughter talking about 9/11 was a bit of a surprise. I was working late at the office on that fateful day, but my wife and Ryo were at home, watching TV, and they saw the live coverage in all its horrifying detail. Ryo apparently broke down in tears. Yet in all the months since, she'd never once offered any special thoughts or reactions when the subject came up in conversation.

"You mean, because the paints take so long to dry?"

"There's that too, but it's more about painting as a medium of expression being out of whack with the pace of things these days."

As a matter of fact, the terrorist attacks had brought a change in mood at my modest little enterprise as well. I sensed a certain tautness in the air that I'd never felt before, and the staff seemed more focused somehow in carrying out their daily tasks.

"Though I'd think being out of whack with the times might actually have an appeal of its own to an artist . . . So is that why you switched to manga?"

"No, no, it's not like that. I never decided manga was going to be my new thing. I'm really only exploring the possibilities for now. But the kids drawing manga at my school have a lot better instincts than the goody-two-shoes in the art club, and they're a whole lot more stimulating to be with. I have no regrets about quitting the art club."

"What about your butting heads with Mr. Agata? I normally wouldn't want to say anything bad about your teachers, but from what Mom's told me, I'd say there are some serious areas of concern in the way he treated you."

"I'm not going to talk about that," she said, her face suddenly going blank.

"Well, I won't insist. But whether teen rebel's the right term or not, you've certainly been going through some changes recently, and I can't help feeling that the art club business had something to do with what triggered those changes. The timing certainly fits.

Mr. Agata is supposed to be a responsible adult, and when somebody like that tramples on the principles of fairness and impartiality, and rips you and your work apart, you have every right to get angry.

"But what we have here is also an age-old pattern that's been repeated over and over since forever. The younger generation gets mad when the older generation lays down all sorts of rules and then ignores their own rules. In my day, kids rebelled violently against their elders by throwing stones and swinging clubs. These days kids who want to rebel turn to crime, but back then they seriously thought they could start a revolution and change the world.

"I get the feeling you've lost faith not only in Mr. Agata as an individual, but also in your school and in society and in the entire older generation. And I feel your anger directed at your mother and me, too. It's like you've moved away into a different world that older folks like us can't even see into."

"You're jumping to conclusions." Once again, Ryo dismissed what I'd said. "Quitting the art club and finding new friends outside school might have happened around the same time, but that's just coincidence, and my art teacher has nothing to do with it. Though it's true I detest him. You and Mom don't have anything to do with it either, and the whole thing about the older generation and whether or not they follow their own rules never once entered my mind. I just prefer to hang out with my new friends away from school because I'm more comfortable with them, that's all. The time I spend with them is more meaningful to me. That's really all there is to it."

The earnestness in her words nearly won me over, but part of me also wondered if the insistent tone wasn't just a bold front to hide how helpless she felt.

"Well, I've actually had all kinds of stuff going through my mind about this."

"That's why I said, I'm sorry if I made you worry."

"In that case, how about you let me tell you some of what I've been thinking?"

"Like what?" she said, looking at me warily out of the corner of her eye.

"Like about why Mr. Agata behaved so badly in your case. I want to see if I can explain, at least in my own way, what his motivation was for treating you so unfairly. Maybe it'll only come across as a bunch of mumbo jumbo to you, but if that's the way it is, that's the way it is."

Our eyes met. She held my gaze for a moment, then gave me a small nod. I began to speak.

Ogita's easy laugh had a way of infecting everyone around him. Over dinner at an Italian restaurant located inside a hotel, I enjoyed unusually large quantities of both wine and laughter as we progressed from steamed vegetable appetizers through a main course of veal steak.

He wanted the scoop on all the recent developments at his old company, including what the Polka-Dot Killer and various other former bosses and colleagues were up to. He showed a particular interest in the New Ventures Office I now belonged to. But what he seemed to enjoy most of all was talking about himself—about his divorce from Momo, and the younger woman he'd been going out with lately, and his coups as a management consultant.

His ears pricked up again when we moved into the lounge after dinner and I finally broached the subject I'd asked to see him about—though when I first launched into my spiel about "unified marketing packages that encompass both product and corporate image, blah blah blah," his eyes seemed to glaze over. I wondered if he might have had too much to drink, but he denied it; he said he simply had no particular expertise or interest in that side of things. He wanted me to go straight to the guts of my proposal.

I filled him in on the problems I saw in the way the brand he'd helped develop was currently being handled and what it meant for the line's future prospects.

"So what do you propose to do about it?" he asked.

I explained that I wanted to jump-start a revitalization effort for the brand and use it as my ticket out of my current dead-end situation. "There are a number of different approaches I'm considering, and I want your advice as to which of them you think has the best chance of success."

He lowered his eyes and sat thinking for several moments, then looked up again and broke into one of his trademark smiles.

"Whatever the approach, I think I'll probably be able to help."

I nodded. This was exactly what I had hoped to hear.

I laid out for him my three alternatives.

The first was to urge the overseas manufacturer to put together its own plan for revitalizing the brand in Japan and press my company for action. The plan would stipulate that I be placed in charge of the effort.

The second was to have the manufacturer actually change importers. There were officially still several years remaining on their contract with my company, but they were allowed to terminate it at any time by giving one year's notice. If they could lay out a concrete plan for freshening up the brand, they should have no problem finding a new company interested in taking on the account.

The last was to create a new Japanese company under the brand's name. This could be done either with the help of my present employer or as an all-new independent venture.

The first approach was the most sensible, while the third would probably be best overall—though it was a considerable long shot in terms of actually coming to fruition (it wasn't until several years after this that one major international brand after another began setting up its own stake in the Japanese market). The second would involve the greatest disruption, not to mention risk. Success would mean being marked as a traitor.

When I was finished, Ogita tilted his head in thought for quite some time before speaking.

"What're your reasons for finding the sensible approach objectionable?"

The way he asked the question struck me as a bit odd.

"I think the chances are pretty slim that I'd actually be let out of the New Ventures Office and put in charge of things. Also, I don't think fundamental change is possible as long as the company has a hand in it. Not under the present management."

Ogita nodded. The air between us had grown heavy.

"You can rule out the last approach," he said without meeting my eyes. "If it weren't for the money they make, they'd just as soon not be doing business in Japan to begin with. I consider the owner a friend, as you know, but somehow, even though he never says it, I always feel like he's looking at me thinking *You poor bastard, what a shame you had to be born Japanese.*"

My heart sank. I knew it would have been tough to pull off, but the idea of creating a new company had excited me the most.

"So that leaves number two," he said. "The issue then becomes finding a new importer. Did you have somebody in mind?"

I gave no answer except to flash him a smile. In the research I'd done to lay the groundwork, I had identified a candidate that I thought would be interested in taking on the brand.

He returned my smile. It was a smile that made the air around us grow even heavier.

"The owner told me once that a number of other Japanese companies had approached him with feelers. He mentioned one that offered very attractive terms, but he turned them down because the guy they sent had bad breath."

He took a small handful of red-skinned peanuts from a glass bowl. As he started rubbing off the skins from several nuts at a time, he looked up at me again.

"If your idea is to take the brand rights with you to another company as a kind of getting-acquainted gift, I think you're overlooking something. The gift comes with some extra baggage. You get what I'm talking about? You. Just put yourself in their shoes for a minute. All they really need is the gift. Nobody trusts a traitor—on either side."

"To my mind, it's not just some lousy gift," I said. "By doing this, everybody wins. And I'm not just saying that to be funny or to put a nice face on it. First of all the brand gets a new lease on life. The new importer makes money. I get liberated from the New Ventures Office. And the company? They avoid getting egg on their face from letting the brand go to pot and being cut off by the manufacturer for cause. They can play the victim, saying they were betrayed by the French and a rogue employee."

"Very clever," Ogita laughed.

"The only reason they're still making a profit is because we laid such a solid foundation at the beginning, and all the people who've been in charge since then have carried on what we set up. At this point everything's starting to look pretty long in the tooth and needs to be updated, but without personnel who have the experience and know-how to do that, just switching to a new import agent isn't going to do much good. I'm not just taking it along as a gift, nor am I tagging along as excess baggage."

"You sound pretty sure of yourself." He wasn't smiling anymore. "I'd say you're on the right track. It always comes down to your people in the end. All the advice I give my clients begins and ends with that. But there's still a crucial piece missing in your plan. You were only involved with the brand briefly a long time ago, and you've been out of the loop ever since. So the question becomes: why you? If the know-how's been passed down like you say, then wouldn't whoever's currently in charge of the account be a better bet?"

I shook my head. We'd come to the most delicate part of my plan.

"As you said yourself, it's about the people. There's simply no one else besides me who can draw up a workable blueprint for this. You can check it out. Needless to say, I can't do it alone. I'll need your help for sure, and there's one other person who's absolutely crucial. Without that kind of support, there's no way I can put it together."

"Is this other person someone I know?"

"No. And I can't tell you who it is yet. For one thing, you haven't even said whether you're in or not."

"That's because you didn't ask."

I studied his face, but I couldn't read his expression.

"And if I did?"

"I imagine I'd say I want to see the blueprint."

"A good bit of it you've already heard."

"Uh-huh," he said, looking me in the eye. "All right, I'll give it some thought. Keep me posted. I think I can probably be of service."

I nodded and reached for the bowl of peanuts. Once you started eating them, you couldn't stop. We continued silently rubbing the skins off the nuts and tossing them into our mouths until the bowl was empty. I said goodbye to Ogita at the hotel entrance as he climbed into a cab.

I didn't feel as though I'd been talking all that long. Ryo had listened attentively all the way through. I noticed there were quite a few more clouds in the sky. The shade of a nearby tree now fell on the bench where we sat, and I could feel a chill wind on my back. When there'd been more sunshine, the slope rising behind the bench had served as a windbreak, but somewhere along the way it had turned into a chute that funneled the wind right to where we sat. No one was playing in the park anymore; the only figures left were of people hurrying across it as a shortcut on their way to somewhere else.

Ryo had hardly uttered a word as I spoke. I felt even more sheepish going on about fairness and love with my daughter than I had with my wife. As I was nearing the end, I hesitated for a moment over how I should wrap up my discourse. Since I'd promised not to lecture her, I needed to steer clear of anything that sounded too preachy.

"So, anyway," I resumed hastily, realizing I needed to keep the ball rolling, "by analyzing the situation this way, I'm not trying to say that we should forgive Mr. Agata, or that we should even make certain allowances for what he's done. If anything, the more I think about it, the more unforgivable it seems to me. There are certain responsibilities a person has as an adult. All the more, when you're a teacher . . ."

I stopped, unable to go on in the same way I had when I'd spoken to Asako. At my sudden silence, Ryo turned an inquiring eye my way.

"I've said pretty much all I have to say. Once you get into the whole area of responsibilities, I'm not sure I want to sound off too much. It gets to be like spitting at the sky. Mom was doubtful whether I could get through to you by putting things like this— whether I could really reach you deep down in your heart. And I have to admit, it sounds overly analytical even to me."

"But actually," she replied, "you do have an argument, I think."

You do have an argument . . . ? Is that the sort of thing young people say to their elders? I felt like I'd been jolted awake. Yet I could think of no good reason why they shouldn't say it. As my mind began to drift, Ryo went on.

"From what I gather, the art club before I came was like the Agata Clan or Syndicate or something. You know, with a big boss who holds total sway at the top, and all his underlings meekly following his orders. Pretty unusual, I'd think, for a high school art club. But it wasn't like Big Boss Agata was forcing everybody to fall in line; more like they all got in line just because it felt good to them. I think it's probably because of the love thing you were talking about. Plus if they could catch the boss's eye, he might open doors for them to get into the art school they wanted to go to, too. Then along I came and disrupted their whole world order, like some kind of foreign body gumming up the works. It threw the boss-man teacher for a loop."

"That doesn't justify squeezing you out. You're not some foreign body."

Ryo shook her head, but with a look of helpless resignation tugging at her eyes and mouth.

"Don't make faces like that," I burst out.

"I don't know what kind of face I'm making," she said, breaking into a smile, "but I'll make any face I want."

"Listen, Ryo." I put a hand on her shoulder. "The whole art club thing is over and done with. We can just put it behind us. I'm more worried about the place you're at right now. And no matter where that is, my sincere hope is that you'll come on back home. That's what Mom wants, too."

As I said it I thought, Sheesh, if this is all it boils down to, that whole, long, drawn-out argument was nothing but a waste of breath.

"Yeah, Dad, I hear you," she said. "So, shall we go?"

We got up off the bench and started walking.

"The stuff you said was really interesting, Dad, and I think I learned something from it," she offered. I couldn't help thinking that she was just saying it to make me feel better.

I walked slightly ahead of her. She had grown past one meter sixty and was still growing. It felt to me as though the distance that separated us now was greater than it had been before our talk.

In the days following my secret meeting with Ogita at the hotel, I worked on writing up a concrete business plan for rejuvenating the brand in question with the help of an associate who worked in the office that handled the account. For the time being I'll simply call this person X. We produced two versions of the plan, one with full details, the other an abridged edition holding key elements back, for use in negotiations with the prospective new importer. We referred to these collectively as simply "the plan."

Two weeks after our meeting, Ogita called to say he was in. He named a firm that he thought would be a good candidate for the new importer. It turned out to be the same company I'd been thinking of. After that we got together several times, each roughly a week apart. We arranged to meet as far away from my building as was practical, and we kept our rendezvous brief. We did not have dinner or go out drinking together.

I gave Ogita a copy of the abridged version of the plan so he could initiate negotiations with the target company. He wanted to know who my associate was, but I was not yet ready to divulge that information. X was the key to the plan's success, but also its most vulnerable link.

Then came the decisive moment. Ogita let me know the date and time when we were to meet with representatives of the target company.

He told me I should bring X along. I balked. It was still too soon. And besides, unlike myself, I couldn't say whether he'd be available on the specified day without asking him first.

"Look, if you want to know their true colors," Ogita said, "all they're really after is the brand. From their perspective, you and Mr. X look like excess baggage. So you need to think of this as your opportunity to sell yourselves."

When he put it that way, there was little I could do but agree. But I told X he should plan to arrive late. Although I was already past the point of no return myself—as far as I was concerned, I had no future with our present employer in any case, so all I could do was charge full speed ahead—I didn't want to expose X until his future job security could be assured. My strategy would be to meet the other party and size things up first, and if I had any doubts about the situation, I would call and tell him not to show up.

But Ogita phoned at the last minute to say the meeting was off. Something had come up that forced the other party to cancel. He promised he would get right back to me with a new date and time, and hung up.

A week passed, then ten days, and I'd still received no further word. I tried but couldn't get hold of him from my end. He didn't respond to e-mail, either. I contacted Momo and learned that he was out of the country for a while. It gave me a bad feeling.

After waiting another full week, I decided to phone Ogita's office. We had agreed not to call each other at work in connection with the plan, but he'd left me no other choice. His assistant answered. When I said my name, I caught an almost imperceptible moment of hesitation, then the sound of a muffled voice in the background. There could be no doubt: Ogita was in the room. But she came back on the line to say that he was away on a business trip. I asked when she expected him back in the office. She answered that she didn't know yet, but she would make sure he called me when he returned.

I had no idea what was actually going on, but one thing seemed clear: I needed to be prepared for the worst. I immediately got in touch with Takahiro Ishikura, alias X.

Ishikura and I almost never exchanged a word at work. He was the most junior member of the group that handled the account for the brand I wanted to reenergize.

The office was headed up by a fashion-plate dandy with a snappy mustache who spoke fluent French. The person in charge of PR and other outside contacts was a well-sculpted glamour girl who'd belonged to the swim team and worked as a magazine model on the side when she was in college. Next to colleagues like these, Ishikura seemed utterly colorless. He wore plain, dark suits and quietly kept his nose to the grindstone. But when you talked to him, you quickly sensed that he had an extremely solid grasp of his job. By contrast, the others on the team were all show and no substance.

Ishikura had first sought me out in the days before I was exiled to the New Ventures Office. He was carrying out his tasks as instructed by the more senior members of his group, but he sometimes couldn't figure out why certain things were done the way they were, and he rarely received satisfying answers when he asked.

"I started poking around on my own," he said, "and I found out that our procedures are all based on what somebody named Ogita and his team, including you, put in place about ten years ago. Since this Mr. Ogita apparently isn't with the company anymore, I thought maybe if I asked you, you could tell me why we do things the way we do."

I didn't think it was a good idea to discuss the matter openly within the confines of the office. There were too many jealous ears. When I suggested we get together later, he understood immediately. We met after work and talked over drinks.

I hadn't had anything to do with the account in quite a few years, so I started by asking him to update me on its present status. To my surprise, I learned that their current procedures weren't merely based on what we had set up all those years ago, they remained exactly the same. What I had trained my successor to do at the time I was transferred to a different post was being repeated to this day in fossilized form. The client's conservatism was no doubt a contributing factor as well, but it appeared that the successors to the team I'd been part of had basically done nothing but coast. Ishikura presented me with one shocking example after another.

After this, Ishikura and I continued to meet and talk outside the building. His attitude toward me remained unchanged even after I was reassigned to the New Ventures Office. Without this ongoing contact, it's doubtful I could ever have come up with a workable plan. But it wasn't solely to talk about the project that I continued to meet with him. I had found him to be of surprisingly delicate sensibilities, and I hoped that our conversations might in some small way help ease the stress that he had to contend with at work. I suppose you could say that I'd come to regard him with a measure of paternal affection.

Because Ishikura was always deferential in his behavior, people often took him to be something of a weakling. But in reality, if he believed he was in the right, he had an inner strength of purpose that allowed him to see things through.

We had already gotten to know each other quite well, when he complained to me one day how everybody saw him as a meek sort of person, and said he hated himself for it.

"Don't you think it's pathetic," I responded, "when people look at your title or face and suddenly puff themselves up or start to grovel? Why should you care what people like that think of you?"

"That's how I used to feel about it, too. But then I began to wonder if maybe I was wrong. It struck me that with some people, it's only because they think I'm weaker than them that they let the bullying side of their character come out. If they saw me as stronger to begin with, they'd probably treat me more normally all along. Instead, when I don't just lie down and take the abuse like the pushover they think I am, they get mad and try to put me down again, and things just go from bad to worse between us."

"That's because they're a bunch of shallow-minded jerks."

"But in point of fact, we both lose out by my being so self-effacing—both me and them. I can give you an example," he said, and then mentioned the name of the former model who handled PR for his group. "When I overheard two of the new girls talking about her in the cafeteria one day, they were both going on about how thoughtful and generous she is. I couldn't believe it. She's never been the least bit thoughtful or generous to me. She's so quick to fly off the handle, and she's even downright mean. When you see somebody who shows two distinct personalities like that, you naturally assume the nicer side is a wolf in sheep's clothing, and the mean side is her true self, right? But I'm starting to think that's not necessarily so. Maybe it's that the new girls draw out her good qualities, while I somehow bring out the worst in her."

Seeing him take the entire burden onto his own shoulders this way, I seriously wondered how long he would last with the company. In fact, with sensibilities like that, it would be difficult for him to thrive in any group. I decided I needed to do whatever I could to protect this sensitive young man who tended to overanalyze things to his own detriment.

And yet, in spite of myself, I had dragged him into my scheme. It had been too long since I'd moved on to other things for me to put the thing together entirely on my own.

I now told Ishikura that I wanted him to forget the plan ever existed. No matter what happened, he should profess ignorance. I would figure out something for myself (not that I actually had any idea yet what it would be). Since nobody else knew about our connection, he ought to be safe if he just went on working the way he always had as though nothing had changed.

He smiled gently in his usual fashion and shook his head. "I don't care if I lose this job," he said without the briefest hesitation.

"I've long since come to terms with that in my mind. Even before you brought up this idea, I was already laying the groundwork for quitting."

"Laying the groundwork?"

"I've been studying to become a certified tax accountant," he said. "Maybe not right away, but I should eventually be able to pass the exam."

It struck me that the fellow might actually have his head screwed on even straighter than I did. Be that as it may, I told him again that under no circumstances was he to volunteer any information about our plan.

The day after I rescued her near midnight in Shibuya, Ryo got home from school earlier than usual. As it happened, I was able to finish things up at the office relatively early that day as well, and we sat down together for a rare family dinner a little before eight. It seems I was lost in a world of my own, however, and offered only sullen, mechanical responses to my wife and daughter's table conversation. They both became irritated with me.

Ryo excused herself and went up to her room as soon as she was finished eating. Asako promptly turned to me with daggers in her voice.

"Are you upset about Ryo's boyfriend?"

That was of course part of it. What father anywhere on earth would be smiling happily after finding his daughter with a boy like Yuta? But that was not all.

"I never had a chance to mention it yesterday, but I heard from Momo. Ogita—that double-crossing Ogita—apparently has cancer. She said they give him six months to a year."

My wife stopped stacking dishes and dropped her hands into her lap. She sat silently staring at me, obviously not knowing what to say.

I had long since filled her in on the entire history of events that resulted in me leaving my former company. There could be little doubt that she, too, blamed Ogita's betrayal for the various hardships she had had to suffer at that time—from the shock of her husband suddenly losing his job, to living with the fear that his new start-up might not survive, to the lost opportunity for her daughter to go to private school.

"Ogita asked Momo to tell me he wanted to see me. I feel kind of torn. I'd just as soon never have to see his face again, but when it comes to a dying man's wish . . ."

Still saying nothing, my wife abruptly rose from the table and fled into the kitchen.

Uncertain what to make of it, I quickly followed.

In the unlighted kitchen, she stood with her back to the sink wiping tears from her face with both hands.

What're you crying about? I almost blurted out, but I held my tongue. The sight of her standing there weeping had made me choke up myself.

Why? . . . I could think of no good answer.

I put my left hand on her shoulder.

"I don't know why I'm crying," she said.

We remained like that for several moments, neither of us saying a word.

Sensing someone's eyes on us, we both turned toward the dining room. Ryo was standing in the doorway staring this way. I dropped my hand from my wife's shoulder.

Ryo's face began to contort. It was like when a small child who's been hurt but isn't immediately sure what's happened suddenly realizes at the sight of blood that she's in pain, and her face falls to pieces.

"What?" she croaked in a voice that sounded as though she'd barely been able to squeeze it from her throat. "Are you out of work again, Dad?"

I felt awful about the uncertainty my family continued to live with. My business had actually been doing very well lately, yet I discovered from my wife that both she and Ryo remained deeply apprehensive about the status of my work. They'd simply been biting their tongues so as not to burden me with their fears.

"When Yuta called me on my cell phone today he wanted to know if I thought your business was doing okay," Ryo said. "Like he was worried for me."

No offense, the boy had apparently said, but from the moment he saw me walk in, he thought I looked pretty down at the heels for someone who ran his own company. I made him think right away of the collapse of the Internet bubble . . . And then after sitting down, I had this troubled expression on my face that wouldn't go away, and he thought he saw me hesitate before I finally picked up the bill with trembling fingers. He also couldn't help wondering if the truth wasn't actually that we

132

couldn't afford to take taxis. No offense, he'd apologized again, but the way it all seemed to add up, he couldn't help being a little concerned.

"Even after Yuta listed all those things, I really didn't think there was anything to it. But then you seemed to be in a bad mood again at dinner, and now I come down to the kitchen and find you and Mom standing there like you're both on the verge of tears, so . . ."

My wife came out of the kitchen and rejoined our conversation.

"Is this by any chance the same Yuta Iwamoto who was in your grade school class, dear?"

"He wasn't in my class. He was a year ahead of me."

"Is that right? I remember he was a wonderful soccer player. Everybody knew him."

They both looked at me as if expecting me to agree, but I had no recollection of the boy from back then.

"I guess he lives in Eifukucho on the Inokashira Line now," I said. I turned to my daughter. "When exactly did he move away?"

"When I was in seventh grade."

"So he hasn't lived near here since then, but you happened to run into him again somewhere?"

Ryo didn't seem interested in answering the question.

"If I recall, his mother had to go into the hospital and Yuta and his father went back to live with his grandparents, isn't that right?" Asako said.

Ryo straightened up and looked at her.

"Where did you hear that?"

My wife looked as though she'd rather not have to answer. "Didn't you know?" she finally said.

"I knew his mother had to go into the hospital. I heard about that when I was still in junior high, from my friend's big sister. Yuta was her boyfriend then."

I looked back and forth between them, not quite sure what this all amounted to.

"There was some talk about his mother that went around the grapevine," my wife said as if to make excuses.

"She had to be committed, because of a nervous breakdown," Ryo now said plainly. She seemed to have decided that there was no point in hiding the truth.

"But she's better now, right?" my wife said.

"I haven't heard. Yuta lives with his father and stepmother now."

There was an awkward silence.

"Does he still play soccer?" I asked in an effort to keep the conversation alive.

"No, he quit when he switched schools. He didn't get along with the new soccer club."

So much for my attempt at keeping the ball rolling.

"How did you happen to meet again?" Asako asked. "I'm curious."

I shot her a look. A question like that could easily rub Ryo the wrong way.

"You really want to know? I think I'm blushing," she said, seeming actually pleased to be asked. My own talk with Ryo on New Year's Day had by all indications failed to strike any kind of chord with her, yet mother and daughter were apparently still able to freely communicate their feelings over a shared wavelength. I was envious.

The chance encounter between Yuta and Ryo had taken place at a well-known CD shop in Shibuya. Ryo had skipped school that day so she could go to the public library to look up about the high school equivalency test. She hadn't actually made up her mind to drop out yet, but she wanted to be prepared so she could withdraw at any time. She decided to stop at the CD shop on her way home.

As she browsed about the store, she thought she noticed a boy watching her. It might be awkward if their eyes met, so she made a point of ignoring him as she went up and down the aisles, but eventually he came right up to her and said, "Ryo Yajima, right?"

Who was this creep? She'd never known any punks like this before. He sported the usual bleached hair, pierced earrings, and baggy clothes.

"I'm Yuta Iwamoto," the boy said.

Ryo recognized him the instant he said his name.

"Oh, sure, I remember you. You were ahead of me in school."

She was surprised how pleased he appeared to be when she said this.

And she was surprised at herself as well. Yuta Iwamoto hadn't crossed her mind once since junior high. And yet, images of him as a dashing grade-school athlete now came back to her as clear as day. Once he'd gone on to junior high, he'd become nothing more to her than her friend's sister's boyfriend; his soccer-star swagger annoyed her and she could hardly have cared less about him. She had found herself in the same group of people chatting together perhaps two or three times, but they'd never actually spoken.

In her surprise, she hadn't even realized she was staring at him. He sheepishly turned away. Girls seem to think it's cute when street punks and their ilk get that look on their face. It's not even a question of how well they were raised. Apparently.

"So what exactly was it about Yuta that tickled your fancy?" Asako asked.

"Oh, I don't know," Ryo said vaguely, avoiding an answer. Then as her mother was about to say something more, she made a sour face and hurried up to her room. Perhaps she thought she'd let herself get a little too familiar with her parents.

"What do you plan to do about Ogita?" my wife asked.

"I might actually have some room in my schedule tomorrow afternoon, so maybe I'll go see him." It surprised even me to hear the words coming from my mouth.

I went to my room and sent off a quick e-mail to Momo:

I'll visit him tomorrow.

Nearly two months went by before I finally heard from Ogita—by e-mail:

I decided on a change of course for the revitalization plan. Details to follow.

That was all.

Immediately after this, I also heard from Ishikura. Rumors were flying in his workgroup that some kind of major administrative change was brewing, and this had put everyone in a tizzy. Not even their head honcho with the snappy mustache had any idea what might be in store for them.

This was then followed by a second message from Ogita:

I wasn't able to move your plan forward in the way you expected. I'm sorry.

At the very last stage of negotiations, opposition grew to the notion of finding a new importer. In the end, the owner himself made the call to stick with who they had.

So the plan will still go forward, but under your current employer.

Not wanting to overstep, I thought it best to refrain from meddling in personnel matters. That of course means your name has never been mentioned. The client side fully recognizes the merits of your plan, so it's still possible for me to bring you to their attention as its author and recommend that you be transferred to the group handling the account. Let me know what you think.

I did my best, but I'm afraid I fell short.

I hope you can think of it this way: your brainchild is indeed coming to life. Your employer has been spared the stigma of being cut off by the manufacturer. Profits can be expected to rise over time. Your vision for breathing new life into the brand is sure to be realized. Needless to say, I'm also pleased to have my efforts as a consultant produce such favorable results. Everybody wins out.

If necessary, we can get together sometime when you're free and I can explain everything.

I wrote a single line in reply:

I want your explanation and apology NOW.

I stayed home from work for the next two days, ignoring the summons I received from Polka Dot. I claimed I had a cold and shut myself up in my room. But I could barely sleep. Nothing I ate had any taste. I worried about what might happen to me. Even more, I seethed over what had already happened.

Ogita had taken the document that Ishikura and I produced straight back to our own superiors. It would be patently obvious that nobody could have put together such a scheme without the help of someone on the inside. Since Ogita was involved, it was a foregone conclusion that suspicion would fall on me.

The question was, did Polka Dot intend to discipline me for revealing internal secrets, or was he so impressed with my plan that he wanted to put me on the team? I found it difficult to take the more optimistic view.

Another message arrived from Ishikura. His group was in an uproar. They were being force-fed a plan that had been developed completely outside their control, and they had to swallow it or the client would walk. Anybody could see that it had been produced with inside help. My name had quickly surfaced as the obvious culprit and become the target of indignation.

Along with their outrage came mutual suspicion. Even I couldn't have gotten such a thorough grasp of the situation without the help of someone currently in the group, yet nobody had the first idea who the informer might be. None of the staff had any connection with Ogita or me.

Meanwhile, Ogita sent no reply.

I decided to face the music: I went to see Polka Dot. He wore a broad, contented grin on his face. Beneath this grin jiggled his familiar double chin. But I noticed for the first time that he actually appeared to have lost a little weight since being named to the board of directors.

"Looks like you've been outfoxed at your own game," he said. I cocked my head but said nothing. "I always thought you and Ogita were friends, but I guess I was wrong. He stabbed you in the back."

I shook my head a bit.

"You leaked corporate secrets to the outside. It's a firing offense. But it's pretty plain that you had help from an ally within the unit. If you'll name that person, I'd be willing to see what I can do for you."

"It's no particular secret who my associate is." I handed him an excerpt I'd photocopied from the more detailed plan. "That's a section of the full version of the plan he wrote. What you got from Ogita is only a crude outline. Though, actually, even that's pretty darn good."

As he studied the document in his hand, he held a finger from his other hand to the temple of his glasses.

"You won't have to look very long or hard to figure out who in the group is actually capable of putting together a document like this. So there wouldn't be any point in trying to keep it a secret."

Polka Dot raised his head to look me in the eye. "So he has the rest of the document?"

"No, I have the only copy—though I imagine it's basically all in his head. I think you might want to know that the person in question already intends to leave the company. I'd advise you to identify him quickly and do everything you can to keep him from quitting. There aren't very many men of his caliber in the whole company, let alone in that group."

Our eyes remained locked together for what must have been a full ten seconds. He was trying to hold his self-satisfied grin but without as much success as before.

"Write up a letter of resignation and bring it to me," he said. "We can handle it as a voluntary resignation. Also, this document belongs to the company, so I want to see the rest of it on my desk ASAP. Understood?"

Without saying another word, I gave a little bow and withdrew.

When I left the building a short time later, I thought I would go directly to preparing for my next job. But as I walked along, I felt a deep despondency spreading into every corner of my being. Dark thoughts swirled about my head as the rest of me seemed to grow lighter and emptier by the minute. It was all I could do to stay on my feet. When I came to a park, I sank onto a bench in the shade.

I had joined the ranks of the mid-life unemployed at the worst possible time, smack in the middle of a recession. I did have some idea of the career change I wanted to make, but given how hollow I felt at that moment, it loomed as an impossibly distant dream.

Pigeons were cooing nearby. Grubby as they were, I wished I could join them and just fly off into the sky somewhere. Someone who's never worked for a corporation can't know what it means to be an organization man. But even for the person who has, the true meaning only becomes clear at the moment he loses the protection of his company. How was I ever going to look my wife and daughter in the eye again?

I knew no way to save myself. I could rely neither on my own devices nor on anyone else. I had no god to whom I could pray. How very small my world had become! . . .

It was going to take some time for me to get back on my feet. I waited for my strength to recover. But when I finally hauled myself up off that bench again, I was no longer the person I'd been when I sat down. Never could I return to the man I'd been before, in body or in spirit. Almost overnight, liver spots appeared on my face, and wrinkles formed where none had been. Gray hairs stood out on my head. I had frequent palpitations, and found myself tiring quickly. In a word, I aged. And to this day, I remain unable to refill the void that opened inside me that day.

I knew long before being exiled to the New Ventures Office that I'd been bumped off the corporate ladder. Nevertheless, I had continued to carry out my assigned tasks quite respectably. The successes I achieved within the New Ventures Office are already a matter of record. At no time did I ever sink into despair over my situation.

But in the days after I penned the standard "For personal reasons, I hereby tender my resignation" letter and submitted it to Polka Dot, thereby relinquishing my status as corporate employee (though to be precise, the man had no interest in seeing me again once he knew I wasn't going to cough up the information he wanted, so I actually handed the letter to his secretary), I found myself facing one situation after another in which my confidence was shaken and my dignity offended. I had gained my freedom, yet I was in danger of losing the ability to exercise that freedom.

First of all, I was stunned by the paltry size of my severance payment, which came to a fraction of my annual salary. I was sure there had been some mistake, but when I checked with accounting and learned the specific formulas by which the payment was calculated, I discovered that the figure was correct. For those who had done all the right things along the way, there were various allowances that could be added to the base amount, but I qualified only for the bare minimum. Since I needed funds for the new business I was planning to launch, this represented a major setback for me before I could even get started. I had failed in the all-essential "primitive accumulation of capital." As if that weren't enough, I still owed a large balance on my home mortgage. It was only a matter of time before we would feel the pinch.

The loss of long-standing relationships came as another serious blow. I was eager to discuss my new business plans with many of the people I'd known through my old job, but once they learned that I'd resigned, they became reluctant to even meet up. I had never been anything more to them than a representative of my company. During my long years as an employee, I'd always thought that I didn't really care all that much what others thought of me. It turned out I'd only had that luxury because I'd been under the corporate wing.

Of course, not everyone treated me that way. There were those who lent an ear to my plans with genuine interest. But it always complicates matters when money is involved. As important as I knew the money was, I had a difficult time broaching the subject with the people to whom I felt closest. It was a real dilemma. Momo was naturally among those I spoke with. She introduced me to a number of her acquaintances. But I couldn't bring myself to ask Momo herself for money. And most of the people she hooked me up with took the attitude that they were only talking to me as a favor to her.

I decided I would have to set aside this ambition of mine for the time being and look for a regular job. But none of the firms I applied to felt like a good fit.

One day, after yet another disappointing interview, I trudged up the sidewalk along Koshu Kaido Avenue to the south entrance of Shinjuku Station. I had intended to go on from there to check in at the job office and collect my unemployment, but my legs refused to carry me in that direction. Instead, they took me through the ticket gate and down the stairs to the Saikyo Line platform.

What could I be trying to do? I seemed to have a route to Yokokawa mapped out in my head . . . and from there a hike up to that tunnel by the double-arched brick bridge. Apparently, I wanted to see my uncle.

To find him, I would make my way into the tunnel and disappear into its darkness . . . My wife and daughter would be left with the house and the land on which it sits. For better or for worse, I'd been unable to get my new business off the ground, so the only debt I had was the mortgage on the house.

Before getting onto the train, I stopped at a kiosk on the platform and bought a can of beer. I popped it open as soon as I found a seat at the end of the nearest car.

I paused to buy a second beer when I was changing to the Shin'etsu Line at Takasaki. Two men dressed in suits and ties sat nearby, to all appearances traveling on business. Every so often they burst into easy laughter, as if they didn't have a care in the world. At least that was how I saw them.

The train had almost reached Yokokawa Station when the cell phone inside my briefcase started to ring. It was my first cell phone, bought the day after I quit my job. I still had a habit of leaving it at home, or, as on this day, forgetting that I had it with me even when I remembered to bring it. A group of high school students within earshot eyed me with curiosity. Cell phones were still an unusual sight at the time.

"Hello?"

It was Momo. Hearing her voice snapped me out of my beer-induced haze.

"I have a great lead on financing for you. Can we meet, like, right away? I think we should strike while the iron's hot."

"You're in Tokyo?"

"Uh-huh."

"Then right away won't be possible."

"Why? Where are you?"

"Yokokawa. Near Karuizawa."

"You mean the place with the famous clay-pot lunches? That Yokokawa? What're you doing way up there?"

"It's a long story. Anyway, that's where I am."

"In that case, come to my office at seven tonight. You can make it back by then, right?"

I looked at my watch. It was now half-past one. I had plenty of time.

"I'll bring you a pot lunch," I said.

I got off at Yokokawa but stayed on the platform and bought two of the local specialties at a kiosk. Since I never actually left the station, the image of Yokokawa preserved in my memory remains as it was when I met my uncle there as a teenager just after he'd come back from London. I know, though, that the new bullet train service to Nagano has in the meantime transformed Yokokawa Station from a famous stop on the old trunk line to the last station on a local branch line out of Takasaki.

The traffic was stop-and-go as the taxi slowly made its way toward Ogita's hospital. Since it was only about a fifteen-minute walk from the station, if it hadn't been for the rain I would have gone on foot. I felt like someone trapped in the cabin of a boat going nowhere.

At the entrance, the taxi drove up to a wall of people standing like a colony of Antarctic penguins at the edge of an ice shelf. They stood shivering in the cold, held up by the unexpected rainfall.

Taking a deep breath, I headed across the lobby. I had no cause to be nervous, but I could feel my pulse quickening as I made one wrong turn, then another in search of Ogita's private room.

I heard a clamor of voices at the end of the hall and realized as I approached that the room it came from was Ogita's. The door was all the way open and the space inside was filled to overflowing with visitors. Most of them were middle-aged men, but there were also a couple of older women and some young people of junior high or high school age. I gathered that a large group of relatives or acquaintances from back home had come up to Tokyo together to see him.

I climbed the stairs to the top floor and killed some time in the snack bar over a weak cup of coffee. Outside the window, the view of the distance was lost in a rainy haze, and a heavy gloom hung over the nearby warehouses.

When I went back, there were just three visitors left—a middle-aged man and two women, one probably in her thirties, the other somewhat younger. They seemed to be having trouble keeping the conversation going. I stepped into the doorway.

Ogita noticed me right away, before I could even open my mouth. "Hey, there you are. It's getting late enough, I'd started to think you might not make it today after all."

"I was here a bit earlier, but you had such a crowd I decided to have a cup of coffee and come back later."

I'd found an e-mail from Momo on my computer at work that morning, saying this would indeed be a good day to visit Ogita because he didn't have any tests scheduled. As she'd said before, she wouldn't be able to get away herself. But if it was all right, she'd let him know I was coming. I gave my assent, and told her what time I thought it would probably be.

The two women quickly took their leave as I entered. The man sat down on a small sofa in the corner without a word. Ogita made no effort to introduce us.

I stood next to the bed and looked at him. The head of the bed was raised behind his back. Momo was right: he didn't look the least bit like a sick man. Clean-shaven and in fresh pajamas, he might even have been described as the very picture of health. He did show his age, however. The years since I'd last seen him had left their mark in new wrinkles on his face.

Ogita spoke first. "You're looking old, Yajima."

"I didn't really expect to hear that from you."

"So how old would your little Ryo be by now?"

"Sixteen, I guess. She's in tenth grade."

"The last time I saw her would have been before she started grade school."

I vaguely recalled having Ogita over to the house once, but I couldn't remember how old my daughter was at the time.

"How's Asako?"

"Fine, thanks."

The room fell silent, and the click of heels passing in the corridor echoed in my ears.

"When Momo called to say you were coming, a picture of you with Ryo and Asako popped into my mind. It's been a long time since I saw Asako, too."

"Uh-huh," I said. I really wasn't in the mood for small talk. I contemplated cutting my visit as short as possible, but then remembered the colony of penguins I'd waded through at the hospital entrance.

"Now that I see you in person, I'd say the man I knew hasn't changed."

"Sure I have. I've been through some pretty rough times, as you well know." I deliberately fixed him with a glare as I said it.

Ogita turned his eyes away. As I gazed at him, I noticed that there was a certain underlying dinginess to the tone of his otherwise healthy-looking tan.

"You're head of your own company now, right? In that sense, I suppose you have to have changed. I never pegged you as having that kind of ambition before."

"I'm both the boss and the gofer," I said. "I have ambitions, all right, but not quite like you. I imagine that explains why I'm such a wimpy kind of boss."

"Well, whatever ambition I may have had, my body's decided to pack it in."

There was a despondent note in his voice that I could not remember ever hearing from him before. He looked me in the eye as he said it, and I was surprised to see his eyes blazing with anger. As if he found it utterly intolerable that a man with a great thirst for life faced death, while a man who was content just to set up a tiny company of no consequence got to live happily on.

I felt my blood rising, too. I had never forgiven Ogita. To my mind, he owed me an apology before he died. But it's difficult to stoke one's rage in front of a man close to death.

"I debated whether or not I should come," I said, intending to waste no time in getting to my final farewells.

"I actually didn't think you would," he immediately broke in. "You're such a cold fish."

"Cold fish?" I said, taken aback. "I don't think I deserve that from you."

His face suddenly changed, and he tried to put on a friendly smile.

"Momo was saying the same thing, you know. She said in some ways you seem to go through life holding people at arm's length."

"Momo said that?"

"Don't worry. She wasn't saying she didn't like you for it. I suggested you were the sort of guy who never even thinks of a woman again once you've broken up with her, and she was basically just agreeing that I was probably right. But when I went on to say that I wasn't like that, I almost always stayed friends with any woman I'd known, she really blew her stack. Which was totally understandable, considering all that we'd been through. I let myself get a little carried away."

The man on the sofa stifled a laugh. If it hadn't been for my past history with Ogita, I imagine I would have found the story funny too.

"You certainly haven't changed," I said, my eyes drifting to the orchid someone had placed behind his bed. "At this rate, I'm sure you'll get through the surgery just fine."

"Didn't Momo tell you? The surgery's completely pointless. And as if that weren't bad enough, some of the procedures I have to go through to prepare for it hurt like hell."

"Yeah, she told me. But I don't think surgery's ever completely pointless."

"They told me my chances of living a little longer *might* go up ten percent. How much point is there in that? Anyway, I figure you actually have to be kind of pleased that this is happening to me, aren't you?"

I was caught off balance by this unexpected jab.

"Pleased? Hardly. Though I can't say I'm especially broken up about it either. We've known each other a long time. It's not an easy thing to come to terms with."

"Sure it is. I'm going to die. You're not. At least not for a while. The same for Momo. I've already accepted it. Go ahead and rejoice."

Refusing to take the bait, I chose my words carefully. "I didn't come here expecting this kind of talk," I said.

"Then what did you come expecting? I don't imagine you came only as a favor to Momo. It was more than that, right?"

His words brought me up short. Why, indeed, had I decided to come? . . .

"I can't say I had any particular expectations," I said. "It seems unlike you. The Ogita I knew would have just assumed that I'd come to see him like everybody else."

He shook his head.

"As I was leaving the house this morning, Asako made a point of reminding me that this was a sick call, and I should behave accordingly. So I told her, 'I promise I won't pull the plug on his life-support system—though I wouldn't mind yanking an IV or two.' She gave me a stern look and said, 'That's not funny.' So I get here and there's not an IV in sight, let alone anything else. Instead, you've got a whole crowd of visitors whooping it up around your bed. What a relief. I was saved from turning to crime."

Ogita made a sour face but said nothing. Seeing his expression, I wondered if maybe I'd said too much. But I can't deny that I also felt a little twinge of satisfaction.

"I think I'd better be going. When I'm out of the office, there's no one to take care of all the little odds and ends."

"Say hello to Ryo and Asako for me, will you?" Ogita said, not quite meeting my eyes.

As I strode out the door, the man in the corner got up noisily from the sofa. I was almost at the nurses' station before he caught up with me.

"Excuse me—Mr. Yajima, I believe it was?" he said.

"Yes?" I replied, slackening my pace a little but not stopping. Maybe it was precisely this sort of thing that prompted the accusations of holding people at arm's length.

"My name is Sawamura, and I'm a longtime acquaintance of Mr. Ogita's. Might I ask what your connection with him is?"

"We went to college together."

"So you've known him for a long time, too."

"Yep," I said curtly. His cloying tone irritated me, and I wanted nothing to do with him.

"All the more, then, wasn't that awfully insensitive—what you said in there a minute ago? You must be aware of his condition. You mentioned his upcoming surgery. And yet you joke about pulling out his life-support system and IVs? That really crosses the line in my book."

I stared at his face. He looked dead serious. He had apparently decided it was his duty to punish me for my bad behavior. What a pain in the neck.

"It's really none of your concern."

"I'm afraid I can't accept that. The poor man's already in a shaky state, thinking about the operation. The sort of thing you said could make him hit rock bottom."

Sawamura had moved half a step ahead of me, glancing over his shoulder as he spoke.

"I'd like you to go back and apologize to him."

"Mind your own business."

"That's exactly what I'm doing. I consider Mr. Ogita my benefactor, and when my benefactor is ill and someone insults him, I can't just forgive and forget."

"I see no reason why I should need your forgiveness."

Sawamura trotted out in front of me and blocked my path. His sturdy build suggested someone trained in judo. I could be in real trouble if he decided to take me down. But I felt remarkably calm. No matter who he was, he couldn't very well start a serious fight in a hospital hallway. He had to be counting on someone stepping in before it reached that point.

Without another word, I started to move around him. He shot out a hand to grab me by the shirt. I swept my right arm around to brush it aside.

"Let's not have any rough stuff in here," came a reprimand from the nurses' station.

A middle-aged nurse fixed us with a stern gaze. There was no anger in her voice, however, nor did she appear particularly alarmed at our little scuffle. Women in white and pink and sky blue uniforms cast disapproving looks our way. A number of patients and visitors had noticed the disturbance as well and eyed us with curiosity.

I moved to step around Sawamura again.

"I want you to apologize," he said, remaining rooted to where he stood.

"What would *you* know?" I spat out as I slipped on by.

Here's what Momo had to say over our clay-pot lunches in a conference room at her office.

In the plane on her way back from Germany, she happened to run into an old friend of hers (and Ogita's)—the president of Handa Enterprises. Given the opportunity, she realized, she should see if she couldn't sell him on investing in my new company. After all, I had effectively been *his* company's savior once upon a time.

After listening to her, Handa looked for a moment as though he'd been put on the spot, but then almost immediately said, "Since it's for you and Yajima, I'll see what I can do."

"If it was this afternoon, I could have gone with you to see him," Momo told me. "Too bad. But I suppose from your perspective, that would've been me sticking my nose in too far. Anyway, he said the day after tomorrow looked good—in the evening. Be sure to give him a call."

I felt tears welling in my eyes and had to blink them back. My feelings of despair began to fade as I munched on my food. I was saved.

"What were you doing up in Yokokawa anyway?"

"I have an uncle there. It's not like he can actually do anything to help, but sometimes when I'm in a tough spot, I like to go see him."

Momo looked me straight in the eye. Her lips thrust forward as if she were about to say something, but in the end she remained silent.

I barely slept a wink between the time I got home that night and two days later when I arrived at Handa Enterprises to give my presentation. I threw every waking minute into reworking my business plan and polishing up the supporting documentation. With Handa Enterprises as my prospect, I had a good feeling about how things would turn out. It was during these two days that Yosuke Yoshida's Internet Emporium, better known simply as YY, took its place in my plan.

Among the various possibilities I'd explored after being shuffled off to the New Ventures Office was the idea of doing business on the Internet, which the Japanese public was finally beginning to warm to around that time. There was nothing particularly original about the basic idea, of course, but I think very few people believed, as I did, that "high quality" could be a selling point even on the Internet.

It was an era when most opinions about the Internet inclined to one of two extremes. Some said it opened up a whole new world in which traditional business models would be completely superseded. Others insisted that the idea of making a profit there was nothing but a pipe dream.

I tried out the Amazon.com online bookstore a number of times in the course of gathering information. The American site's careful design along with the measures it took to set the user's mind at ease and simplify the buying process made a strong impression on me, and I became convinced the same methods could be adopted in launching a new Web-based business in Japan. But before I got to any concrete development, my old company had thrown me out on the street. So I decided to pursue the idea on my own. Except that, from the very beginning, my plan was not to set up an independent site that I would own myself, but rather to manage a cybermall belonging to a site owned by someone else. I didn't think I had it in me to handle the reins of a large business. My love was not big enough.

I surfed the Web in search of a suitable partner. I was looking for a site that was a bit rough around the edges, like they were just faking it, yet where I could sense a certain underlying energy and backbone. It was by applying my expertise to transform a site like that into an attractive, high quality experience that I could add value. If instead of erasing every trace of the site's original crudeness, I could preserve some of those characteristics as part of its personality even after the makeover, all the better.

On the day I made my pitch at Handa Enterprises, I hadn't yet had any contact with Yosuke Yoshida, but I claimed that I'd already negotiated a preliminary agreement with a well-known e-tailer. I also touted Amazon.com to the hilt, enthusing over all the attention its methods were receiving in the United States and talking up the advantages of introducing those methods to Japan before anyone else, presenting for their examination only such data and information as was favorable to my case. Anybody who wanted to check would have immediately learned that Amazon had yet to make a single cent in profit at that point. But I was presenting to three top executives—the founder and chairman of the board, his son the current president, and a managing director I'd worked with while at my old company—all of whom were still completely dependent on assistants even for handling e-mail, and they raised no questions at all.

As a matter of fact, it may not even have mattered to them what I proposed to do. Momo had effectively twisted the president's arm, and although his father the chairman was famous for being a tightwad, he never forgot a favor: if it was for someone he owed, he was quite willing to ignore the question of profitability—at least so long as the amount involved was not too large. I returned from my presentation with an informal promise of financing, and I immediately called Momo to thank her.

Next came YY. It took some effort, but I managed to get an appointment with Yosuke Yoshida, and when I met him I took the liberty of upgrading the informal promise of financing I'd obtained from Handa into a close business alliance with them.

I had worn my hair fairly long ever since college, but on the day before the YY meeting, I had it cut short. I squirmed a little inside when I saw how much older it made me look, but reassured myself that it also gave me more of an air of authority.

When I think back on it now, it was quite a high-wire act. And as it turned out, the precarious tightrope walk continued for a time even after the business was officially off the ground. Recalling some of the deceptions I got away with makes me break out in a cold sweat—though I also find it quite amusing.

It was still raining, but at least half of the penguins crowded around the hospital entrance had apparently plunged into the ocean, and the taxi queue was a good bit shorter as well. As I stepped toward the end of the line, a black Mercedes pulled up, and I heard a voice shout "Yuki!" I turned to see Momo peering through the open rear window.

Opening and closing her own door, she came trotting over to where I stood.

"You're leaving?" she asked in her usual relaxed manner.

"Uh-huh. Did your stuff wind up early?"

"I just slipped out for a bit. I'll run up to say hello and come right back, so can you wait? I have use of this car for as long as I need it."

She threw a look toward the taxi queue as she said it. The weather was not especially cold for this time of year, but waiting in line would still be a drag.

As I sat on a waiting-room sofa at one end of the lobby, I felt my spirits sagging. I regretted letting myself be persuaded to come see Ogita. And I bristled at having had to deal with the likes of that Sawamura character, even if only in the briefest of encounters. At the same time, I found myself thinking that there was indeed something to what he'd said, and squirmed uncomfortably at my own suggestibility . . .

Barely ten minutes later, Momo was back. "Why the dismal look?" she said.

I got to my feet without a word.

"Did something happen up there?" she asked as we walked toward the entrance. "He didn't mention anything."

"Not with him," I said, and then briefly recounted for her the incident in the hallway. "Do you know this guy named Sawamura?"

"Only by sight. I've seen him here several times, but I don't know who he really is. There've always been some pretty dubious characters in Ogita's circle. He's not at all picky about who he deals with, you know."

When we got to the car, Momo climbed in first and told the driver, "We'll be going back by way of Shibuya. Near the expressway ramp on 246."

"No, no, just drop me at the nearest station," I said.

"It's hardly even out of my way."

Traffic was backed up from the hospital clear to the main road. As I stared ahead at the unmoving line of cars, I yawned. Low barometric pressure always makes me sleepy. When I lowered my hand again after covering my mouth, I brushed Momo's arm.

Our eyes met, and a smile spread across her face like a flower slowly unfolding. The wrinkles around her eyes only made her look all the prettier.

"The truth is, I got kind of worried. I know how Ogita can be, especially now, and you're not as unflappable as you look, either."

"I don't know how I look, but I'm the epitome of unflappable."

A twist of sarcasm came into Momo's smile. "In case you've forgotten, back at the old company, you butted heads with the higher-ups more than anyone."

"No way."

"I guess you weren't aware of the effect you had. You may not remember it, but I promise you, your former bosses do. You should ask them."

If she was right, I could understand that it would not have endeared me to them as an employee.

"So were you worried more about me, or about Ogita?"

"Both. You can both be as stubborn as little kids. I know you only came because I begged you to. I'm sorry if it left you with a bad taste in your mouth."

"It was no problem at all," I said. And sitting there next to Momo, I started to feel that was really true.

"Looks like it's letting up," she said. But out the window on my side, the rain appeared as heavy as ever.

The driver seemed to be taking an inordinate interest in me in the rearview mirror, and it was starting to irritate me. Did I make him curious because I looked like a different breed from his usual clientele? Or was he maybe imagining something improper between Momo and me? I'd have thought such an obvious show of curiosity would be taboo for the driver of a chauffeur-driven luxury car. Such thoughts played through my mind as I began paying closer attention to him, when suddenly I noticed that he appeared not to be human. To judge from the way his mouth and nose thrust forward in a snout, he must be a deer or a bear, or some other creature of that type. But his fingers were extraordinarily long, and as if that weren't spooky enough, there was a short little tongue waggling from beneath each of his claws. Maybe the limo company was trying to hold down costs, but even so, wasn't it going a bit too far to hire drivers like this? For that matter, wasn't it outright illegal to employ anything but a human as a chauffeur? I turned toward Momo intending to draw her attention to this, but she had disappeared from the seat beside me, and I had an unobstructed view of the scene beyond her window. A fake, cardboard sun hung beneath a gray sky that seemed to threaten snow at any moment. This sun must have been what fooled Momo a while ago and made her think the rain was letting up . . .

I felt my shoulder being shaken and pushed my eyelids open to see Momo peering at me. She looked a little annoyed. I suppose I really shouldn't have fallen asleep.

"You seem pretty worn out," she said gently. "Do you think maybe you're working too hard?" Apparently she wasn't annoyed with me after all.

"Mmm, yeah, well, I don't know . . ." I decided to let her think it was indeed too much work. I couldn't very well tell her I'd simply drifted off because of the low pressure system. I wasn't some house cat.

The forbidding but familiar streetscape formed by the crush of buildings that flanked Route 246 and the elevated expressway came to a halt outside the window. Several buses roared noisily by one after the other. The rain had stopped.

"I'm so glad you came. He's determined to put up a strong front, but it had to be really eating at him that he couldn't see you."

"Well, I thought it was something I ought to do—to visit him at least once. Even if I didn't really want to."

The driver had circled around the car and was waiting to open my door. He looked more like an over-earnest penguin than a deer or a bear.

Momo extended her hand. "Anyway, thank you," she said.

"Don't mention it," I replied. "And thanks for the ride."

I took her hand, and she gave me a squeeze back.

When I finished up for the day and emerged from the building a little after eight, air thick with moisture hung softly over the darkened city like an invisible mist. It was a balmy evening, suggesting the arrival of spring.

On my way down Dogenzaka I saw the woman I thought was probably Chinese roving the sidewalk in her usual white down coat. Wasn't it about time I actually said something to her, I thought. Besides, I hadn't been able to shake off the blue funk I'd been in since visiting Ogita, and I needed something to lift my spirits.

With this double motive providing the wind at my back, I began steering my way through the crowds of pedestrians who jostled up and down the hill, catching one current, resisting another. The down coat gradually drew nearer. I was within only a few meters of the woman's back when with perfect timing she turned around. In the artificial light falling on her from every direction, she broke into a friendly, easygoing smile. A second later, from some other direction in the crowd, I felt another set of eyes staring at me.

"Hey there, boss. Is it just going to be straight home as always today?"

My smile froze beneath the surface of my cheeks, and the greeting I'd intended to offer in the interest of international friendship shrank back deep into my throat. I was afraid Ryo might be watching.

But when I turned my head to look about me, the feeling disappeared and did not return.

I asked my wife about Ryo when I got home.

"She came home earlier than usual saying she wasn't feeling well. But she ate a normal dinner, so I think she's probably okay. How did your visit with Ogita go?"

I told her how he hadn't looked the least bit sick, and about my encounter with Sawamura. I chose not to mention running into Momo, though I'm not quite sure why.

During the day, Asako had apparently found her mind drifting repeatedly back over the years since we'd been married.

"I was thinking how, compared to the Ogitas, it must look to others like we've had a blah and boring life, but it certainly hasn't been an uneventful one."

"You mean like me losing my job, and then going into debt to start my own company? Those were tough times all right. If you hadn't taken it all in stride, at least as far as you let on, I might well have thrown up my hands along the way."

"I was worried, but I had this vague feeling that we'd come out okay in the end. I wasn't just putting up a good front."

"So I have your vague feeling to thank."

"But things really did keep working out, right?"

I had never told my wife about that day when I'd given up hope.

"I wonder if I ought to visit Ogita, too," she said.

"He asked me to say hello to you and Ryo." I didn't think I wanted her to go.

"Ryo was still in kindergarten, so I guess it's been over ten years since she and I last saw him."

In the days that followed, there were several more times when I felt someone's eyes on me as I headed down toward Shibuya Station for lunch or on my way home after work. I wondered if maybe Yuta Iwamoto was watching me, but I never actually caught sight of him anywhere.

Meanwhile, Ryo remained in school and went there faithfully every day, but she was also constantly staying out late, and at home she seemed to be avoiding talking to her mother and me even more than usual. Asako had been right: the long talk I had with my daughter in the park on New Year's Day had failed to connect with her in any significant way. Life went on like this with little change until near the end of winter term.

Going home after eleven one night, I spotted Ryo riding in the same train car. The car was too crowded for me to move to where she was. Our eyes met once, so I was pretty sure she'd seen me, but then she avoided turning my way again. From the side, the look on her face seemed to express not so much defiance as hopelessness.

Her door was closer to the head of the stairs when we reached our station and she went on down without waiting for me. I saw her disappear into the ladies' room near the ticket gate. Passing on through the gate, I waited for her on the other side.

She had apparently anticipated this. She walked toward me with her eyes averted, brushing her hair back with one hand.

"Sorry I'm so late," she said before I could open my mouth.

"Looks like we'll have to give you a curfew," I said coldly.

She let several moments go by before responding. "Fine, give me a curfew, but I want to get a job. I know the school says we're not supposed to work, but it'll be okay if it's close to home."

Why had mentioning a curfew made her bring up getting a job? I certainly wasn't going to give her permission to work late at night. As I puzzled over what the connection might be, I turned to look her way and a passing breeze brought me a whiff of her hair and clothes. Mixed in among the smells of greasy food and cigarette smoke and perfume I recognized another very distinct odor that took me back to my youth. A languorous, sweet-smelling smoke. There could be no mistake. In my college days, one of my friends lived in a dorm where they secretly grew pot, and I had been a regular beneficiary. My good fortune lasted for about a year, until a feud between different factions of leftist extremists culminated in a murder at the dorm and the entire place was shut down. I knew that smell too well to mistake it.

"Look, Ryo, you're not old enough yet to be staying out to all hours of the night. Especially if you're doing things that are against the law. That's not something I can just look the other way about."

She turned to me as though taken aback, but immediately looked away again. Fixing her eyes straight ahead, she started walking faster.

"It's marijuana, right? I recognize the smell. Are you into harder stuff, too?" I lowered my voice to avoid being overheard by other pedestrians walking ahead and behind.

"I've never touched it myself," she said in her normal voice.

"But you were there when others were doing the stuff? That's not good either."

"You did pot when you were young, right?" I was caught off guard by this comeback. "I mean, that has to be how you know the smell. Yuta had you pegged. He said you were definitely the type."

"I don't want to see you get arrested."

She shot me a withering look that seemed to say, *So are you telling me I just have to make sure I don't get caught? Like you didn't get caught?*

When we reached the house, Ryo started to go straight to her room, so I called her back. She sat down at the dining table with a sullen look on her face.

I asked Asako to come, too, and announced that Ryo would have a curfew of seven from now on.

"*SEV-en?* No way! That's not fair! My manga and graphic arts groups meet after school. I can't possibly be home that early."

I shook my head.

"You'll be home by seven, and dinner will be at seven-thirty. If I can't be here, you'll sit down with your mother."

Ryo's face grew darker, but she raised no further protests and simply gave a small nod. Then she turned to her mother and asked, "May I go now?"

"Yes," she said.

I felt my gorge rising, at both of them, but if I objected at this point, it would undermine the appearance of a united parental front.

After Ryo was gone, Asako said, "I don't have a problem with giving her a curfew, but I wish you'd consulted me first. And I hope this means that from now on you're going to call and tell me whether you'll be home by seven thirty. Otherwise, I won't know how much dinner to make."

"Of course," I answered, but I groaned a little inside. That was something I hadn't thought about.

After that, Ryo stopped staying out to all hours. But she observed her seven o'clock curfew only in the loosest sort of way, thinking nothing of missing the mark by twenty or thirty minutes. As the one dealing with this on a day-to-day basis, my wife had to wage a constant war with her. My work generally kept me too busy to get home for dinner with them.

Momo kept me updated on Ogita's condition by e-mail, informing me that his operation had gone well and, a short while later, that he'd been discharged from the hospital. His mother came up to Tokyo to see to his needs during his recovery, and Momo had been wheedled into getting things set up for mother and son's "new life together" after his discharge—almost like a doting parent helping to set up a pair of clueless newlyweds in their first marital home. A son over fifty and his mother in her mid-seventies were now living together under the same roof for the first time in decades, with the added complication that the son was gravely ill.

> I don't know how many times Mrs. Ogita has come crying to me that her son was a fool to split up with such a devoted wife.
>
> Her opinion of me seems to have gone up quite a few notches since when we were married.
>
> But it's only because we're not married anymore that I can do things for him without all the emotional baggage, so I still think it's good that we got divorced.
>
> Though I have to admit, I'm totally baffled sometimes why I keep going to such lengths to help him out.

The messages from Momo broke off once mother and son had settled in together. I gathered that Ogita's cancer was in remission for the moment. But the next time he went into the hospital it would mean that death was near. Ogita had asked Momo to go ahead and make hospice arrangements, but she'd told me she couldn't bring herself to do it because she knew how fiercely his mother would object.

So I pretty much assumed that my next message from Momo would be when Ogita's cancer came roaring back.

One day after six, I realized I hadn't called my wife yet, but decided to check my e-mail first and found a message from Momo in my mailbox. I thought it had to be about Ogita, and a chill went through me.

Dear Yuki,

I know it's short notice, but could we meet tonight? I'm feeling down. And annoyed. If you can do dinner, call or text my cell by 8.

Momo

She'd sent it from her phone. A picture of Momo in a fit of pique rose before my eyes.

I looked around the office. None of my staff had gone home yet. The one person not present was out on a sales call.

Just then the door opened and the missing Hashida entered. "Boss," he said as he hurried in, omitting his usual greeting and hurrying straight up to me at the big desk. He leaned close to my ear. "There's a weird kid hanging around outside the door."

"A weird kid . . . ?"

"He was standing there in the hall, and when I came this way he asked if this was Mr. Yajima's company. I asked who he was, but he just walked toward the elevator without saying anything, so I let him be. He looked like a high school kid."

I immediately got up from the desk.

"Be careful. He could be dangerous," Hashida warned. "You can never tell what kids might do these days."

"I think I know who it is. He's okay."

I found Yuta Iwamoto standing by the elevator with his head turned the other way.

"Did you want something?" I asked.

Still avoiding my eyes, he bobbed his head in a little bow. He seemed wound up pretty tight about something.

"I wanted to talk with you. I mean, that is, there's something I wanted to tell you. But it can wait till you're done for the day."

"Okay, but you can't be hanging around out here in the hallway." Even as I said this, a woman who'd emerged from another door on the same floor was giving us strange looks, glancing back and forth between us. When I smiled and said, "Have a nice evening," she cocked her head a little uncertainly and replied, "Thank you. You too."

I went back into the office with Yuta. We drew even more quizzical looks from my staff than we'd gotten from the woman outside.

"He's the son of an acquaintance of mine," I announced by way of explanation.

I led the boy into my private office and told him he could wait for me there, motioning for him to have a seat on the sofa. I left the door ajar. Ayumi thoughtfully took him a canned coffee drink.

I looked up at the clock on the wall. Almost six thirty. Momo had said to let her know by eight. How long was this talk or whatever with Yuta likely to take, I wondered. Dialing my home number, I told Asako she didn't need to prepare any dinner for me. I could tell by her voice that she wasn't happy about it.

"Is Ryo home yet?" I asked.

"Uh-huh," she said. "For the last week or so, she's been quite a bit earlier."

"That's a surprise."

"I don't suppose you could have noticed . . ."

Pretty much as soon as I got off the phone, my staff started wrapping up for the night and taking their leave. By ten of seven, Yuta and I were left alone.

"Have you had dinner?" I called to him from the desk in the main room.

"No, but I'm not really hungry," he said.

Picking up my mug of green tea, I went into the smaller room and sat down at my own desk.

"So what is it you want to tell me? Something about Ryo? Or something unrelated?"

He looked at the floor. A feeling of weariness came over me as I recalled the barrier of silence he'd maintained the first time I met him. He claimed he had something to tell me, but I couldn't be sure he even knew how to talk.

Still avoiding my eyes, he raised his hand to touch his silvery blond hair several times in a kind of nervous tic before finally opening his mouth.

"Um, I'm not sure what I should call her when I'm talking to you, but I hope just Ryo is okay. If I said Miss Ryo or Miss Yajima, it'd feel like I'm talking about someone else."

"That'll be fine," I said.

"Ryo suggested I should come up here once to see what your company is like."

"Why is that?"

"I don't do it myself, but the other kids I hang out with, they sometimes call Ryo 'the boss man's little princess,' not in a bad way, you know, but when they say things like that, Ryo, she usually just laughs and ignores them."

He glanced up at me for a second as if to get my reaction, but I offered no response.

"And, um, since I started going out with Ryo, my buddies, they've been teasing that I'm not as much fun to hang out with anymore, but I never let it bother me. Until the other day, this chick who's a couple years older starts razzing me, saying Yuta has this thing for rich girls, that's why he picked Ryo, because she's the boss man's precious little princess, and she starts laughing at me with this other chick. Actually, the other one, she was somebody I'd turned down once when she wanted me to go someplace with her, and I think she still can't get over it. Her dad owns, like, a whole bunch of buildings in Ikebukuro and Omiya, and he's super rich."

He looked up at me again. I didn't like the direction this was taking, but I continued to act as though I had no reaction at all.

"I was just going to ignore them, but they turn to Ryo, and they go, 'We see your dad a lot on Dogenzaka, you know,' and they start making snide remarks about how the girls touting for customers call out to him like they know him, and he doesn't seem to mind at all, and they want to know, 'If your dad's got his own company, why doesn't he come to work in a car?' These chicks, themselves, they never show up at the club except in some guy's wheels or a cab, and I figure her old man wouldn't be caught dead going anywhere all by himself on his own two feet, but what's it to them what anybody else does? So I finally yelled at them to give it a frigging rest. Well, they glared at me for a minute and then went off somewhere else, but . . ."

He broke off.

"But what?"

"Well, I thought I was standing up for Ryo when I said what I did, but all of a sudden I find out Ryo's pissed at me, too. I couldn't figure it out. That's when she told me, 'You should go visit my dad's company sometime and see for yourself.' Then she gets up and stalks out of the place."

He looked at me with a *What was that about?* look in his eyes. He apparently thought I might be able to explain why Ryo had blown up at him. Well, he'd have to ask her. I had no idea, either.

"Okay, that explains why you came. So, now that you're here, what do you think? You've seen pretty much the whole works. Besides these two rooms, all we have is a bathroom and an office kitchenette."

"It may be small, but I think it's cool. I'd like to have a company like this someday, too. Forget the big corporations. Not that they'd have me, anyway, I guess, but . . . The people you have working for you seem nice, too."

"They do, don't they," I said with a smile.

Friendliness first; everything else will follow—that was our company's motto. Keep the office tidy at all times. No one should have to break the bank on clothes, but always maintain a neat appearance. Be friendly to one and all.

"Ryo told me about what a tough time you had getting this place going . . . Anyway, sorry if this seems pushy, but I wanted to tell you a little about myself. From what Ryo's said about you, I figured you'd understand."

"You think *I*," I said, pointing my right index finger at my chest, "will understand you?"

"I know I might look that way, but I'm not just a goof-off, and I think I've been treating Ryo with respect. Since she said you gave her a curfew the other day, I've been trying to make sure she gets home on time. Though I've also been wondering if the whole curfew thing isn't my fault to begin with."

I glanced at my watch. It was already half past seven.

"Hold on, will you," I said. "You're a friend of Ryo's, so I want to hear you out. But if you'll wait just one second, I need to send off a quick e-mail."

I went to my computer in the other room and sent my regrets to Momo:

Sorry, it'll have to be another time.

Sitting face-to-face, just him and me, I found that I wasn't as put off by this boy as I had been before. I gathered he was quite popular with the girls, and I could sort of see why. Though, actually, that was one thing that still rubbed me the wrong way about him, too.

"I imagine Ryo's told you about my family?" he said.

"Some," I answered. "I know your mother got sick, and that you and your father moved back in with your grandparents. I guess that's about it."

As if to brace himself, the boy drew in a deep breath and then slowly let it out.

The story Yuta told about his family was a grim one. A city boy of good birth and good heart fell in love with a pretty, innocent country girl, also of good birth. They got married and in due course had a baby boy and girl. For a time they were the very model of the happy family. Although friction between the young Mrs. Iwamoto and her mother-in-law remained a headache while they lived under the same roof, once the newlyweds moved to their own house in the suburbs, even that problem appeared to have been resolved. But as it turned out, that was precisely when things began to fall apart for the young family.

Mrs. Iwamoto was unable to adapt to life in her new surroundings—a recently developed upscale subdivision. As a stay-at-home mother, the isolation unnerved her. Insulated as they were from any major traffic artery, she found herself frightened by the extreme quietness of the neighborhood, broken only by the occasional sound of a child practicing the piano. Before long, she was on the verge of a nervous breakdown. Her husband's first response was of unconcern. But then, as time went by, he grew increasingly annoyed at her gloominess and endless grumbling. He began staying out later after work, and on his days off he found excuses to visit his parents so he would not have to remain at home. Occasionally, he even raised a hand against his wife. All of this deepened her loneliness, and she began taking her frustrations out on the children. Yuta said he remembered almost nothing of his family from his preschool years.

This first period of difficulties fell behind them about the time Yuta entered first grade and his sister started kindergarten. Yuta excelled both in the classroom and on the playground, and his mother made friends with other mothers at the kindergarten, which brought a period of respite to her battle with loneliness.

But the good times did not last long. They came to an abrupt end when his mother injured a neighbor's child while driving her car. Although she'd barely touched the girl, it was enough to knock her to the ground and break her arm. The ensuing barrage of blame was more than Mrs. Iwamoto could cope with, and she found herself isolated again. Her husband blamed her as well, and things snowballed from bad to worse.

"In the space of just one week, it was as if blinds had been pulled down all around our house and we were suddenly living in total darkness," Yuta recalled.

His parents now yelled at each other in an unending series of arguments. His little sister woke up one morning with a rash covering her face and arms and legs. She was treated for atopic dermatitis but failed to respond well, and her mother sank increasingly into depression again. Exasperated by her relapse, Yuta's father returned to his former ways, hitting and kicking his wife even more violently than before. Yuta also felt the brunt of his punches as he tried to shield his mother from this abuse.

There were many nights when Mr. Iwamoto failed to come home at all. As before, he would say that he had to look in on his parents in Eifukucho, and on weekends he sometimes took Yuta and his sister with him, but most of the time he was actually at a mistress's house.

Although the family managed to cover for Mrs. Iwamoto in the presence of other people, by the time Yuta entered junior high it became increasingly clear that her deteriorating mental condition required professional attention. Her husband and mother-in-law were concerned about appearances, however, and refused to let her be seen by a psychiatrist.

Yuta threw himself into his schoolwork in an effort to make at least that part of his life a more positive experience.

"I played the model student—the best I'd ever been," he said.

From his youngest days he'd been a natural athlete, and when he joined the soccer club in junior high, he quickly established himself as a player to be reckoned with. He often stayed on after practice to run through some more exercises by himself. This was his way of avoiding what awaited him when he got home—the dismal look on his mother's face and her litany of woes. In her clashes with his father, Yuta always sided with his mother, but it was difficult to suppress his loathing for her when it was just the two of them. He hated feeling that way, but he couldn't stop himself from feeling what he did.

Yuta didn't witness the incident himself, but he learned that his mother had tried to kill herself when she was alone with his father. She was obviously close to the breaking point. His little sister was sent to live with their grandparents.

The rest of them continued to live as before for a while longer. The curtains stayed closed even during the day and a gray mood filled the house. It pained Yuta to see his mother spend whole days at the kitchen table doing nothing but chew on her nails.

One fateful day, Yuta's father told him he had to make a decision. Although he knew his father was at least half to blame for what had happened to his mother, he felt he had no choice but to go with him.

His mother moved back to her parents' home in the country, where she was admitted to a hospital. The divorce became final a year later. So far as Yuta knew, she remained under treatment even now—though not once in the intervening years had he personally ever heard from her.

A year after the divorce, his father remarried, giving Yuta a new mother. She supposedly was not the former mistress, but his father never offered any details about her.

"She's not a bad person. In fact, she's cheerful and friendly and my sister's very attached to her. They're such good friends it almost seems unnatural."

But Yuta's relationship with his father remained difficult. Thinking about his mother brought pangs of guilt for having abandoned her, which in turn triggered hostility toward his father. When he was with his family, he felt like he had no place there. Meanwhile, school had become a drag. He began spending his time wandering about town and acquired a new group of friends on the street—which might make him look like a delinquent to someone like me, but he'd never done anything that could actually be called a crime. Getting into fights was about the extent of it.

"Believe it or not, I'm pretty fast on my feet," he grinned.

When I didn't return his smile, he quickly wiped the grin off his face.

"I've been careful to treat Ryo right. I know she's not the kind who'd normally hang out with guys like me or my buddies, and she's smart enough not to get in too deep. I mean, I've never said this to Ryo, but the problems she thinks she has, if you ask me, they're really not anything to get all that worked up about—though I know everybody's sensitive about different stuff, so it's no big deal. What I'm trying to say is, you run into all sorts of people in Shibuya, but I think maybe grown-ups tend to see only the bad side, only outer appearances, so even though I don't normally care if people understand me or not, I wanted you to know that that's not all I am, I have good points too, and, I mean, I absolutely do not believe I've ever strayed onto the wrong path. I hope you can believe that."

I looked at my watch. It was now after nine. I was famished, but I had a question or two I wanted to put to the boy.

"You said Ryo knows enough not to get in too deep, but she came home with a rather distinctive smell on her the other night. I didn't figure it was anything regular with her, but still, wouldn't you say that qualifies as getting in pretty deep? Or does pot not count as getting in too deep for you?"

Yuta dropped his head. "I wasn't there that day," he said. "I'd told her before not to go to parties like that, and I really didn't think she would, but I guess they managed to sweet-talk her into tagging along. She swore she didn't do any herself, though."

I had to consciously hold back a sigh.

"How about you? Do you often go to parties like that?"

"I wouldn't say often . . ." He was still looking at the floor. "Recently, not at all."

"Look at me a minute," I said and he finally raised his head. "If you want to continue going out with my daughter, then I want you to promise me you won't go to parties like that or do pot anymore. Not by yourself, and not with your buddies. I assume you understand why I insist on this—considering that you made the effort to come and talk to me as Ryo's father."

He replied with a firmness that surprised me. "I won't go, sir. And I promise I won't do the stuff by myself, either."

For several moments we held each other's gaze. I started to say something but hesitated, and then Yuta seemed to do the same. In the end we both said nothing.

He got to his feet. "Thank you for your time, and for hearing me out."

After stepping out into the hallway, Yuta turned to make a little bow. Then he pulled a cell phone from his hip pocket and flipped it open with the urgency of a desperately thirsty man offered a cup of water. When the elevator arrived, he dipped his head in another little bow as he stepped inside, but his eyes never left his phone's display.

I had listened attentively to everything he said, but at the same time, like a tongue involuntarily probing a swollen gum, my mind was poking through some long-forgotten memories of my own childhood and adolescence.

For example, I found myself recalling a scene from sixth grade.

My class was scheduled to leave for several days of Seaside School, and we'd been told to assemble on the playground, but I arrived late (I'd acquired a tardiness habit in kindergarten, which I never managed to kick until I started running my own company). I had reached the street that skirted the playground, when I saw one of my classmates coming toward me from the direction of the main gate, hand in hand with his little brother, walking away from school. It puzzled me for a moment, but then I understood.

The boy was an unruly kid who was forever getting into trouble. His clothes were always dirty, he seemed to rarely take a bath, and he smelled bad if you got too close. Everyone in the class knew that he belonged to the handful of students exempted from paying the monthly lunch fee. To participate in Seaside School, we'd all been told to bring a small amount of money, something like a hundred yen, to cover the cost of cooking ingredients (we would prepare the food ourselves), but the boy's parents had apparently been unable to let him have even that much. Although quite a few other parents had trouble paying their kids' lunch fees on time, I'm pretty sure this boy was the only one who didn't get to go to Seaside School.

Our eyes met. A sad smile flickered across his lips. I hurried past him to the gate. He and his brother trudged on down the road next to the playground where all our classmates were assembled.

It was an era when the curse of poverty was a serious concern. This state of affairs went on for a good many years, but then somewhere along the line it faded from people's consciousness. Which is not to say that poverty actually disappeared—merely that no one but the poor themselves considered it a pressing issue anymore. (The classmate who was too poor to go to Seaside School grew up to become a reasonably successful builder in my hometown. He later went bankrupt, but I understand that in his more prosperous days he was a big spender who was popular with the local bar girls.)

Yuta's troubles came not from poverty but from family dysfunction—the problem that afflicts our own era. Children are cooped up inside. Neither parents nor children are really plugged into their community or wider society. It means that when difficulties arise at home, the children have nowhere to go. Once they feel there's no place for them at home, they lose sight of anything to live for. They may withdraw even further, shutting themselves up in their own rooms. Or if they're strong enough to fly out of the coop, they may seek new ties outside the family.

At this point, my thoughts take a leap. Family problems will surely continue to arise until the end of time. But will the day come when people no longer regard family dysfunction as a serious concern, even though the problems it creates never actually go away—much as poverty stopped being regarded as a pressing issue over the course of time? This possibility actually strikes me as reason for hope. But how could I explain this in a way that those actually affected by it would understand? . . .

I found myself recalling, too, my first love. For this reminiscence, I return to the summer vacation I spent with my uncle in the farm cottage.

After dinner one evening, my uncle went off with our landlord to a bar in Karuizawa.

The study material I'd brought with me from home had not once seen the light of day since I arrived. I decided to get it out and start on my summer assignments, spreading my notebook open before me. It was a cool enough evening to leave me feeling a little chilly in my T-shirt and shorts. I switched on the radio, which my uncle kept tuned to the Far East Network. Flying insects that had found their way in through a tear in the screen were crashing into the light fixture and the ceiling overhead.

"Hello! Anybody home?" I heard Kanoko call from downstairs.

"Come right on in," I yelled back the way my uncle always did. She'd said she was going to bring me some watermelon.

I heard light footsteps ascending the stairs. She was apparently alone. I glanced down at my English text. I hadn't read a single line yet.

"Oh, are you studying?" she asked when she appeared in the open doorway. On her tray were four large half-moon slices of yellow watermelon.

"I was getting ready to, but I hadn't actually started."

"Is it okay if I join you?"

"Sure," I said.

Setting the tray down on the table I was using as a desk, she spread some newspaper she'd brought with her on the tatami. Then she took a slice of watermelon and sat down cross-legged in front of the paper.

"Would you like a spoon?" she asked.

"No, thanks," I answered as I followed her example and folded my legs under me on the floor.

Kanoko bit into the middle of her watermelon slice, then she pointed her lips, opened just a little, and began spitting out seeds one after the other, *pfft pfft pfft*.

I gazed raptly at her as she ate—at the glossy skin of her calves protruding from her denim cutoffs; at how terrific she looked sitting there with her legs crossed beneath her.

"I suppose you're thinking I have no manners," she said a bit impishly.

I shook my head.

"Well, I admit it. I have no manners," she smiled. "But it just so happens watermelon tastes better when you eat it like this."

I started on my own slice, spitting out seeds as I went.

"Is this the American armed services station?" Kanoko asked, her watermelon still in hand.

"Uh-huh. We get some interference, but it's not unlistenable."

"You understand the English?"

"I can catch the titles of songs I know. The rest of the talk is basically gibberish, so I can ignore it. That's what I like about it."

"Hmm. I don't go in for foreign music so I never listen to it."

"Too loud?"

"No, it's not that."

I couldn't keep my gaze from drifting back to her face, and our eyes met.

"What?" she asked. There was a softness in her expression.

"Oh, nothing," I said. "I'd started to think you didn't like me."

"Huh?" Her normally not particularly big eyes popped wide open. "Why in the world . . . ?"

I felt a bit of a jolt at her obviously unfeigned surprise. It meant she hadn't been bothered in the least by the things I'd said.

"It's just, I thought maybe you would come along to Usui Pass with us, but then you didn't." I said it lightly, so as not to betray how heavily it had weighed on my mind.

"That's because I was up there just last week. With your uncle. Didn't he tell you?"

This came as another jolt—a bigger one.

"He told me it was his second trip, but he didn't tell me he'd gone with you," I said. "Was it just the two of you?"

She nodded. "Your uncle's so cool. I started wishing he were my dad, and I actually looped my arm through his as we walked along. Even though I wouldn't dream of doing that with my real dad."

The jolts continued. I could no longer taste any sweetness in the watermelon.

"But then things got kinda scary. You probably went to that abandoned tunnel, too, right? Well, he started trying to get me to go inside with him, and the next thing I know I'm screaming, 'Stop it!' You might laugh when I say this, but I'm actually a little bit psychic, and the place was giving me the creeps. It was scary enough just standing at the entrance. No way was I going inside."

"Did you see anything?"

"No, I only feel things. But your uncle, he stands there staring into the darkness for a while and then suddenly says, 'Ah, there she is.' He claimed he saw a woman, and she turned to look this way, and their eyes met. When he told me that, I decided I'd heard enough, and I ran back a ways from the opening. But your uncle wasn't the least bit fazed. 'She looks like someone I used to know,' he tells me. 'She must've come here to see me.' That's what he says. And then, when he finally turned to come home, he raised his arm to wave good-bye to her."

"Wow."

"What was it like when you went?"

"I didn't see a thing. Nor feel anything, either."

Kanoko finished her slice of watermelon and put the rind down on the newspaper.

"You're so different from your uncle. He's been keeping it low-key up here, but I know he usually lives a pretty wild life. He's the kind who's too busy having a good time to get married. But you're the quiet type. The complete opposite. So the mystery is why your uncle asked you to come. Do you two even have anything to talk about?"

"It's not really a question of having things to talk about. We have kind of a special relationship."

I turned my head so she could see the left side of my face.

"See the dent on my ear, near the top?"

She leaned over for a closer look. The fresh smell of soap and shampoo hovered about her. I willed her to come even closer, but to no avail.

"Yeah?" she said. "Does that have something to do with him?"

"Uh-huh. He's the one who put it there, by crushing my ear between his fingers. It was just after I was born."

I told her the story of how my uncle grabbed my ear so hard that it left a permanent mark. It was the first time I'd ever told anyone.

"So that's why, for him and me, it's not a matter of having things to talk about. It's like we're father and son."

"That's a great story," she said, sounding as though she really meant it.

It was because of this deep bond that my uncle had seen fit to tell me his own curious story. He seemed to be convinced that he was going to die—sometime in the not too distant future. I could see well enough that he wasn't quite up to par, but it certainly didn't look to me as if anything life-threatening was going on . . . He ultimately died two years later—in a car crash, not from any illness. Most of the family believed it was suicide.

Kanoko took a second slice of watermelon in her hands. "And just so you know," she said, "you're wrong about me not liking you."

I nodded. Needless to say, I was ecstatic.

"In fact, if anything, I'd say I like you quite a lot," she added casually, almost as if she were talking about something to eat.

I was so startled I almost dropped the watermelon I was holding. In my surprise, I heard myself saying something I'd normally never have imagined coming from my lips.

"Well, if you want to know how I feel, I like you a lot, too, but I think what you mean when you say if anything you like me a lot and what I mean when I say I like you a lot must be totally different."

Now *she* seemed startled, looking at me with her head cocked a little to one side and puzzlement on her face, not saying anything. The space inside my chest felt like it was exploding in a ball of fire. Why had I said that?

I took three bites of watermelon and spat out a dozen or so seeds. The watermelon still had no taste.

"I know you have a boyfriend," I finally said. "And you've been seeing him even while you're here, right? My uncle told me. He comes to get you on his motorcycle in the middle of the night. I heard the engine, and your footsteps."

Kanoko set her watermelon down on the newspaper.

"That's not me," she said evenly. "It's the girl from the next house over. Maybe you didn't know, but they have a daughter in her early twenties who works at the farm co-op. She sneaks out their back door and crosses through our lot to get out to the road. You really should give me more credit, you know. I suppose you can't see from here, so you couldn't have known, but I think this is what's called giving someone a bum rap."

A ray of hope lit up my heart.

"If what you said a minute ago was supposed to be a declaration of love, well, then I'm flattered," she went on. "But in case you didn't know, people fall in love more easily on vacation. And vacation loves are also the easiest to forget once you go your separate ways again. That's what your uncle said. Where you are affects how you feel. I've noticed that much myself . . . Well, I'd better be going. You have assignments you're supposed to do during vacation, right? I do, too, actually, but I left all my school stuff back at home."

Ear-grating static suddenly started breaking up the radio signal. I did an about-face and reached to adjust the tuning.

I felt a light tap on my shoulder. Turning back, I found Kanoko's face right in front of my nose. I thought she was going to say goodbye, when instead she closed her eyes. Without even thinking, I touched my lips to hers. Then, in the brief instant it took me to consider *What next? Do it again, with more feeling,* her lips were already moving away.

"See you tomorrow," she said with a smile sweet beyond compare.

It was after midnight when my uncle came home. Though in high spirits, he seemed rather worn out. After a quick dip in the bath, he immediately got out his futon and lay down. But as I was lighting a mosquito coil, he started up a conversation.

"Kanoko was planning to come over, as I recall. How'd it go?"

"We just had some watermelon and talked."

"Likely story. Though I guess that's about your speed, so I shouldn't be surprised. And I went to all that trouble to let you have some time alone with her."

I stood up to turn out the light.

"She said she went with you the last time you hiked up to Usui Pass. Why didn't you tell me?"

"Ah, she told you, did she? I thought you might be jealous."

"Why should I be jealous?" I said, putting up a bold front.

I could see dimly that he was looking at me with his head propped up on his elbow.

"She also told me that the motorcycle in the middle of the night isn't coming for her, it's coming for the girl in the next house over. You didn't know what you were talking about."

"It's coming for Kanoko all right," he said emphatically. "I went outside and checked with my own two eyes, so I know. The other girl's a whole different size and shape from Kanoko—there's no way I'd confuse the two."

"Are you saying she lied to me?"

"I suppose that's what it comes down to."

I was skeptical. But my uncle had no reason to be lying either.

"Why would she lie?"

"Everybody does it sometimes. She probably just didn't want you to see her darker side. I'm pretty sure her uncle knows all about it, too—that she's been sneaking out at night. But he keeps his mouth shut because he remembers what they say about fools who stand in the way of love. Plus, apparently, Kanoko's starting to lose interest in this biker guy anyway. Putting his foot down right now could backfire, so he's biding his time."

I had a sudden urge to tell my uncle that I'd kissed her. But before I could open my mouth, the sound of a motorcycle engine approached. It came to a halt in front of the house and *vroomed* lightly a couple of times.

Silence returned all around. Even the insects seemed to have fallen still. The suspense mounted.

The engine revved two more times, a little louder than before. Still no footsteps came.

The bike continued to idle, its rumble rising and falling slightly as if the engine were being adjusted.

Suddenly the engine cut off. We could hear the rider whistling some tune. The Tigers' "My Marie." What a wimpy song.

The whistling stopped and the insects resumed their keening.

"I was going to tell you . . . ," I began to say.

"Shh!" My uncle quickly silenced me.

The rider kicked the starter once, twice, three times, and the engine roared back to life. With a big burst of the throttle, the bike sped off. After fading into the distance for a time, the sound began rising again. We heard it decelerating as it reached the house, but then the biker gunned his engine loudly a couple of times and drove off at top speed.

"What were you starting to tell me a while ago?" my uncle asked.

"I kissed Kanoko tonight."

My eyes had grown used to the dark, and I thought I saw him smile.

"Well, what do you know?" he said. "You're no stranger to lying yourself."

Over the next two days, Kanoko and I started from just getting to know each other and moved bit by bit toward seriously falling in love. The jerkiness of our progress between those two points owed strictly to my own inexperience. Somehow, I thought the only way to cross that short distance was through a great number of small steps. Meanwhile, Kanoko behaved with utter self-assurance and seemed to be deliberately adjusting her pace to mine. It took me two full days after our first kiss before I kissed her again.

That night, the motorcycle returned once more. He stuck around quite a bit longer this time. The wait roiled me as I listened, and even after he had finally gone, I remained unable to fall asleep until the sky turned pale and the birds began to sing. I realized it still bothered me that Kanoko had lied.

The next day, Kanoko and I planned to go into Karuizawa after lunch, just the two of us. But everything came to a screeching halt right after breakfast.

Kanoko got a call from home. Then immediately after that, my uncle received a call from work. What exactly was said in those two conversations is of no concern to me. What matters is that, shortly afterwards, Kanoko boarded a train at Yokokawa Station and left for home, while my uncle and I got into his Peugeot 204 and headed back to Tokyo.

"My leave of absence is over," he said. "It's such a shame. Especially for you. Sorry."

Kanoko and I exchanged addresses and promised to write. "We'll see each other again, okay?" I said, and she nodded in assent as she squeezed my hand. But I never wrote a single letter, nor did I ever get one from her. And I never told my friends at school or anyone else about the girl with whom I'd shared the most fleeting of summer loves.

A suspicion crossed my mind. I called my wife and asked if she could put something together for me to eat when I got home.

"So long as you don't mind leftovers," she replied.

Arriving home, I changed out of my work clothes and sat down at the table. Asako went to the refrigerator to get me a can of beer. She said Ryo hadn't been out of her room since dinner.

"Never mind the beer," I said.

"My goodness. That's unusual," she said, returning the can to the shelf.

As I ate my dinner, I filled Asako in on how Yuta Iwamoto had shown up at the office to tell me the story of his family.

"He said he was telling me these things because he knew he was partly responsible for me putting my foot down with Ryo, and he wanted me to understand him better. He also said he had the feeling that I was someone he could talk to."

I set down my chopsticks and took a sip of the toasted green tea Asako had poured for me.

"Talking with him one-on-one, I can see he's not a bad kid. And I think he probably meant what he said about feeling he could talk to me. But no matter how I look at it, there has to be more to it than that. I think he was holding back something crucial."

I had to say it, no matter how much I wished I didn't. I needed to keep my cool.

"I suspect Ryo's pregnant. Not that I have any proof."

Asako remained silent for several moments. "I've actually been wondering the same thing," she said.

"You have?" My spirits sank. I realized that I'd been hoping she would insist it wasn't possible. "Since when?"

"Two or three days ago, I guess. It's not that she's said anything, or that I've seen any obvious signs. It's just a vague feeling. Intuition."

"So you haven't caught her sucking on lemons in the kitchen?"

She gave me a disapproving look. It was a lame attempt at humor, I knew, but I felt like we needed a bit of levity to get us through this.

For a time, neither of us said anything more. Our thoughts turned first, of course, to our daughter's well-being. But almost as quickly we were overcome, both of us, by that aching sense of emptiness that comes from disappointment and failure.

"First we need to ask her," she said heavily, as if prizing open reluctant lips. "I mean, since we don't actually know yet."

"Absolutely. We have to find out. But I was thinking, it'll be easy enough to apologize if it turns out we're wrong, but what if we're not? Then what do we do? We need to be sure you and I are on the same page."

"On the same page?" she said, frowning. "Oh, yeah, maybe so. So what're you thinking?"

"Getting rid of it is out of the question. I think Yuta coming to see me the way he did has to mean Ryo intends to have the baby."

"I agree. But . . ."

Asako pursed her lips and sat looking at me from across the table. But what? Was she still searching for the next words, or merely reluctant to say them?

We could not allow our daughter to get an abortion. That had been my immediate reflex. Asako's instincts had apparently been the same. But did that necessarily mean we both wanted the same thing?

If we viewed the situation in purely pragmatic terms, abortion had to remain an option. Yet we had both rejected that possibility. It was a flash judgment we'd made, but I imagined we would arrive at the same decision even if we stopped to reconsider the question more carefully—because it was driven both by our concern for Ryo's physical and emotional well-being, and by what was presumably an instinctive desire not to destroy an emerging life. For the moment, that was the gist of my thinking. But it seemed rather too flimsy to put into words.

"So, assuming she has the baby, what do we do after it's born? I don't imagine she'll be able to stay in school."

I took a deep breath before answering. "Not very likely. I wonder if they still call it 'illicit consorting with the opposite sex.' At any rate, doesn't the student handbook explicitly forbid sexual activity?"

"Whatever the handbook says, I don't think she'll have much choice but to withdraw. Once it starts to show, they'll tell her she has to leave anyway, so it'd be better to go before that happens."

I hadn't gotten that far along in my thinking yet, but I immediately knew she was right.

"So she'll quit school, and then what? I guess considering what to do about completing her diploma can wait until after she has the baby."

"Either way, we'll obviously have to help raise the child. I mean, since both of them are still children themselves."

"So how's this going to affect Yuta? Does the guy who got the girl knocked up get kicked out of school, too? That doesn't sound like anything I've ever heard."

"In the end, the girl always gets left holding the bag," she said evenly. "It's so unfair."

"I'll give Yuta a good talking-to," I said, not wanting her to lay the blame on men in general. The perpetrator of this deed was specifically Yuta Iwamoto—the boy who came to tell me at length about his own life but neglected to mention the pregnancy. Yet I bore him no ill will. There could well be a lot more to him than I gave him credit for.

"Ryo's sixteen, and he's seventeen," I noted. "They can't get married till after his next birthday."

"Married? They're still children. Everybody knows that teen marriages never work out."

"They have to decide for themselves in the end, so I'm not saying we should force them. But they at least need to seriously think about it—as part of their responsibility to us and to his parents, not to mention to the child they'll be bringing into the world."

"What if they actually say they want to?"

"We'll let them. It doesn't mean they necessarily have to live together. Ryo and the baby would stay with us here, at least for a while. A lot of marriages end in divorce these days. There's no reason we should have to think that far ahead at this point."

A troubled look came over her face.

"Though I guess that would put a lot of the burden on you," I added.

She closed her eyes and shook her head slightly back and forth. Then, as if still trying to convince herself, she said, "You know, this actually isn't a bad thing. It just didn't happen quite the way we might have wanted, and also the timing's a bit early—that's all. That's how we need to think about it. We're going to become grandparents. Right?"

"Well, yeah . . ." I knew that, of course, but to hear it put so directly brought me up a bit short. I was going to be a grandfather?

Asako knocked on Ryo's door.

"Yes?" she responded right away.

"We'd like to talk to you. Dad's here, too. Can we come in?"

This time there was no answer. My wife looked at me and was about to knock a second time when the door opened.

Never had I seen such a grim look on my daughter's face. I realized there was no use in wishful thinking.

As we entered the room, Ryo buried her face in her mother's shoulder and broke into uncontrollable sobs.

"How're we going to talk if you're acting like this," my wife admonished, but the sobs continued. She threw me a look that said *Say something!*

"Ryo?" I tried, but there was no sign that she'd even heard me. I signaled my wife with my eyes that she should be the one.

"Are you pregnant, dear?" she asked point-blank.

Ryo nodded into her shoulder.

"How many months?"

"Three," she squeezed out in a barely audible voice between convulsive sobs.

So she was still under the cutoff for an abortion. She was no doubt tearing herself to pieces over what to do. My heart went out to her.

"I'm glad you haven't done anything rash," I said. "I assume it means you think you want to have the child?"

Ryo nodded again, still not lifting her face from her mother's shoulder.

"This is actually a happy event—one we should be congratulating you for. But under the circumstances, no one can honestly do that. We're too shortsighted. We can't see how this is going to affect us, or those around us, or the child waiting to be born. So we're clueless. You understand that?"

"Uh-huh," she said, sounding like a small child who's cried herself out.

"So here's what I suggest. Try to concentrate on making this experience something you can look back on and say, it might have been awfully hard at the time, but it was the right thing to do and I'm glad I did it. Concentrate on making it that way not just for you and Yuta and the baby, but for me and your mother, and for Yuta's parents, too—for all of us. That means from this point on, you need to make sure you act responsibly in everything you do— both as our child and as your child's mother. Promise us this, and we'll do everything we can to help you and the baby."

Even in a crisis like this, I found myself spouting empty platitudes. I felt disappointed in myself.

Ryo was still sobbing.

"Will you promise, Ryo?" her mother pressed her.

She nodded over and over into her shoulder.

The next morning, Ryo appeared in the dining room with her eyes still a little puffy from crying but her expression remarkably calm. And she remained fully in control of her emotions when, after breakfast, we discussed plans for her to withdraw from school as well as how to deal with Yuta and his family. Not only was she not upset about having to quit school, but when I brought up the question of marriage, she immediately showed an active interest in the idea. I was at a loss to explain the transformation from the night before.

My wife, however, had a rather different reaction—as I discovered when Ryo mentioned that once she had the baby, she wanted to take classes to prepare for the high school equivalency test.

"And who's going to pay for these classes?" Asako demanded.

"I doubt I'll be able to afford it yet, so I'll probably have to ask Dad."

"So you'll just lean on your father?"

She hadn't particularly raised her voice, but the effect on me was like being boxed in the ears.

Seeming not to have noticed the change in her tone, Ryo went on in the same matter-of-fact way as before. "For money, I'll need Dad's help, but of course I'll also need your . . ."

Now seeing the look on her mother's face, she stopped short.

"I can't believe I'm hearing this!" my wife shrieked, her voice rising to a pitch I'd never heard before—and hope never to hear again.

At the same time, she brought her fist down on the dining table with a violence I'd never expected to see from someone who'd always taken such meticulous care of her dishes and furnishings. This, too, I hope never to see again.

"Just so you know, I did not raise my daughter to have a baby at sixteen and drop out of school! You should be ashamed of yourself. How can you sit there acting like it's the most natural thing in the world?"

She shot to her feet and stalked out of the room.

Ryo turned white and looked at me. No words came. I went after Asako.

I found her in the bathroom leaning on the washstand with both hands, her head bent over the sink. The reflection in the mirror did not reveal the expression on her face.

Ryo's flushed face appeared next to her mother in the mirror. "I'm sorry, Mom . . . Mom . . . ?"

Asako did not respond. She remained with her back turned to us, unmoving.

Ryo crumpled to the floor and broke into tears. She wept silently, without last night's racking sobs. It was impossible to tell whether Asako was crying, too.

I stood there awkwardly, saying nothing.

Still keeping her face averted from us, my wife suddenly turned to step into the bath enclosure and shut the door behind her. The hand-held shower came on, and I realized she had started cleaning the tub. She had always kept the bath spotless, but I'd never known her to go at it in her ordinary clothes, not caring what got wet. This, too, is something I hope never to see again.

Dear Yuki,

Ogita has gotten quite a bit worse.

Yesterday, a little before noon, he called asking me to come as soon as I could—actually, he made it sound like an order. I know he feels like his back's against the wall, but as long as he's still trying to boss me around, I figured he couldn't be doing all that badly.

I told him I was in the middle of something so I couldn't get away right then, and *click*, the phone goes dead. I never mentioned it to you before, but he's been doing this sort of thing a lot lately. He's picked up a short fuse.

When I finally went by a little after eight last night, the home health nurse was still there, and she told me he'd gone on quite a rampage earlier. He got into a fight with his mother about checking back into the hospital, and he apparently started throwing books and dishes and whatnot. I guess maybe he felt embarrassed about it afterwards, since he tried to rationalize it by saying it just goes to show how strong he still is . . .

Basically, he wants to stay at home, and his mother wants him to go back. But from what the nurse says, he's pretty much reached the point where he can't get by at home anymore. She asked me to help convince him that he needs to go back to the hospital.

When I went into his room, he didn't seem all that much different from the last time I was there. Our conversation seemed perfectly normal, too. So I was having a hard time bringing the subject up. But then out of the blue he says, I guess it's hospital time for me again. Nothing tastes any good anymore, in fact I don't feel like eating anything to begin with, and when I do I just throw it all up, and now even my mom's ready to keel over . . .

So he obviously knows exactly where things stand.

He used to carry on about being ready to go any time, but now that he sees the day of reckoning actually getting close, I think he's pretty scared.

He moped about never getting to come home again, it was all over for him, so I told him that wasn't true, the whole reason for going to the hospital was to get well enough to come back—trying to lift his spirits, you know? But he just gives me a crooked smile and shakes his head. I couldn't help noticing how shrunken his face looks compared to before. You haven't see him in so long you'd probably think he looks completely wasted away if you saw him now.

They finally talked to his main doctor today and decided he would check back in three days from now. He'll be getting a really expensive private room. He always used to love company, but he insists he doesn't want to be with anyone else.

You're such a tease, saying you have something to tell me the next time we meet. When's that going to be, anyway? I know you must be busy, but you could at least answer my e-mails.

Momo

I found the message from Momo when I checked my e-mail just before heading out to an appointment at Ryo's school. I had no time to compose a reply. After taking care of things at the school, I was scheduled to meet Yuta's father. This was the first time I'd ever taken time off from work in order to deal with a school matter for my daughter.

As I flipped my computer shut and stood up, I saw Hashida looking at me in distress. He'd been dealing with an unhappy client on the phone.

"He insists on talking to the boss," he said.

I had half a mind to yell at him that if I took the phone every time someone demanded to talk to the boss, we'd need a dozen of me to handle it all. But I took a deep breath, glanced quickly at my watch, and accepted the handset. This would almost certainly make me late for my appointment.

Hashida had made a mistake, which is to say, we were at fault. The client incurred no actual damages, as it turned out, but the possibility of damages had been real. Hashida had acknowledged this and apologized. But the client side was unwilling to let it go. They apparently thought they could use the foul-up as a wedge to pry better terms out of us. In the larger scheme of things, their dealings with us had to be a mere drop in the bucket for them, but the person handling our account obviously saw it as an opportunity to earn some points with his superiors. I also got the feeling he'd just been itching for a chance to read the riot act to someone with the title of president. I listened with mounting irritation. This was one seriously twisted fellow. But I bit my tongue. When he finally seemed to have run out of steam, I handed the phone back to Hashida. As I did so, I gave him a stern look of reprimand.

I had driven to work that morning. It was raining, and in any case having my car would be more convenient for making the rounds from Ryo's school to the hotel where I was meeting Yuta's father and to a couple of client calls after that.

The car was a Toyota Prius hybrid that I'd bought used. When I left my old job, I'd decided it would be wise to trade in my Audi A4 wagon for something more economical. For one thing, maintenance costs were going to be a struggle now, and for another, the car was still new enough to bring in a nice chunk of change on the trade. The Prius was not only fuel-efficient and very well built, it was fun to drive because it sometimes switched over entirely to the electric motor—and since they weren't very popular among used car buyers, I got a great bargain, too. I joked to Asako and Ryo that, naturally, I was making the switch purely out of concern for the environment, but it failed to get a laugh out of them.

Pulling up to the main gate at Ryo's school, I told the attendant the purpose of my visit. He politely directed me to the visitors' parking area. My connection with this school was about to come to an end.

Inside the building, prim-looking teenage girls in sailor-style uniforms greeted me with *Hellos*. I returned the greetings but felt intensely out of place. I actually thought I might get a case of the runs. My school jitters apparently still hadn't changed, even after all these years. If someone told me they could send me back in time to any age I chose, you can bet I'd stay away from any of the years I was in school, from kindergarten through college.

Ryo's tales from school had always centered on her art teacher and the brassbound principal or vice principal. So when I spoke with her homeroom teacher, I was pleasantly surprised by what a nice man he was. About forty, he was the well-built athletic type, and he had an amiable smile that never seemed to go away. He breezily brushed aside my apologies for arriving ten minutes late. When I told him that after discussing it as a family, we'd decided the best course for Ryo right now was to withdraw from school, he said he was sorry to hear it and that he felt like he must have come up short in some way, sounding as though he truly meant it. I began to feel as if I were being deceptive. As a matter of fact, I suppose I was.

It all went much more smoothly than I expected. As I started to get up after receiving the forms required for processing the withdrawal, the teacher turned off his ever-present smile and said, "I had a number of chances to speak with Ryo, but she never really opened up to me."

"I'm afraid she has a bit of a difficult streak."

"Actually, I heard that she was skipping classes to hang out in places like Shibuya, so I asked her about it the other day, and warned her that if the behavior didn't stop, I'd have to call in her parents."

"Is that right? She didn't mention anything to us."

"The thing is," he said, his amiable smile returning, "your daughter isn't the only one who skips school, and with things the way they are these days, trying to put a stop to it all would be futile. It's just that there are so many dangerous temptations out there on the street, and I really hate to see kids losing their way."

I had the feeling that this teacher was aware of Ryo's condition.

"From my perspective," he went on, "I think it really is our loss to see Ryo leave. A school like this is in many ways a closed community. I've always looked for the students who join us at the beginning of the high school years to bring in some fresh air. Though maybe that's a burden the kids themselves don't really want to shoulder. I thought Ryo was a very good stimulus to the other students in that sense. I'm repeating myself, but I really am sorry to see her go."

All I could do was bow my head.

Yuta's father, Hidenori Iwamoto, was a manager in the Materials Department at a major appliance maker. He self-deprecatingly joked that he expected to be put out to pasture at one of their subsidiaries any day now, but he apparently owned several properties in Tokyo and lived very comfortably. We were the same age and had finished school the same year. Of average height and build, his balding pate made him look old for his age—though he spoke smoothly and with great energy. His appearance made me feel like I was talking to someone considerably my senior, and I found it hard to identify with him as a member of my own generation. As part of the group that came after the first big wave of baby-boomers, though, you could probably say that one of our key identifying characteristics was precisely that we didn't have a strong sense of mutual identification.

This man and I were now going to be connected by marriage.

Worrier that I am, I had fretted en route that I might wind up being the first one there, or that if Yuta's father failed to volunteer an apology I wouldn't know how to proceed. But Mr. Iwamoto was waiting in the appointed hotel coffee shop when I arrived, and he stood up to greet me as I approached, immediately following up with an apology for the trouble his son had caused. It only bothered me that it came across as somewhat perfunctory, as if he was merely going through the required motions.

He proceeded to remark on how his divorce and all the attendant circumstances had left a good deal to be desired in the way his son was raised. Seeming quite ill at ease, he asked if I minded and lit up a cigarette.

"These days even my own home and office are off-limits," he said, blowing a stream of smoke down to one side. "But I have no intention of giving it up at this point. It won't be all that much longer now before I wrap up my career, and I can't see that there's a whole lot I have to look forward to. I figure I'll at least hang on to the pleasures of smoking."

Hmm. If I'd remained at my old company and carried on in good standing, I suppose I'd be entertaining similar thoughts about now. As it is, I'm a long way from wrapping anything up, that's for sure. I've still got boatloads of worries.

"Then again, I suppose if I'm going to have a grandchild, I'll have to reconsider. I certainly never imagined I'd be talking about one this soon, though."

My grandchild would also be this man's grandchild . . . This went without saying, of course, but it hit me in a different way to hear it from him. I had already made it clear over the phone that we were absolutely opposed to an abortion, and Yuta and his father and stepmother had all expressed their support for that decision.

"There's certainly the baby, too, of course, but the first thing we need to talk about is the parents," I said, steering the conversation in a different direction. "I stopped by my daughter's school on the way here and informed them she'll be withdrawing. Naturally, I avoided any mention of the pregnancy. I guess at a lot of places these days you can take a leave of absence to have your baby and return to school afterwards, but we always knew they wouldn't allow that at Ryo's school."

Silently, Iwamoto lowered his head.

"My daughter ultimately wants to take some art classes and study for her equivalency test so she can get into art school. I'd like to make this possible for her if I can. It means she and the baby will have to live with us at home. That's the only way she'll be able to study and take care of a child at the same time. I assume you have no objection?"

Iwamoto nodded, as a pensive look came over his face.

"What does Yuta want to do? From what Ryo tells me, I understand he plans to start up a game software company with some older buddies of his."

Iwamoto shook his head. "That's basically just an excuse to skip school—nothing but a pipe dream. Actually, this whole thing seems to have shaken him up a bit and, commendably enough, he came to me with bowed head the other day saying he wanted to be able to raise his child properly, so could I please support him while he finishes school. I'd personally like to see him go on to college as well, and I think he probably has the necessary motivation for it now. So realistically speaking, it makes sense for the child to live with your daughter for the time being."

I nodded. "They're still high school students, so they'll have to accept that they can't live together as a family, but to just leave it at that seems a bit wanting somehow. If I'm not mistaken, I believe your boy turns eighteen this year?"

I waited for him to confirm this and then asked him what he thought of having Yuta and Ryo get engaged for now, and then marry once Yuta was past his birthday.

He looked perplexed. "Of course, since they're going to have a child, it's natural enough to think about marriage, but I'm afraid they're just too young. They have no means of supporting themselves. This is the time of their lives when you want to see them studying, not working. I'm inclined to think that forcing them into marriage at this point would be counterproductive." He studied me as though taking my measure as he spoke. "It seems to me the question of marriage is something the two of them need to consider for themselves after they have their diplomas. Actually, I was talking about all this with my wife. If they decide to get married when they're in college, maybe they could set up house together in an apartment I own right near our place. My wife could lend a hand with childcare to make things easier on Ryo."

I shook my head. "They made the mistake of creating a child when they had no means to take care of it. Mistakes ought to have due consequences. I'm not saying they need to be punished. But if they've failed to get a clear sense of family and society into their heads, then it's our duty as parents of minors to impress on them the existence of such things. Whether they actually get married or not is for them to decide. After all, it says in the constitution that marriage must be based on mutual consent. But what's important is for them to think about it properly once, so that they become aware of themselves as part of a larger society that has this institution called marriage. If they decide it's a silly institution and they don't want to be tied down by it, then they need to spell that out for us in their own words."

I could see Iwamoto turning this over in his mind. He seemed surprised that a father faced with his daughter's pregnancy would raise such abstract concerns. But in the days since learning that my daughter was carrying a child, I'd watched her complexion, her facial expressions, and her mannerisms all undergo a rapid series of changes that reminded me of nothing so much as when my wife was pregnant with her, and while on the one hand the physical actuality of it threatened to overwhelm me, on the other I felt my convictions (if you can call them that) growing stronger than ever.

Iwamoto finished an entire cigarette before he finally spoke again. "So if they decide they do want to get married, we would accept their decision. But for the time being they would live separately?"

"Yes. At least until Ryo is ready for college."

"I agree, that seems best. I hope you don't mind if I say something that might seem a little crude."

The tone of his voice had changed abruptly to that of someone much surer of his own mind.

"I can't remember if somebody told me this or I read it in a book, but I heard that the leader of the Indian nonviolent resistance movement, Gandhi—what was his other name? Mahatma? Anyway, according to Indian custom, he married very young, I don't think he was even fifteen, and the story is that he became completely obsessed with sex and spent all his time in bed with his wife. Day in and day out, nothing else. It's my own son we're talking about here, but I'm a man, too, and I can't help being a little worried about that sort of thing. I'm sorry if my bringing this up makes you feel uncomfortable."

I was at a complete loss for words.

"I wonder if they have even the slightest clue about what marriage entails," he said, his voice barely above a murmur.

"That's exactly why we have to make them think about it," I replied, but even to me the words sounded empty.

I have a tendency to forget that institutions and laws are merely a thin outer shell covering the living bodies and myriad desires that lie underneath. But not everybody forgets.

When we got up to leave, Iwamoto asked if I'd like to go for a drink somewhere, but I made the excuse that I was driving.

My next stop was a seedy-looking building on the edge of Kanda, where Yosuke Yoshida maintained an office. YY chaired the firm that was my company's most important client—or perhaps it should be described as our de facto corporate parent. The firm itself had offices in another building nearby, but YY insisted he felt more at home in the "back alley" atmosphere of the separate, shabbier premises where he did his work. As usual, he held forth with great animation, taking an occasional swig of bottled oolong tea as he spoke.

"My hat is off to you for coming up with the idea of building a quality, upscale shopping mall on the Web long before the Internet bubble even got started. I mean, I was pretty skeptical at the time, but I figured it was worth a try, and although there was a period there when I thought I'd been had, everything turned out well in the end.

"Anytime you make quality your selling point, things like the seller's depth of experience and taste and reputation come right to the fore. This is no different whether you're talking about the Web or about conventional brick-and-mortar stores. That's common knowledge these days, of course, but so far as I'm aware, the only place you'd have seen anything like that stated back then was in books about Amazon.com. There I was, a sucker for anything new, catching the computer and Web bug at an age when most people thought I ought to know better, like a fool letting myself get sucked into the strange world of e-tailing, basically just hoping I wouldn't lose my shirt, but also thinking maybe if I was lucky I could get a little something to bloom. As you well know, nobody was making any money on the Internet in those days.

"Then this perfect stranger walks in the door, and it's you, and just like that I find myself completely revamping my site the way you tell me to. My online department store had been like Akihabara's old black-market stalls, and you turned it into something much classier, not quite up to the Ginza or Omotesando, maybe, but at least up to the level of, say, the Aobadai neighborhood along the Den'entoshi Line. I updated all of our code. I mounted a serious push to bring higher-quality merchants into the mix. And whaddya know?—all of a sudden I'm making a profit. Me and my staff, we could never have pulled off a transformation like that by ourselves, not in a thousand years.

"To be honest, once the money started rolling in, I used to think, man, Yajima could have all the profits for himself if he did this on his own, thank goodness he's got modest expectations. Heh heh heh.

"You seem happy just to play the coordinator for my shopping mall. You take a remarkably unenterprising stance, preferring to stay a step back from the rough and tumble of the Web as much as possible.

"But sad to say, the time when a distinctive personality was enough for an e-tailer to attract customers on the Web is quickly coming to a close. Or at the very least, I think we've run out of room for growth.

"The biggies don't have any taste, but in the sense that they've become household names on the Web, they have the power of their own brands and their reputations to carry them. With the huge selections of merchandise they offer, the shopper has no reason to go looking for a specialty mall unless he's an absolute stickler for quality. Taste that's not driven by brand consciousness easily caves in to practicality or versatility or low price. At least on the Web. Probably in the brick-and-mortar world, too. At this point, the biggies are leaving everybody else, including us, in the dust. The guys who've already made a pile keep raking in more and more, and we're approaching the point where they'll be taking it all.

"Of course, thanks in good measure to you, we've built up a loyal customer base, so we can probably go on muddling along. We get M&A feelers all the time, and everybody says it's our unique blend of old black-market charm and slick, modern style that caught their fancy. They're looking to tap into that combination and want to acquire the know-how. That's what they say. Virtually none of them knows anything about you. If they did, I suppose they'd be knocking directly on your door, so in a sense I guess you're getting your wish. And it works out nicely for me, too.

"I could just sell the whole operation off without giving you a second thought if I wanted. There's no telling when we might wind up going belly-up down the road, but if I sell now, I can sell high. In the Internet world, a man my age is like a hundred-year-old geezer, so it's a good time for me to retire. I've made a nice bundle, after all. But somehow, I still feel this seductive pull, you know? From the money and the business, both. Heh heh heh.

"Anyway, the latest feeler I got isn't for a merger or acquisition, but for what could be a very attractive alliance. We're being courted to sign on as one of the marquee merchants at a major shopping portal. We'd retain control of our own business, but it'd be tough to handle it all with our current workforce. What we've got here is something on a whole different scale. They suggested they might buy up this other outfit, one of those total crap online sales sites you find dangling from every branch of the Web these days, but if we have to babysit a bunch of losers like that, they're likely to drag us down with them. So I told these people we wouldn't sign on unless they took that outfit out of the picture. Needless to say, I was counting on you being part of our lineup when I did this.

"You can see where I'm going with this. What I want to do is bring you all the way into the fold. There aren't all that many people working in the Web space who have your instincts. Of course, I can't guarantee it's going to pan out. You hear no end of stories about people buying into some big scheme that goes bust, or at least busts them. That's true for brick-and-mortar and the Web, both.

"Now, I know you never make a move unless you think it's rock solid. If I recall, there're just five of you in your shop right now, right? Oh? So three of them are officially only part-time? That's pretty amazing. Anyway, here's what I propose. We'll buy you out. Your whole crew, including the part-timers. We'll negotiate a purchase price that makes you and your family secure for life. You yourself will come on as director of website operations.

"To anybody else, this would be an irresistible deal, but I know you don't see it that way. That's the problem with you. You have this idea, you've said it before, that you don't have a big enough love to bring more people under your wing. But trust me, as a director, you'll do just fine without that. With the power of your position, you can just crack the whip. The employees might not like you, but that's what you're getting paid for.

"Just so you know, if you turn me down on this, I won't say I'm going to sever all dealings with your outfit, but you should assume the special relationship we've had until now will be a thing of the past. The shops you brought in can say good-bye to preferential treatment, and standard tenant fees will apply. That may change the character of our site, but I figure being with a major sales portal should make up for that. Is this a threat? In a way, I suppose. If you decide to throw us over and look for a new meal ticket somewhere else, I won't try to stop you. I couldn't do it, anyway. But I'm sure you're well aware, that's not going to be easy. Especially since you've never ventured out from under my company's wing before. Heh heh heh.

"I'll give you three days to think about it. That's as long as I can wait before I have to make my own decision about the alliance.

"Why the long face? You know I don't really mean it as a threat. What's that? You've got some stuff going on at home right now? Why don't you tell me about it?"

I told YY that I was soon to be a grandfather. He and I rarely had occasion to talk about our private lives, but we at least knew the makeup of each other's family.

"Your daughter would be a junior now, right? Attending a very respectable private school, as I recall. And you certainly don't impress me as the type who'd have a love child hidden away somewhere. She's not getting an abortion?"

YY had always had a good memory, and he never shied away from being direct. I myself come up short on both counts.

"No. We didn't even consider it."

"So I suppose that means she has to drop out of high school? And here I'd always pictured your daughter as the serious, responsible type."

The words "drop out" coming from someone else's lips gave me something of a jolt.

"That's what it means. Unfortunately."

"How old's the father?"

"A year older than Ryo. We'll be urging them to get married."

"You're kidding. I wouldn't advise it. They're too young, don't you think?"

I began laying out for him the reasons I thought they should wed. Before long I found myself repeating much of what I'd said to my wife and daughter about love and fairness. YY listened quietly, without interrupting.

". . . Kids who seek refuge in this 'world without grown-ups' invariably end up having an even harder time of it. And it's ironic how, even as they disdain grown-ups, they're forced to grow up real fast themselves. And they usually turn into adults who don't have anything going for them. I don't want to see Ryo end up like that. I'd rather have her do the grown-up thing as a proper member of society. Then it'll be easier for us to offer help when she needs it. That's my thinking."

"So that's the Yajima brand of love. Or actually, something more than love, maybe. Well, I guess I don't have anything to say about that part, but I do take issue with your argument about fairness and impartiality. I'm not going to say you're right or wrong. I just think you have a critical blind spot."

"Sure, my thinking's probably riddled with holes. But what's the blind spot you see?"

"You said at the outset that you're not addressing the question of absolute justice. I'd say that's wise. But if you're going to consider fairness in a social context, then I think you need to look at its material underpinnings."

"So you're a materialist."

"Well, I gave up being a Marxist, so I don't necessarily think *every*thing can be reduced to material factors, but I also don't have much use for people who think only in abstractions and ignore the material footings on which they're based."

"Which maybe includes me."

He ignored my self-deprecating remark. "You were raised by middle-class parents, and you and your family remain firmly rooted in the middle class today. Fretting about fairness and impartiality is basically a middle-class thing. Think about it. The upper classes are built on sucking wealth out of the rest of society, so there's no concern for justice there to begin with. And whether society is doing the right thing or not makes no difference to them at all. On the other hand, the lower classes know that even if society were fair and impartial, they wouldn't be the ones to benefit from it anyway. In fact, if they're not going to get the advantages of good homes and schools, then it makes perfect sense for them to choose less savory ways of bettering their lot by turning to crime or the mob. Those in the middle are the ones who benefit most from a fair and impartial society. Peaceful communities, stable incomes, happy homes. That's why until recently we had this fantasy of the whole country turning into one big middle class. It wasn't a bad fantasy as such, but too many people were fooled into actually believing it. How stupid can you get? Like insisting that this country is classless. Well, if you're going to define class according to what you find in England, then of course Japan doesn't have any classes. But that doesn't mean we don't have our own equivalent, because we do. So let me ask you this: what do you think the future has in store for Ryo?"

"Has in store?"

"Do you think she'll be able to keep up a middle-class lifestyle like you?"

An image of Yuta rose up in my mind, and then one of him and Ryo and the unborn child as a family.

"It's not too likely, I suppose."

"Not a chance. To begin with, we're headed for a shakeout of the middle class. The middle class as we know it today is going to disappear. Guaranteed. A new middle class will probably emerge in its place, but it'll be more like today's lower middle. The world's long since changed. The last ten years have brought us deregulation and financial reform, not to mention a complete overhaul of the tax system to favor the wealthy whether you're talking about income or property or inheritance. The effects grow clearer each year. Just look at how much richer the rich have become. And at the fact that today's middle-rankers are now little more than reserves for the poor class.

"So in other words, you hold your daughter's fate in your hands. If at this point you join the ranks of the rich, she doesn't have to take a step down. What I'm doing, in effect, is offering you that opportunity."

"Your analysis may be correct," I told him, "but I'm reluctant to buy into it. Though I'll give your proposal some serious thought, I'm not inclined to accept it just to win at the game of getting ahead. Even if it has *Do it for your family* written all over it. As you say, the world has changed. I need to protect myself and my family both materially and financially. And I've got no one to rely on but myself. For that, I'll even turn mercenary when I have to. But I still want to believe that a fair and impartial society is possible in this world. Otherwise, I'd have a hard time getting up in the morning. The thing is, whether Ryo and her family end up poor or not, if they have to live in a world where anything goes no matter how outrageous, then she's not going to have a happy life. If what you predict is inevitable, I'll definitely be very sad."

"I'm not predicting anything. I'm describing present reality."

"Even if that's true, the world could change again, at least so long as some of us believe that a just society is possible. When there's no one left who believes that, then the world will be a much worse place than it is now. If we get to that point, there'll be no way for it to change for the better anymore."

"But you'll continue to believe it, I imagine."

"Yeah . . . I imagine so. Like an idiot."

"From my perspective, I'm glad there are still people with that kind of faith. Makes it that much easier for me to rake it in."

YY got up from the sofa and reached out his hand.

"I'll look forward to an affirmative reply,"

I stood up and shook his hand with a little nod.

I had to make one more client stop before returning to the office. When I finally sat down in my usual spot at the big desk, I found a note waiting for me. It was in Ayumi's hand.

"Sorry we're all leaving before you get back. You've been looking pretty stressed out lately. Are you getting overtired maybe? We thought you could use an energy drink, so everybody chipped in to buy you one of the expensive Yunkers. Hashida says they really work. From all of us."

I may have said my company was a bit short on love, but that didn't mean there was none at all.

Dear Momo,

I got your message when I was on my way out the door, so I couldn't reply right away. I just now got back to the office after going to four separate appointments.

The news I mentioned is too big to waste on an e-mail, so you'll just have to wait. It involves my daughter.

My company has come to a crossroads.

I rarely hear directly from YY, but last week he called to say he wanted to talk with me, and I went to see him today.

He was pretty tough on me. He says my business is at a dead end.

So basically he wants me to work for him—though I can't offer any details yet.

YY's an interesting guy, but I don't think I can trust him completely.

There've been times when he's put one over on me, or at least tried to.

I can't say I was especially surprised by the direction the conversation took. He'd dropped some hints about it before, so I'd done my homework before the subject came up for real today.

I didn't answer on the spot, but I'm pretty much resigned to the inevitable.

You're a busy woman, and Ogita seems to have plenty of money, so maybe you shouldn't let yourself get dragged into doing so many things for him (if you don't mind my butting in from the outfield).

Hope to see you soon so we can catch up.

Yuki

I brought in Takahiro Ishikura as a consultant for the negotiations involved in YY's outfit taking over my own.

Ishikura had soldiered on at my old company for three more years after I left. Then, after getting his license as a CPA rather than as a tax accountant, he joined an accounting firm. He was now well on his way to establishing himself not as a mere bean counter but as a top-notch analyst. Polka Dot had apparently tried very hard to retain him when he tendered his resignation.

No doubt because of his newly gained confidence, the impression of weakness Ishikura used to give people had disappeared. When I approached him for advice, he quickly offered his services, even though his firm did not normally take on such small assignments.

He remained single and apparently had no plans to marry. Back when we were still colleagues, I remembered telling him about my bachelor uncle, and he responded in all seriousness that he admired a man who lived that way. As it happens, the two men could scarcely have been more different. My uncle was unafraid of ruffling feathers, and was sometimes outright combative, as he established a way of life true to his own inclinations— though he came to grief in the end. Ishikura, on the other hand, just floated lightly on the wind. Perhaps it was a difference of the times in which they lived. To me, Ishikura seemed the lonelier figure.

He came to see me one evening, and Ayumi was the only other person still in the office when he left.

"He's a sharp-looking guy, huh?" I said, almost as if it were to my own credit.

She agreed, and then added, "He's gay, right?"

As a matter of fact, I had long assumed the same. But it wasn't something that had ever been of any concern in my relationship with him, nor did I expect it to be in the future.

Ishikura warned me that letting my business be acquired by YY's company entailed substantial risks to me. Certain things he'd found out about YY's operation raised red flags. I already had my suspicions, but even so, seeing the evidence laid out plainly in front of me proved quite a shock. Like when you go in for a physical because you're vaguely concerned about certain symptoms you're having, and the lab report comes back with exactly the results you feared.

Having said this much, he added that in his opinion it was a risk well worth taking. This was an opportunity for me to put myself—and what I'd achieved thus far in the marketplace—to the test, and the potential returns were commensurate with the risk.

I sighed. "Since it's really not what I'm cut out for, I'll probably wind up getting cancer from all the stress."

"Your tendency to get cold feet is another of the risks," he said without cracking a smile.

I explained YY's proposal to my employees and asked them each to let me know in private what their wishes were. They all said they wanted to move over to the new company with me.

For them, there would be virtually no difference in job security between working for me and working for YY's company. But the culture would be different. Having grown used to my way of doing things, they were likely to find YY's methods less agreeable. I would need to find ways to cushion the impact for them—though there was really no telling whether that would be possible. Then again, since YY had always been our most important client, they had presumably taken the difference in culture into consideration.

"I'll go where you go," Hashida told me.

"I want to continue working with you," Ayumi said.

The votes of confidence were good for my ego. But a certain burden came with them as well.

My wife left on a weeklong trip with an old college friend. They would visit Shizuoka first, and then go on from there to Kyoto.

I myself had been away from home on business trips many times, the longest of which had sometimes stretched to more than a month, but I had almost never been at home with my wife away. Since her parents lived right here in Tokyo, she could visit them without having to stay over. Just once, she had taken Ryo to Izu without me to spend several days at the vacation home of some relatives.

She offered no special reason when she told me she was going on this trip. She merely said she'd squirreled away a bit of money that she would use to pay for it. I asked no questions.

Instead of seeking any further explanation, I found myself remembering the night we first learned that Ryo was pregnant. Not my daughter's tears or my wife's fit of anger, but the silence Asako had fallen into after saying "I agree. But . . ."

Neither of us subscribed to religious beliefs that pronounced abortion a sin. That didn't mean we lacked moral scruples. Far from it. But when I asked myself why it was, at root, that I didn't want my daughter to have an abortion, all sorts of things began welling up. Perhaps my wife's silence that night came from an underlying murkiness in her own thinking much like mine.

Words fail me when I try to articulate my reasons. All I can do is wish you a good journey. That's the kind of half-baked man you're looking at. But I love you.

Dear Yuki,

I haven't written in a while, but Ogita is really starting to struggle now—though I don't think he's actually approaching the end quite yet.

His cancer is spreading. The tumor that began in the peritoneum is apparently starting to reach over the small intestine in a way that hinders proper digestion, triggering severe reflux and frequent vomiting.

Even when he's asleep, sudden attacks wake him up. He can't get a decent night's rest without heavy-duty sleeping pills.

When he's awake, though, he's completely lucid. He just feels a constant pressure in his stomach, and queasiness. I suppose the blessing is that he's not actually in a lot of pain.

It's not so much that I took your advice to heart, since mainly I'm just too busy at work, but I've substantially cut back on my visits lately—both how often I go and how long I stay. It's also partly because I felt that the more time I spent with him the less I liked him.

Kind of a weird thing for a divorced woman to be saying about her ex-husband, huh?

The whole ordeal has turned him into a different man. Though actually, I guess he's probably still about 80% the same. I think the continuing physical toll and the approach of death are changing him a little bit at a time.

I remember when your father died from a brain tumor, you said afterwards that, besides the sense of powerlessness, the hardest part was having to watch him gradually becoming not himself anymore.

At some stage he was still 70% himself, you said, but then after a while he was only 60%, then 50%, and after that he went downhill really fast. But even then, on days when you happened to be feeling good yourself, you said he still seemed 70% like the father you knew, or 60% okay again.

You laughed that it sounded like you were debating whether the amount left in your glass was ONLY this much or STILL this much. It struck me as just the sort of thing you would say.

Now I actually know how you felt. Though in Ogita's case, it's not his brain that's under assault, so I suppose I can't really compare him with your father.

The trouble is that the 20% of him that's vanished must be where most of the things I liked about him were, and the things that always bugged me are still there in the 80% that's left.

I've heard this is what typically happens when people get old or sick. I don't recall hearing the other way around much.

I wonder why it's never the good parts that remain and the bad parts that disappear.

I had a call from Mrs. Ogita yesterday begging me to come see him. Just listening to her made me start to cry.

I suppose she phoned partly because she's so exhausted from being there all by herself, but I think mostly it was because Ogita was moaning and groaning about feeling so lonely.

So of course when I went to see him today, I met the 80% of him that I don't like. Oh well. Fume, fume.

Now here I am, moaning and groaning myself.

I actually have something else to tell you, but I guess I'll stop here for today.

That's a teaser—just like you.

So let's get together soon.

I know you don't have time, but it's the same with me.

We're not getting anywhere sending e-mails back and forth, so expect a call at your office.

Momo

Ryo had recently begun painting pictures of a blue cat. She said the cat was her. Its face and belly were swollen. The color reflected her own mood.

"Talk about cliché," she said self-mockingly.

But she had obviously grown quite fond of the blue cat as a subject. When the smell of the oil paints bothered her, she would switch to gouache or pastels. She said it wasn't a problem that someone else out there was already painting blue dogs.

As I stood beside her watching her work at the canvas, the lines of an old poem tumbled out of the recesses of my memory and I began reciting them aloud.

> *It is good to love this beautiful city.*
> *It is good to love the buildings of this beautiful city.*

"What's that?" she wanted to know.

"The beginning of a poem called 'The Blue Cat' by Sakutaro Hagiwara. I'm pretty sure that's how it goes."

She cocked her head. Apparently she had never heard of the poet.

"What comes next?" she wanted to know, but I couldn't remember.

I went to my bookshelves and dug out a compact paperback of *The Poems of Sakutaro Hagiwara* that I'd bought when I was in high school. With its yellowed cover and pages, the book looked like a rectangular piece of mummified pastry. I found the poem, but the type was small and the print beginning to fade. It would be a struggle to decipher without my reading glasses.

I held the book out to Ryo, half expecting her to make a face at its moldered condition. But she took it without the slightest hesitation and began reading the next lines.

It is good to come to this city and rove its busy streets
in pursuit of all the sweet women,
in pursuit of all the high life.

She stopped reading and made a pout with her lips as she looked up at me.

"I can understand him wanting 'sweet women,' but why 'all' of them? One woman should be plenty, don't you think? Even if he's some lech who wants to fool around with more than one, '*all* the sweet women' is a bit much."

"I think he's just letting his fantasies run wild, probably. Hence the exaggeration. You have to consider the times he lived in, and the fact that he was a country boy. He had probably picked up the idea that extravagant rhetoric like that was what made a poet."

"Then what about the 'high life' part? Does he want to become some kind of big shot?"

"I think it's more that he aspires to the spiritually elevated life of a poet."

"But he says 'all' again."

"Uh-huh. So I suppose it includes the feeling that he wants to be recognized by the world and become somebody. But if I remember how the rest of it goes, he turns a soberer eye on himself after that. Something about 'this beggar of a man.' Not that the rhetoric isn't still pretty exaggerated. But it's people like him, like the country-born Hagiwara with all these fantasies and inferiorities swimming around in his head, that make up a big part of the city's population, right? No city's made up only of people who were born there. And yet the place is beautiful. He's able to get past his own illusions to appreciate that. At least that's how I see it."

Ryo began reading again.

> *Asleep in the night of this sprawling city*
> *is the shadow of a lone blue cat.*
> *The shadow of a cat telling the sad story of humanity.*
> *The blue shadow of the happiness we never cease to pursue.*

"I like this part," she said.

I considered what I myself had been pursuing over the years on my way to where I was today. "Sweet women" were not what you looked for in the big city, and going after "the high life" had never even entered my mind. "The revolution" had more appeal than that. I wouldn't even say I was pursuing happiness. *The blue shadow of happiness* . . . Back in the 1970s, we'd talked about self-actualization and finding our own identities, but at this point, no matter what I might personally want, my family and my employees were too much a part of my life to ignore. I was born ten years too soon to shrug them off like some disaffected punkster saying,

"What do I care?" Or maybe it's actually more like twenty years too *late*, I thought, as an image of my uncle rose up in my mind.

Ryo brought the book back to me the next day. Her assessment: "He's a chauvinist and a stalker and he's kind of heavy on the depression, so I can't really go along with a lot of what he says, but I did like some of the poems. All in all, I'd say he's pretty interesting."

After that, Ryo always gave the shadows in her pictures a bluish tone, no longer painting them in simple monochromatic grays.

Ryo and Yuta got engaged, exchanging silver rings they'd made for each other by hand. They had in fact already planned to get married even before I brought it up. As soon as Yuta turned eighteen, they would go to the ward office to make it official. At that point they would establish their own family register, and enter the new baby in it. But actually setting up a household together would wait until Ryo entered college.

Unfortunately, almost as soon as they'd swapped rings, Ryo was hit with the engagement blues and pregnancy blues and a whole bundle of other blues all at once. She got into fights with Yuta every time they got together. She complained that he was constantly saying insensitive things.

"He tells me with a straight face that he envies me not having to go to school," she fumed. "Doesn't he realize how scary it is to have to drop out and be stuck at home in total isolation?"

Now, wait a minute, I thought. *Before any of this happened, you were talking about dropping out entirely on your own.* But I decided this should remain unsaid—especially since Yuta was not without fault. True enough, he'd gotten a buzz cut, removed his piercings, and apparently hadn't missed a day of school since their engagement, which to his mind probably amounted to a considerable sacrifice. But as I saw it, his inability to sense how miserable Ryo might feel at being barred from school represented a lack of imagination or compassion or both. It just went to show how immature he was.

Whenever Ryo and Yuta had some kind of disagreement, it was easy for everyone, including me, to blame it on their immaturity and drop some remark about them still being kids. But even if they were still no more than children themselves, they were going to have to take responsibility for raising the child they had created.

No doubt they both regretted what had happened and wished they could extend their childhood a while longer. But they were simply going to have to take this experience as an opportunity to grow up. They could not become parents and remain children at the same time.

Once again, I was spitting at the sky.

I was taking my car to work more frequently now. I liked not having to fight the crowds on the train coming home. Since it was usually quite late by the time I knocked off for the night, traffic on Expressway 3 tended to be pretty light.

On Friday night, the day before we were all supposed to meet Yuta's family for lunch, I ignored the ring of the phone at nearly midnight and descended from my office to the underground garage. A dull ache had lodged in my lower back and both of my legs felt a little numb. At my age, the long hours took a toll.

As I was driving along in the passing lane on the expressway just past Sangenjaya, a Mercedes S Class and a Lexus LS came racing up hard on my tail, and I quickly took refuge in the cruising lane. Then not too long after crossing the Tamagawa River, I saw an overturned vehicle ahead with flames coming out of it. I wondered momentarily if it might be one of the earlier speeders, but I was wrong: it was a van with a business logo on its side. The fire appeared to have just started. Thinking I might be able to help, I pulled onto the shoulder and stopped.

As I started toward the burning van on foot, there was a loud *boom* and a huge ball of flame erupted from it. In the blinding light, I could see the black silhouette of the driver hanging inside. It was impossible for me to get any closer.

I went back to the car to get my cell phone but couldn't find it. I'd apparently left it at the office.

Doofus, I muttered. It was what the older guys used to call me at the warehouse where I worked during college.

Suddenly feeling sick to my stomach, I got out of the car again. But when I tried to throw up, nothing came. As I sank onto the shoulder and sat there feeling sick, a truck driver wearing a blue jump suit came up and asked if I was all right. All I could manage was a nod.

Three police cars arrived, but we were still waiting for the ambulance and fire trucks. I couldn't help feeling it was my fault.

One of the cops came over to say I needed to move my car farther away, and asked me what I could tell him about the accident. He also took down my name and address.

"So you didn't actually see it happen," he said as if to confirm what I had told him.

I mentioned the two speeding cars that had overtaken me earlier. I couldn't give him either license number.

"All right," the cop said. "You're free to go."

"I'm feeling sick, so can I just sit here a bit longer?"

Several fire trucks and an ambulance arrived. Traffic was starting to back up as passing drivers slowed down to rubberneck. With the help of one of the cops, I slid my Prius into the slow-moving line of cars.

It was nearly two by the time I reached home. Asako was waiting up for me. She seemed not just unhappy but furious.

I drank a glass of water and told her I'd left my phone at the office. Then I recounted what I had seen on the expressway.

"But I couldn't call you because I didn't have my phone. Sorry."

Her expression softened. She still wasn't smiling, but I could relax.

"Ryo was feeling so bad today that we almost went to the hospital," she said. "But she's okay now. No need to worry. Though emotionally she's a little bit wobbly. You know, it really feels like the whole family is stretched to the limit right now."

When I went into the bedroom after taking a shower, Asako's raspy breathing told me she was already sound asleep. I turned out the light and got into bed. I didn't feel the least bit sleepy. Apparently my adrenaline rush had not yet completely subsided.

Even with the curtains closed, light from a nearby streetlamp filtered through the darkness of our bedroom. I lay gazing at my slumbering wife's profile for a very long time.

When we arrived at the restaurant fifteen minutes early, the proprietress greeted us at the door and told us she had already seated the Iwamotos. This was to be the first full meeting of our two families, and in view of Ryo's condition, we had agreed to get together for a casual lunch at an Italian restaurant just down the street from our home. As we were led between the tables toward a private room, I became aware of the noise my shoes were making on the wooden floor. I realized I'd never worn hard-soled shoes here before.

When the proprietress opened the door, the four Iwamotos all stood up at once, filling the tiny room with the sound of scraping chairs reminiscent of the end of class in junior high.

The first greetings we exchanged as we faced each other fell somewhere between those of old acquaintances meeting after a long absence, and those of two families still bewildered at being bonded together by their children's unexpected union. Asako and Mrs. Iwamoto then went through the usual formalities of two women meeting for the first time, and Mr. Iwamoto introduced Yuta's younger sister. She gave the impression of a modest and studious girl—the exact opposite of her brother. She spoke in a tiny, almost inaudible voice.

In the lull that followed, I suggested we all sit down.

Yuta exchanged a quick look with Ryo. "We have something we'd like to say first," he said.

His hair remained very close cropped, but it seemed to have been dyed a deep chestnut color. He had on a three-button suit of the kind the younger generation wears almost like a uniform these days, but in a bit of a surprise, the fabric was a silver-gray color with a sheen to it rather than the more typical flat black or charcoal.

"Ryo and I realize this whole thing came as an unwelcome surprise for everyone. We want to apologize for that." He lowered his head. Ryo quickly followed suit, but I sensed something half-hearted in the way she did it. "It makes us really happy to have our two families get together like this in support. Thank you." This time they both lowered their heads together.

It called for a response. "I hadn't expected you to say anything like that. I appreciate it," I said. "Anyway, why don't we all sit down."

As we took our seats, the proprietress and a server, who'd been standing by the door, passed out menus and placed glasses of water on the table.

To keep things simple and healthy, we ordered the same full-course menu for everyone and agreed to forego alcohol.

Mr. and Mrs. Iwamoto asked Ryo how the expectant mother was doing. She mumbled in an uncharacteristically timorous voice that she was fine now.

Asako quickly stepped in to elaborate on her answer. "We thought it was just a bit of a cold until she started feeling nauseous and then threw up a couple of times. Fortunately, half a day of rest was all it took to settle that down. She's also been a little more high-strung than usual, but she's young and she's pregnant so that's to be expected. We don't think it's anything to worry too much about." Her smile and easy manner helped relieve the tension that tends to prevail at meetings of this kind.

For the most part, Mr. Iwamoto sat gazing out the window. Each time our eyes happened to meet, an awkward smile came to his lips.

Ryo and Yuta were talking in voices too low for me to hear. They hadn't gotten together last weekend because he needed to study for a test, so it had been almost two full weeks since they'd last seen each other. Ryo was in a bit of a sulk, and Yuta seemed to be trying to soothe her feelings.

Mrs. Iwamoto remained silent. She merely nodded from time to time as my wife rattled on about restaurants and bakeries in the area. It wasn't until the subject of household pets came up that she finally opened up. She said she had a white Siamese named Mimi. It was a house cat, but from time to time it managed to escape somehow. If she had to search all night to find it, she would. The cat had been hers since before they were married.

Yuta's sister responded with a monosyllabic yes or no to everything she was asked, never adding anything more.

"It's been about three years since I was back here," Mr. Iwamoto said to me in a low voice when he was finished with the pasta course. His family apparently had a rule not to talk about the days when they used to live nearby, especially in the presence of Mrs. Iwamoto. They had returned today to a part of town filled with memories of his first wife.

"On the whole, the neighborhood doesn't seem to have changed all that much, but didn't this place use to be a French restaurant?"

"They turned it into Italian about two years ago," my wife replied.

"Times just keep on changing, don't they? Even what looks the same turns out to be different.

We finished the meat course. Ryo left half of her small steak uneaten. A silence as sharp as a knife descended on the table.

"If I may," Mr. Iwamoto spoke up in a voice that filled the room. "From what Yuta tells me, the two youngsters have decided not to have a ceremony. But . . ." He stopped to clear his throat once, twice. He didn't actually seem to have anything caught in his throat; he was simply feeling awkward about what he was preparing to say. "I'd first like to ask Ryo if what Yuta said is correct, and I'd also like to know if this is something her parents are aware of."

Her parents? Thinking he had chosen a rather distant way of referring to us, I waited for Ryo's response, but she gave no sign that she was about to say anything. As I was preparing to prod her, Yuta spoke up.

"It's what I told you, Dad, of course it's correct. It's not anything you should have to bring up here."

"I didn't ask you," Mr. Iwamoto said, his voice taking on a sudden edge.

"Yes, my wife and I are both aware of that," I said.

Right from the start, Ryo had never even considered a wedding. But Yuta came to her one day saying he was making plans for a party to announce their marriage to their classmates and friends before the baby was born, and he had even picked out a convenient date. She hit the roof—*You never asked me! You're not even thinking of the strain I'm under!*—and adamantly opposed the idea. She made him promise that they would not have a wedding or any other kind of party with lots of people. My wife had been the first to hear about this little spat, and she had relayed the story to me.

"It does seem a bit strange to be talking about putting on a big fancy wedding for teens who are still in school and have absolutely no financial means. My wife and I both agreed with Ryo."

"Is that right?" Mr. Iwamoto said, sounding distinctly let down. Clearly, he hadn't wanted to believe what his son had told him. "It's just that more modest weddings actually seem to be the trend nowadays, and although I do understand what you're saying about them still being in their teens, surely it's one of those milestones that really ought to be marked somehow. My wife's been so looking forward to seeing our son's bride all decked out in her wedding gown. I feel the same way, actually. The other day we were talking about how Ryo, too, must be dreaming of putting on that wedding dress."

He glanced over at his wife, who nodded twice in affirmation.

"I couldn't care less about putting on a wedding dress," Ryo said flatly.

Mrs. Iwamoto gave a startled look but, as before, remained silent.

"Is that right?" her husband said, heaving a sigh and looking up toward the ceiling. "The fact is, my wife has been saying she already thinks of you as if you were her own daughter, and she really was counting on seeing you all dressed up as a bride."

I was beginning to feel sorry for Mr. Iwamoto even more than for his wife. I wished Ryo hadn't felt it necessary to be so blunt with him.

The server came in carrying a large tray laden with a selection of cakes and gelato. The room fell silent again until after she had served everyone their choice of coffee or tea.

"I guess more people these days feel wedding ceremonies and receptions are meaningless formalities that aren't worth the trouble," Mr. Iwamoto spoke up again, this time in a more direct tone—one I imagined him using with his employees at work. "But I think exchanging wedding vows and celebrating their marriage at a reception with lots of family and friends and colleagues from work to witness it helps press home to the couple that this is something you can't easily undo—as a matter of appearances, if nothing else. After all, it's never an easy feat for two complete strangers to join their lives together. When you go through a rough patch somewhere down the line, the memory of having put on a proper wedding in spite of all the trouble it was can sometimes help you overcome whatever problems you may be having, I should think. An awful lot of marriages end in divorce these days."

He paused to look around the table, but no one ventured a word either in support or disagreement.

On the way home from the restaurant, Ryo walked in slow, short steps like an old lady on the brink of exhaustion.

"Are you all right?" her mother asked.

"I'll manage," she replied.

"You need to make more of an effort to get along with Yuta," I said.

"We get along fine," she answered.

Ryo's face and stomach were noticeably filling out now. In the days immediately after we learned of her pregnancy, a certain aura had come over her that I remembered from when my wife was pregnant. But now her entire figure had been transformed into that of an expectant mother, and even her constitution seemed to be changing. When I first became conscious of this, I felt sorry for her all over again. She was so heartbreakingly young. But at the same time, naturally enough, I found myself eager for the day to come when I would finally get to see my new grandchild's face.

"Fluid's collecting in his abdominal cavity now," Momo reported. As usual, we had agreed to meet at Cascade, but this time neither of us reached for a laptop. "I wasn't able to get to the hospital the last few days, and when I finally saw him again today, his stomach was so distended you couldn't miss it."

"Because of fluid collecting inside his belly?"

"Uh-huh. I guess it was already collecting before, little by little, but now all of a sudden it's a whole lot more."

"Is it a bad sign?"

"Yup. It means he doesn't have much time left."

"How much?"

"Two weeks, maybe. A month on the outside, but that's the absolute longest."

I nodded, but found myself at a loss what to say next.

I still remembered the shock of hearing right out of the blue that Ogita had only six months to live. To have that now cut down to two weeks or a month hit me with a different sort of weight.

"But at this point he's still lucid, right?"

"Yeah, he can still talk fine, and he understands what you're saying, too, but . . ." She stopped and fell silent. After reaching for her teacup, she held it in her hand for a long time before finally taking a sip. "You know, the tea here really isn't very good. I think the same thing every time I come."

"Oh? Their coffee's not so bad, I don't think."

I reached for my own cup to take a sip and see. It actually wasn't very good either.

"The last time I visited, the room smelled awful. Like an old-fashioned drop toilet gone sour. Apparently he'd had a major bout of vomiting and they'd just finished cleaning it up. I pretended not to notice, but it wasn't easy, let me tell you. The thing is, I don't think it even entered his mind that I smelled anything. You know how he used to be—always so concerned about impressions. The first time he went into the hospital, he kept wanting to know, did he look sick, did the room smell funny? The day you visited, he actually asked the other people planning to come that day to show up at about the same time. He wanted you to see that he got tons of visitors. His mother let me in on that little secret a while back."

"Wow, I never would have guessed."

"But that person is completely gone now. Once the cancer gets this far, you don't have the energy to keep up appearances, and you can't really even see what's going on around you anymore."

"Because of what the sickness takes out of you?"

Momo nodded. "But I have to tell you what happened the week before last," she said.

When Ogita was back at home after his first stay in the hospital, his mother arranged for various practitioners of folk remedies and alternative therapies to see him. Although he was skeptical about them all at first, some of the folk medicines and the *qigong* actually gave him a measure of relief, and he became convinced of their efficacy. He especially began to put a lot of trust in his *qigong* doctor, even declaring that for the first time he'd found a true mentor in life—a guru.

Momo, however, was getting a far more dubious impression of the man. His visits had taken on a noticeably more religious slant as he became surer of his sway over Ogita. Convinced that she knew what he was up to, she told Ogita of her suspicions. His immediate reaction was to blow up at her, demanding that she stop casting aspersions on his teacher, but as a matter of fact—and this was hardly surprising for someone with no previous religious interest—he had started to have doubts of his own.

Then one day the man suggested that in due course he'd like to look after Ogita's mother. In essence, he was saying he wanted to "manage" Ogita's assets. Ogita erupted with an intensity that no one would have guessed his ravaged body capable of and drove the man away, yelling that he never wanted to see him again.

Momo had visited him shortly after the showdown. She found him looking even more worn out than usual, but he launched into his tale of valor with a degree of animation in his voice that she hadn't heard in quite some time, painting himself as the hero who saw through the pious fraud and escaped his clutches by the skin of his teeth.

"Doesn't that sound just like him?" Momo said. "As soon as he decides he doesn't like someone, he makes a complete about-face and forgets that he was on such good terms with him barely a second before. I could see that the Ogita I knew still survived somewhere inside, and it gave me a tiny little bit of joy."

Whether by coincidence or not, Ogita's condition began sliding rapidly downhill after the *qigong* doctor's visits ceased. Mrs. Ogita regretted her son's outburst dearly. As far as she was concerned, no price was too high to pay for treatments that helped him, and she was in no condition anyway to be thinking about what she should do with his assets after he was gone.

"It made me stop and think about what really was the right thing to do, and what makes people happy," Momo said. "Especially since it wasn't only his physical condition I was concerned about, and I could definitely tell he was feeling more depressed and lonely as time went on."

"To hear you say the Ogita you knew still survived makes me happy, too," I said. "Though I'm not sure how convincing that sounds from someone who was actually glad when he originally heard about the cancer."

She dropped her head. "I think it's only natural for you to still feel bitter about what he did. Ultimately I hope you can find it in yourself to forgive him, but I honestly don't feel I can ask you to do that yet. I know all too well what you had to go through."

"Let's not talk about it anymore. Why don't I tell you that bit of news I've been dangling in front of you for so long."

"Oh, yes, do!" she said, her face instantly lighting up.

I filled her in on Ryo's pregnancy and engagement, adding that it was a very odd feeling, not being able to decide whether I should be embarrassed or happy.

"Oh, but I think it's wonderful!" Momo said. "People say that teenage marriages never last, but there're plenty of marriages between full-grown adults that end in divorce, too. If you ask me, when it comes to kids, it's best to start early and have lots of them if you can."

Momo would probably never have any children of her own, but I'd had a hunch she might approve of Ryo's pregnancy. It was gratifying to hear her say it was a good thing.

I went on to relate how Ryo and Yuta had squabbled at the meeting between the two families. I'd started to wonder whether they would even make it to their wedding day. But then, the following weekend, Yuta had come over before lunch and stayed until after dinner, and they'd been so lovey-dovey it was almost annoying to watch. The difference had brought me up short, and I was surprised to find myself picturing Yuta as a doting father.

"We may still think of them as children, but after all, we're talking about the attraction between male and female. You can never really tell from the outside what makes two people click."

Our conversation was rudely interrupted at that point by a voice from the counter. "You two there. We're closing, so we need you to leave." The fellow seemed to be a part-timer.

It was 10:25, five minutes before closing time, and we were the only customers left.

Momo picked up her purse and stalked over to the counter. "'You two there'? That's a fine way to address your customers. Not to mention it's not actually even closing time yet."

She was obviously furious, but she kept her tone even. The blood drained from the part-timer's face.

As we exited after paying the bill, I turned to Momo. "Feisty," I said with admiration.

She laughed as she answered, "You can't make it as a woman on your own if you're not willing to be a bit feisty now and then."

"You haven't coughed up your little secret yet, so I guess we'll have to make another stop."

"That's why I said we should go to a bar to begin with."

"But I'm driving," I said. "Wait right here."

In the parking garage I put the top down on my new blue Peugeot 307CC. I pulled up to the curb where Momo was waiting.

"What's this?" she squealed.

"YY says if I'm going to be on the board, I can't be driving an old car, so I bought a brand-spanking new one. It may be a convertible, but the top goes up and down at the touch of a button, and it seats four, so it's actually a deceptively practical choice."

"Wow, it's as if the bubble never burst."

"It wasn't as expensive as you might think. It's not really a luxury car—just unusual."

"I thought the IT industry was supposed to be struggling."

"Some easy pickings came my way. The winners are still making good money."

I headed for a hotel in downtown Tokyo. The entrance to the parking garage eluded me at first, forcing me to drive around a bit. Momo sat in the passenger seat humming a tune under her breath. I couldn't hear it very well, but I thought it might be one of Yumin's songs.

I remembered my uncle's battered Peugeot 204 as a cute little car. Beyond that, I had no special interest in or fondness for Peugeots. With its hard-shell retractable top raised, the 307CC merely looked like a somewhat oddly styled two-door sedan. That's what appealed to me about it. I wasn't looking for a flashy sports car that flaunted my success, or for a more practical car that simply had a high price tag. The upshot was that Ryo had begged me to never drive with the top down in our own neighborhood.

It was a bar, but I was driving and couldn't drink, so even though she didn't particularly like alcohol, Momo ordered a glass of wine.

She raised her wine and I raised my iced *pu-erh* tea for a toast.

"Okay, so out with it," I demanded, eager to hear whatever it was that she'd been withholding from me. Even now, recalling the moment makes the blood rush to my face.

Momo brought the glass to her lips and let a sip of wine slide slowly down her throat.

"I've decided to get married."

The bombshell left me agape for a moment.

"Huhhh? . . . You're not talking about remarrying Ogita by any chance?" Nothing could have been more unwelcome from my point of view.

She closed her eyes and shook her head. "No. Though his mother did beg me to a couple of times. Meanwhile, because of everything I've been doing for him, his aunt accused me of trying to worm my way back into his good graces for his money and told me no way was she going to let us get back together. Well sheesh, I never wanted that in the first place."

"Okay. So who's the lucky guy?" I found myself rejoicing at being spared the most crushing of blows.

"A guy at work. By the name of Nick."

"Where's he from?"

"Germany. But I actually met him in America, back when I was in grad school. He was kind of a jerk. A notorious playboy. He hit on me once, too, at a party, but I gave him the cold shoulder. Now all of a sudden that same Nick comes to the Japan branch as my boss. Makes you wonder if our small world isn't maybe a little too small."

"That's some coincidence all right. So this Nick character figured he'd pick right up where—?"

She closed her eyes again, but this time shook her head more slowly.

"When I was in America, he knew me as Momo Ogita. Since I've gone back to using Kurihira as my last name, he didn't know until he arrived that I was on his staff. When he saw me, his first word was, 'Surprised?'"

"*He* said that to *you*?"

"He was in a wheelchair. Just before his thirtieth birthday, he'd been in a skiing accident that damaged his spine and left him paralyzed from the waist down. We'd been told beforehand that our new boss would be in a wheelchair, but I never imagined it would be the Nick I'd known in grad school."

She stopped and glanced at me with upturned eyes.

"You said he's paralyzed below the waist?"

She nodded. "That's how it is."

I nodded, but I wasn't sure what I meant by it.

"He's an amazing guy, Yuki. For someone like that, just coping with his own situation is hard enough, but he worked his way up to be a manager in a major corporation, and to be sent halfway around the globe to run the Japanese office."

"Yeah. That's pretty impressive."

"He's scheduled to be transferred back to the main office in Germany by the end of the year. When he found that out, he asked me if I'd go back with him and be his wife."

I nodded gently again.

"It was a really hard decision," she went on. "Remember the e-mail where I said I had something more to tell you, but that

I'd call? I was hoping to use you as a sounding board that day. Wouldn't you think most guys who got a message like that would pick up the phone right away themselves?" She smiled a little mischievously.

The reason attentive guys are so popular with the ladies isn't only because of their attentiveness, I found myself realizing after all these years. It's also because they tend to find more opportunities to seize. By no stretch of the imagination, it seemed, did I have "hidden talents in the ways of love."

"Still, the way I see it, you're actually part of the reason why I decided to say yes."

"How's that?"

"Well, back there after you quit your old job, you kind of got stuck for a while. Then thanks to a purely accidental meeting, I wound up being able to help you out. It made me really happy. After that, I thought, this is what it's all about."

"This is what it's all about? Meaning . . . ?"

"When you live by yourself for a long time, you kind of lose sight of what you're doing, and what your life amounts to. Especially when you go through some kind of hardship. I know it sounds trite, but you start wanting something to tell you that you're an indispensable part of this world, or that you're making a valuable contribution to others. So what are you supposed to do? Volunteer? Join a religion? I tried stuff like that, but I couldn't really get into it. But when I wound up being able to help you out that time, it gave me genuine satisfaction."

Looking me straight in the eye, she dropped her head in a little bow, as if to say thank you. I returned her bow.

"That's when I realized: you've been an important part of my life for a very long time, and it's when I can do good things for the people who've been dear to me that I feel happiest and most fulfilled. I suppose that's also like saying I realized I don't have a very big heart, but I can't change the way I am. So Ogita goes into the hospital, right? I don't think I have a particularly strong maternal instinct, nor am I helping out because I still love him. Of course, there's an element of that, too, but when I think of some of the things he did in the past, I don't know how many times I've had to fight off the urge to quick, strangle him while I've got the chance— while he's too weak to fight back. And yet, devoting myself to the needs of the man I once called my husband isn't a burden to me at all. In fact, I get pleasure from it, and that's why ultimately I figure it's for my own benefit as much as his."

"All right, I see where you're coming from," I said, and then hesitated for a moment before asking, "So are you saying that you're marrying this Nick as a new act of kindness?"

"No, it's actually the other way around. With Nick, my affection for him definitely comes first. Real affection. Just so you know, he's still not exactly a saint. He's a lot like Ogita on that score. He has some quirks that really get under my skin, and he can be such a hard-ass that some of my co-workers say they'd punch him in the face if he weren't in a wheelchair, or worse, that they'd like to shove him down a hill. But the bad things other people say don't have any effect on me. To me, he's never been anything but charming, and outside the office he's the kindest, most attentive man you can imagine. I really want to share the rest of my life with him. That's why I've decided to say yes. The satisfaction I know I'll get from giving him a helping hand is just a bonus on top of that."

I had no desire to try to change her mind, but neither could I say I was particularly happy to hear what she'd told me. "I see," was all I could manage.

"But," she said with the impish look of a child up to some new bit of naughtiness, "I haven't given Nick my answer yet. I've made up my mind to say yes, but at the moment, you and I are the only ones who know that."

Releasing my gaze, she dropped her eyes to look for her purse.

"Tomorrow's a workday, so we'd probably better be going," she said. "It's hard to believe we used to make nothing of staying out all night even with a full day's work ahead. I assume you can drop me off?"

"Sure," I answered. "But I don't think I'm done talking. Does your condo have visitors' parking?"

"Nope. And they enforce no parking around the clock on the street out front, too. Even in the middle of the night."

"I'll take my chances."

"There's supposed to be a pay lot somewhere nearby, but I'm not sure where," she said. She picked up her purse and started for the door.

The waves were gentle in the small inlet as my uncle swam parallel to the shoreline, lifting his elbows high out of the water in a stylish crawl. I watched his progress on and off as I smoked a cigarette on the beach.

"Aren't you going in for a swim?" my cousin Atsuko asked.

"When I'm done with this," I said, gesturing with my cigarette. She followed my line of sight and picked my uncle out from among the crowd of bathers.

"He swims with such clean strokes," she said. "He's good at everything he does, isn't he? Absolutely everything. My mom says she used to hate him for it, since she was always an underachiever. She mentions it every time he comes up in the conversation."

"Your mother could hardly have been an underachiever . . . But you're right. He's not just a good swimmer, he's a good coach, too. I was in fifth grade when he found out I couldn't swim at all and took me to the city pool to teach me. He had me going pretty good before the day was out."

"Really? He actually taught you how to swim? Everybody's always complaining how standoffish he is to his brothers and sisters, not to mention their kids, but you seem to be special to him somehow. To be honest, I might've been too intimidated to come to the beach with him today if you hadn't been coming along."

"Why should you be intimidated? He wouldn't hurt a fly."

"I'm sure he wouldn't, but there's something about him that makes us all feel kind of stiff, you know. So why are just you so special? Since he's not married, some in the family keep whispering that he's probably gay, but I don't buy it myself."

I didn't really want to explain to her what made me special to him. Fortunately, she didn't seem to want to know all that badly, either.

A thin veil of clouds stretching high across the sky softened the glare of the sun, but the humidity remained oppressive.

My uncle stopped swimming and rolled over to float on his back.

"I'm not very good at the crawl, so maybe I should go ask him for some pointers," Atsuko said.

I stubbed out my cigarette in the sand and lit up another.

Atsuko gave me a disgusted look and got to her feet. She brushed the sand from the back of her bathing suit as she walked toward the water.

I watched as my uncle began showing her clearly and methodically how to correct her stroke, just as he'd done with me. For some reason, I had no desire to join them.

When I learned two weeks later that my uncle had died in a car crash, a picture of him at that beach was the first image to flash through my mind. He appeared as a lone figure in the water, with nobody else around.

That summer, for no particular reason that anybody could determine, my uncle returned to spend his vacation in the old hometown he'd shunned for so many years. This was a big part of why some of the relatives speculated that his death might actually have been a suicide. The theory was that he'd come home to pay his final respects to the family he had been neglecting. It also seemed odd that such an excellent driver would wind up in a fatal single-car crash by his own error; nor could anyone explain why he might have been driving that remote section of highway in the middle of the night, so far from either his home or his office.

The last time I saw my uncle alive was on that day at the beach. I don't remember talking about anything special. Even now, I have no way of determining whether or not his death was a suicide.

But ever since he died, I've gotten into the habit, on various occasions, of putting questions to this man who's no longer with me. I don't ask out loud—nor, of course, does he ever answer.

At this point in my life, I know a great many things that my uncle never knew.

It was through him that I learned about the Marquis de Sade and Norman Mailer and Kenzaburo Oe and Yasutaka Tsutsui. But when I brought up writers like J. D. Salinger or Kaoru Shoji, he showed no interest. And he never knew that Gabriel García Márquez or Haruki Murakami even existed.

There are a great many other things he never knew.

About living with a wife and daughter and grandchild. About living in a fifty-year-old body with a fifty-year-old mind and having fifty-year-old sex. About the IT revolution. About obsessively faddish teenage girls. About Japan's economic bubble. About the religious cults in the news. About the rash of downsizing businesses. About *otaku*. About radical Islamists. And so on.

Would he perhaps brush all these things aside, saying he didn't even want to hear about them? I have to admit, there's not a shred of good news in the lot. My uncle never knew the 1980s. My father died on New Year's Day of 1989—the year Emperor Hirohito died only one week later. You don't normally get to choose when you're going to die, but I figure these two did pretty well. Neither of them had to live through the 1990s, which people have taken to calling the lost decade. Implying that it was a decade that might as well never have taken place,

I suppose. But ten years is too long a period to dismiss out of hand like that.

None of us can overtake those who have preceded us in death.

Momo had continued to keep me informed by e-mail about Ogita's rapidly declining state. His dying hour still lay in the future, however, and I more or less assumed I would hear about that only after it was all over.

Then I got a call from her at work. It was after eight in the evening, and Hashida was the only other person left with me in the office.

"I think this is it," Momo said in a voice filled with urgency.

"I'm sorry to hear—"

"Will you come, Yuki? I need you to come right away."

"You mean to the hospital? Me?"

"Uh-huh. Please, you have to come," she said and clicked off.

I left Hashida to close the place up for the night, and headed for the hospital in a cab. My Peugeot was in the shop for repairs.

Did Ogita have something he wanted to say to me with his dying breath?

The moment I arrived, I understood why Momo had been so insistent. Besides the doctor and several nurses, she and Ogita's mother were the only ones in the room.

Mrs. Ogita was stroking her son's hand as if in urgent prayer— a hand that must already have been beginning to turn cold. She looked so terribly small. Momo stood beside her former mother-in-law, murmuring something into her ear.

Ogita lay without expression, his body covered in a white sheet. His eyes stared vacantly up at the ceiling, the whites standing out against the brown of his skin.

Momo became aware of my presence. Our eyes met for an instant, but she turned away again without so much as a nod.

Even after entering the room, I failed to feel the presence of death. It seemed more like I was watching some abstract stage production on the theme of human mortality. But not because the person about to die was Ogita. I had felt this same way both at the deathbed of my father, when he lay slipping away after a long battle with a brain tumor, and at my mother's bedside, which I reached after she had already succumbed to a sudden subarachnoid hemorrhage. I've never shed a tear when anybody died. Something inside me freezes up at the sight of death.

I decided to step back out of the room. There was a man rushing this way down the corridor. It was Sawamura. I'm generally not very good with faces or names, but I had no trouble remembering this person from the one previous encounter we'd had. His face was streaked with tears. He nodded at me without the slightest sign of recognition as he hurried into the room.

"Mr. Ogita!" he cried out, his voice resounding through the door into the hallway. Then I heard him say something to Mrs. Ogita, followed by a reply from Momo.

When I opened the door to go back inside, Momo came out.

"Are you sure it's safe to be away?" I asked.

"It's okay, I don't think it'll be quite yet," she said, her voice so low I could barely hear. "Thank you so much for coming."

"Why isn't there anybody else here?" I asked, indicating the room with my eyes.

She shook her head with a look of bafflement.

"His mother wasn't in any shape to be making calls, so I phoned his closest relatives, and not one person said anything about coming. I called the day before yesterday too, to say the doctor gave him less than a week, but apart from a cousin who dropped by on his way home from work, all he's had is one visit from his uncle's family. I never had the sense before that he didn't get along with his relatives, but I really don't know what to think . . ."

Momo and I went back into the room and circled around to the other side of the bed. I noticed an odd gurgling sound coming from Ogita's abdominal area.

His mother and Momo called out to him repeatedly, with Sawamura occasionally joining in.

"Please use this to moisten his lips," a nurse said, handing me a cup of water and a cotton swab.

I dipped the swab in the water and reached for his lips, only to stop short. I thought I'd seen a flash of light in his eyes, but since no one else seemed to have noticed anything, maybe it was only my imagination. Damn, I thought. He's not really with us anymore. If I was going to come see him again, I should have done it when he was still lucid—when I could have at least talked to an Ogita who was still eighty percent here. And I should have demanded to know what the hell he actually had in mind that time he screwed me over. How he might have answered didn't really matter.

It was nearly an hour later before he drew his last breath. Death came quietly. When the doctor announced that he was gone, Momo began sobbing. Mrs. Ogita continued to call out her son's name. Sawamura stepped back from the bed and collapsed on a stool in the corner. I touched Ogita's hand, lying lifelessly on top of the sheet. The skin was rough, and already there remained almost no warmth left for me to feel.

I worried that no one would come to his funeral either, but was relieved—not to mention surprised—when I found a crowd of what must have been several hundred mourners in attendance. The seats reserved for family members were filled with the relatives who had felt it unnecessary to be present in his final hour, all looking very solemn. Momo sat quietly in the front row of the open seating area.

The consulting firm Ogita had been working for at the time he was diagnosed took the lead in the ceremonies. Grim-faced men and women in mourning clothes cut as sharply as expensive business suits moved about the hall taking care of sundry tasks.

The eulogy was read by Ogita's boss, the vice president of the firm. I found its content rather curious in many ways, but noticed no sign of surprise from the other people listening.

"Besides being devoted to serving his clients as a consultant, Mr. Ogita felt a strong desire to enlighten others about his profession, which remains unfamiliar to the public at large, and he was preparing to publish a book to this end. In his own description, it was not to be a business publication, but rather a non-fiction novel that presents its truths through the devices of literature. His choice of such an approach seems entirely in keeping with the advice he repeated so earnestly to his younger colleagues, that it is not enough for a consultant to compile numbers, gather information, and present his analysis of the data; what matters most is his own strength of character. Although I never had a chance to read the finished manuscript, he did let me in on his chosen title for the work some time ago: 'A Consultant in Love.' I can hardly imagine a more fitting title, for he was indeed in love with his work as a consultant, passionate about helping his clients prosper, and at the same time he was also a man of many loves in his private life. Sad to say, it proved impossible for the book to appear during his lifetime, but I understand it will be published with great fanfare by a major publisher in a few months' time . . ."

When I asked afterwards, neither Momo nor Mrs. Ogita had heard a word about any such book, and in fact month after month rolled by with no sign of its publication. At this point, I have no way of knowing whether the tall tale originated with Ogita or with the vice president. But let me go on record as saying that I would very much like to read a book called *A Consultant in Love* by this man.

Ryo's due date came and went with no sign of the baby being ready to make its appearance. Meanwhile, preparations proceeded apace for the merger of my company with YY's and the announcement that Yosuke Yoshida's Internet Emporium would join the well-known portal site as one of its marquee tenants. The birth and my big move at work were in effect on a collision course, and I was sorry that I couldn't be there for Ryo as the all-important moment approached.

In my first act as the newest executive at YY headquarters, I was about to address the fifty employees I would be overseeing, when I heard the chirp of a text message arriving on my cell phone. I handed the phone to Ayumi standing next to me and asked her to check the message. It was from my wife.

"Leaving for hospital," it said. Ryo had finally gone into labor a full week after she was due.

"The happy day is here," Ayumi said.

I pictured myself dropping everything and rushing pell-mell to the maternity hospital.

Suddenly everybody in the room was applauding.

I slowly released my breath and looked around the fifty faces of my brand-new staff . . .

It was evening before I finally got to the hospital and met my new granddaughter for the first time. She was, in essence, the typical newborn bundle of wrinkles, and I was not as overcome with emotion as I had expected to be.

Most of all, I was glad to see that Ryo looked strong and in good spirits. She told me that both her mother, who accompanied her into the delivery room, and Yuta, who waited outside, had turned green when she went into the pushing phase. Asako had had to be carried out of the delivery room and put on an IV, and Yuta had spent the time in the men's room losing his breakfast. Ryo herself got through the delivery without incident, but said she was embarrassed afterwards when the nurses remarked that she seemed to have a very sensitive mother and husband—as if in admiration, but half-giggling, too.

Ryo and Yuta named their daughter Yuka. It may sound a little old-fashioned, but they chose the name themselves.

That December saw several departures.

Hashida tendered his resignation as soon as the winter bonuses were paid. He had apparently assumed I would continue running things the way I did before as head of my own company: I'd always been a hands-on boss in everything we did, with the others following my lead. But in my new surroundings, I switched to a hands-off approach in which I issued general instructions— "Don't just rely on the Web, get out of the office and make the rounds on your own two feet"—but did very little more. Some of the staff took advantage of this approach to slack off, and I could understand why Hashida might be pissed with them. But so long as they didn't mess something up really badly, I made a point of not stepping in. There were about three real crackerjacks on the crew, and I knew I could count on them to keep things moving along. Even though my office was located right next door to Website Central, only rarely did I emerge from my inner sanctum or allow any of the rank and file to enter it.

Ayumi settled in as my secretary after the move. She was constantly butting heads with the long-time YY people, who saw us newcomers as interlopers and conspired to drive us out, and this soon led to open warfare. For a time it looked as though she might get bogged down in endless feuding, but she never came crying to me for backup from above. In the end, she managed to defeat the opposing forces on her own. I was pleased, but it was a painful blow when a short time later, in mid-December, ten of the old-timers on the losing side quit en masse and went to work for a rival site. Among the deserters were two of the three people I'd been relying on to hold things together.

Feeling responsible, Ayumi volunteered to help fill the gap. "I'll go work in Website Central, boss," she said. "You don't do much these days anyway, so anybody could be your secretary. There's no reason it has to be me."

I later learned that YY had been alarmed when he first noticed that I had changed the way I worked. But he quickly concluded everything was going to be fine. For one thing, my unit was producing pretty good results. Sales had seen a pronounced spike immediately after the company joined the big-time portal site, and they continued at a very good pace for the most part even after the initial excitement was over. There were any number of routine foul-ups and misunderstandings along the way, but my capable staff dealt more than adequately with each situation as it arose. For another thing, my new style of operating was actually very close to YY's own. He had repeated to me almost like a mantra that businesses where management wastes its time working shoulder to shoulder with the rank and file simply don't last. I figured anyone who bought into that view a hundred percent probably wouldn't make a very good manager, but there was a measure of truth in it.

As expected, Momo departed for Germany with Nick shortly before Christmas. She claimed Nick was the jealous type and declined to introduce me to him before they left.

About a month after Yuka was born, Ryo decided to divorce Yuta. Neither she nor Yuta would say much about it, but the immediate cause was apparently that he cheated on her.

It came to light that, while Ryo was pregnant, Yuta had struck up a friendship with a girl at school, whom he continued to spend time with now. Although he insisted she was "just a friend," Ryo found this impossible to believe.

Even before any of this was revealed, however, she had apparently already concluded that Yuta was neither a suitable husband for her nor a suitable father for her child.

"When it comes down to it, he's just too immature," she told her mother. "Just because you get married, just because you fathered a child, it doesn't automatically qualify you to be a husband or a father. That's what finally dawned on me."

She also put it another way: "I wish I'd met Yuta after he was a few years older. He's got lots of good qualities; I don't dislike him, even now. But I'm not his mother, so I don't have the patience to make allowances for this, that, and the other while I'm waiting for him to grow up."

As late as early November, they were both still looking forward to their first Christmas together with their new daughter, but soon after December arrived, Ryo went to pick up the Divorce Notice form at the ward office.

When all was said and done, the time the three of them actually spent together as a family probably amounted to no more than a few hours.

I met with Yuta and his parents at a hotel to discuss what should happen after the divorce. Seeing the *What did I tell you?* look on Mr. Iwamoto's face as he came in put a sour taste in my mouth. But there was probably no denying that the formal framework of marriage had made all their adolescent emotions and insecurities bump into each other more harshly than they would otherwise have done. Part of the responsibility for placing that framework on them rested with me.

Since two minors with a child of their own were getting divorced, there was the potential for some unusual complications. But I intended to keep things simple. In unilateral fashion, I laid out a number of demands:

Ryo would return to our family register after the divorce. Which is to say, she would cease to be Ryo Iwamoto and once again become Ryo Yajima. There could be no objection here.

We would continue to raise Yuka at our home. Naturally, Ryo would be the custodial parent. But since Ryo, as a minor herself, still remained under the authority of her own parents, we, as her parents, would automatically also have parental authority over Yuka as well.

There remained one problem with this arrangement, however. The Yajima family would have a child with the Iwamoto surname. Our wish, therefore, was for Yuka to take the Yajima surname.

The three Iwamotos frowned, but they had apparently anticipated something along these lines and raised no objections.

There were several possible routes for Yuka Iwamoto to become Yuka Yajima under the current family registration system. We would need to choose one of them.

Looking at Yuka's best interests over the long term, realistically speaking, the options could be reduced to two. Ryo Yajima could establish a new family register of her own, and Yuka could be recorded as her daughter on that document. But if possible, we preferred to keep Ryo on our own register for the time being.

The second option was for Asako and me to adopt Yuka as our own daughter. Adopting a grandchild as a child of one's own was a very simple process as far as the paperwork was concerned, and Ryo had agreed to let us do it. (She did balk when we first suggested the arrangement, apparently feeling as though her parents were trying to steal her daughter from her.)

The three Iwamotos' faces froze.

"I hasten to add," I said, "that just because the family registry says Yuka is our child, it won't mean Yuta and Ryo are any less her true parents. Although Asako and I will take over authority and responsibility as Yuka's parents, an adoptive relationship can be dissolved by the parties involved. Underneath it all, Yuta and Ryo will in fact remain Yuka's parents forever."

This was obviously extremely difficult for any of them to swallow. Mr. and Mrs. Iwamoto would be losing a granddaughter, and Yuta a daughter—both on paper and in substance. But I intended to push this demand through.

I had calculated that they would in fact find it possible to accept this in the end. After all, Yuta was still very young, and he seemed to have no trouble attracting girls. He could go on to have as many more children as he cared to. In the meantime, being unencumbered would open up possibilities for the future that he might not otherwise have.

That we might suggest something like this had no doubt occurred to the Iwamotos even before our meeting. It was a tried and true way of dealing with babies born to underage mothers.

Mr. Iwamoto asked in return that they be permitted to see Yuka as often as possible even after she became our adopted daughter, and the negotiations came to a close. Tears spilled from Mrs. Iwamoto's eyes. She had no children of her own, so Yuka was not of her blood, but the girl had come into this world as her grandchild, and I suppose she looked upon the baby as if there were a genuine biological connection. Meanwhile, I thought I noticed an air of relief in Yuta's manner. I was careful to hold the anger I felt firmly in check.

As I pulled out of the hotel's underground garage, I saw three figures huddled together against the concrete wall. It was only a brief glimpse, but I recognized them instantly as the Iwamotos. Yuta had sunk onto his haunches, his shoulders shaking with sobs. His stepmother was bending over him to offer comfort, while his father just stood there looking on.

I forgive you, Yuta, I murmured to myself. *Ryo and Yuka aren't your family anymore, they're my daughters . . . Maybe I'm the one who should be asking you to forgive me.*

During the last week of December, I had to go back to staying at the office late into the night for several days running. A programming error had resulted in a large number of Christmas orders missing their promised delivery dates, and dealing with the aftermath was taking every minute of my time. When you have slipups like this, "quality merchandise" becomes an empty slogan. I spent my days apologizing profusely to our clients, and at the same time ordered up a complete review of our code to make sure we didn't have some other hidden bug or trap waiting to explode in our faces like a time bomb.

December 29 should have been the first day of our New Year's break, but most of my staff came in as usual. It meant I couldn't very well take the day off myself.

After eight that evening, when the last of the fallout from the programming error seemed to be all but taken care of, Ayumi came into my office.

"You know, boss," she said, "this makes me wonder if your new hands-off policy might not be such a good idea after all."

"It's fine, it's fine," I replied. "A little foul-up like this isn't going to make me change my ways."

"Do you realize I haven't had a single day off this month?"

"The boss takes it easy while his staff takes care of business—that's how a good company works." I patted her on the shoulder. "Tell you what. I'll take you out for a nice, fancy dinner sometime soon. Whatever you like."

"You really have changed, haven't you?" she grumped. "But that's okay. We'll manage somehow by ourselves. Since that's the way you want it. Just remember, if something goes wrong, you're still the one who has to take responsibility."

She fixed me with a look out of the tops of her eyes.

"Absolutely," I replied. "But nothing's going to go wrong, so there's nothing to worry about."

"The funny thing is, I kind of feel that way, too. But if you slack off too much, boss, I may just take over the company myself. Don't say I didn't warn you."

With a hint of a smile tugging at her lips, Ayumi went back to her desk in Website Central, where the clamor of the day had not yet completely subsided.

Near midnight, I sped home in my Peugeot 307. When I opened the front door, the smell of milk hit me in the face. It was the smell of home, where my baby "daughter" lived—breathing, drinking, eating, pooping.

I found a pajamaed Ryo in the living room, feeding the baby a bottle.

I looked into Yuka's deep, black eyes. She didn't smile for me, but I couldn't help smiling at her.

"Just when I finally think she's out for the night, she wakes up again," Ryo said in a worn-out voice.

Asako emerged from the bath, and I took my turn. When I was done, I found Ryo and Asako having a cup of hot chocolate in the living room.

"Would you like some, too?" my wife asked.

I shook my head and went to get a beer from the refrigerator instead.

"We pretty much wrapped things up at the office today, but I still have to go in tomorrow. Yoshida made me agree to have lunch with him. It's not about work, though. He wants to hold a two-man symposium on love and fairness, part two. An exploration of their material foundations."

"Sounds pretty heavy for holiday time."

"It's what YY said he wanted to do, so who am I to argue? The way I figure it, we managed to make it through another year. I owe him this much."

"It's been quite a year."

"That's for sure. And I have a few more gray hairs to show for it."

"Wait a minute, Dad," Ryo said, breaking into our exchange. "Are you saying you discussed the same things you talked to me about last New Year's with your boss?"

"Uh-huh. The conversation happened to go that way one day."

"That sucks," she said, frowning in disapproval.

"Why the sour face?"

"I always thought you'd worked out all that stuff just for me, as something to talk to me about. I don't mind that you also ran it by Mom. But it kind of cheapens it if you went around talking about it with people at work, too."

"You're a fine one to talk. I put my heart and soul into that speech, hoping it might have some kind of impact on you, but I never saw the slightest change in your behavior. Talk about a letdown. That's why you never heard me bring it up again. A big part of why I mentioned it to Yoshida was because I wanted to get a third opinion—whether what I said was really so far off the mark."

"Oh. And here I was under the impression you had total confidence in your analysis."

"What did Yoshida say?" my wife wanted to know.

"That fussing over fairness and impartiality is just a middle-class thing. It makes no difference to the rich or poor."

"I'm not sure I get what that means, but just so you know, I've thought about what you said lots of times over the past year. I really have." Ryo had become quite serious. "Maybe I didn't ultimately live up to your expectations, Dad, but I honestly think the things you were trying so hard to tell me that day gave me strength deep down inside. Like when things seemed to be racing totally out of control, or when I had a fight with Yuta and was feeling low. There were so many times like that this year, you know, and each time I thought back to what you said to me in the park on New Year's Day. I'm not all that smart, so maybe I didn't really understand it all that well, but it's absolutely true that I took heart from it."

Asako and I looked at each other.

"It's gratifying to hear you say that." I felt a little embarrassed, but tried to hide it as best I could. "But compared to any argument I might have patched together with my limited brainpower, after getting stuck in one dead end after another, I think all the things you actually experienced this year, and all the things those experiences forced you to think about for yourself, probably carried a whole lot more weight."

"No way," she said point-blank. "Whatever I experienced, and whatever I thought up in my own head, would never have been enough. For one thing, I didn't even know how to think for myself before, at least not in any proper way. It really was a pretty incredible year, finding out I'm pregnant and getting married and becoming a mother and getting divorced, but about the only thing I'd say I've learned from it all is that I've still got an awful lot left to learn. Even today, I still don't have the first idea where I might be headed."

"Learning that you've got a lot to learn just goes to show how much you *have* been thinking."

"I bet I'll still do plenty of really stupid stuff, though. You can probably count on it. I'm glad we had that talk, but that doesn't mean I'm going to suddenly turn wise overnight."

"Knock yourself out," I said. "The more foolish the daughter the more doting the father."

Asako and Ryo both shook their heads as if to say I was talking nonsense again.

"I think Dad's changed this year," Ryo declared.

"I agree," her mother nodded. "Though not as much as you."

"Huh? What do you mean by that?" I said. "Actually, now that you mention it, one of my staff said basically the same thing to me today. But that was about my management style, which I changed on purpose. I've also been getting a lot of flak that all I do is look out for number one lately, but that's on purpose, too. At least here at home, the only thing that's changed is the car I drive."

"Well, your staff has it exactly right," Asako said bluntly. "You only think about yourself."

"You may think you know yourself, but you actually don't."

My wife and daughter looked at each other and let out little snickers.

The sound sent my pulse racing. I felt as though the two of them had drifted somewhere far away. Or maybe not. Maybe I was the one who had drifted away from them.

Feeling a little dizzy, I closed my eyes.

The Peugeot 204 with my uncle at the wheel hurtled down the old Usui Pass highway kicking up clouds of dust in its wake. The French-made economy car had a habit of throwing its fan belt, he'd told me. The body was susceptible to rust. It creaked and rattled all over. About all it had going for it was its sleek four-door styling and spiffy aqua-blue paint job. Yet with my uncle deftly working the four-on-the-tree gearshift, the three pedals on the floor, and the small-diameter wheel, the car zipped along the road like a nimble sports car. We were traveling much too fast for me to savor the after-glow of my tearful parting with Kanoko only a short time before.

He turned into the gravel parking lot in front of a small road-side restaurant and brought the car lurching to a halt.

"Darn, they're closed," he said, seeing the sign on the door. "I was thinking I should call the office."

This was in the age before cell phones, and coin-operated pay phones were often kept safely inside the host establishment.

"Could you maybe drive a little slower?" I asked.

"Getting car sick?" he said, looking concerned.

"No, I feel fine, but you're scaring me a little."

"Oh. I thought maybe you were going to throw up."

"The car sounds like it might fall apart any second."

He leaned over the wheel with a chuckle.

"Don't worry. It's not going to pieces, at least not in the next few hours."

For my sake, he drove more slowly after that. I thought back over the all too brief time I'd had with Kanoko.

"My leave of absence is over," he said. "It's such a shame. Especially for you. Sorry."

It was as if he'd read my mind.

"*My* break's not over yet," I replied, though I knew it missed the point. Our conversation broke off.

He coughed. It was a light, dry cough. Come to think of it, he'd been coughing like this every so often since we first started out. I just hadn't consciously noticed it until now. Perhaps he wasn't aware of it either.

I looked at his face. When he realized I was staring at him, he said, "Feel free to take a snooze if you want."

"I'm not sleepy," I answered.

"You sleep an awful lot, you know. I chalked it up to your being so happy-go-lucky, but maybe you're actually just that worn-out."

"I'm not happy-go-lucky and I'm not worn-out," I said. If anyone had cause to worry, it was me. But I couldn't bring myself to mention his cough.

Even so, I nodded off almost as soon as I closed my eyes.

I heard a rattling sound as the world around me began to shake.

Was it my uncle's Peugeot 204, finally falling to pieces? The person beside me was not my uncle but my wife. I heard a baby crying. Maybe Yuka had woken up upstairs, and Ryo was getting up to comfort her. I had lived half a century before I even knew it. But this was not yet the end. My "youngest daughter" was only two months old. This was not yet the end.

TRANSLATOR'S NOTE

The translation is based on the hardcover edition of *Aoneko ka-zoku tentenroku*, published in Japanese in April 2006, by Shincho-sha. This was a substantial revision of an earlier work with the same title that appeared in the March 2005 issue of the literary journal *Shincho*.

THE BLUE CAT
by Sakutaro Hagiwara

It is good to love this beautiful city.
It is good to love the buildings of this beautiful city.
It is good to come to this city and rove its busy streets
in pursuit of all the sweet women,
in pursuit of all the high life.
The avenues are lined with cherry trees—
just listen to all the sparrows singing in them!

Asleep in the night of this sprawling city
is the shadow of a lone blue cat.
The shadow of a cat telling the sad story of humanity.
The blue shadow of the happiness we never cease to pursue.
What shadow is it that I seek
in longing for Tokyo even on days of sleet,
huddled cold against a backstreet wall?
What is he dreaming of—this beggar of a man?

After graduating from Keio University, NAOYUKI II made his debut in 1983 with *Kusa no kanmuri* (The Grass Radical), which won the Gunzo Prize for New Writers. His other award-winning works include *Sashite juyo de nai ichinichi* (A Day of Little Importance, 1989), *Shinka no tokei* (Evolution Clock, 1993), and *Nigotta gekiryu ni kakaru hashi* (Bridge Over a Muddy Torrent, 2000). *The Shadow of a Blue Cat* (2006) is his first novel to appear in English.

WAYNE P. LAMMERS has won two awards as well as an NEA Translation Grant for his translations, which include Juzno Shono's *Still Life and Other Stories* and *Evening Clouds*, Mitsuyo Kakuta's *Woman on the Other Shore*, and Aska Mochizuki's *Spinning Tropics*.

SELECTED DALKEY ARCHIVE PAPERBACKS

FOR A FULL LIST OF PUBLICATIONS, VISIT:
www.dalkeyarchive.com

CARLOS FUENTES, *Christopher Unborn.*
Distant Relations.
Terra Nostra.
Where the Air Is Clear.
JANICE GALLOWAY, *Foreign Parts.*
The Trick Is to Keep Breathing.
WILLIAM H. GASS, *Cartesian Sonata and Other Novellas.*
Finding a Form.
A Temple of Texts.
The Tunnel.
Willie Masters' Lonesome Wife.
GÉRARD GAVARRY, *Hoppla! 1 2 3.*
Making a Novel.
ETIENNE GILSON,
The Arts of the Beautiful.
Forms and Substances in the Arts.
C. S. GISCOMBE, *Giscome Road.*
Here.
Prairie Style.
DOUGLAS GLOVER, *Bad News of the Heart.*
The Enamoured Knight.
WITOLD GOMBROWICZ,
A Kind of Testament.
KAREN ELIZABETH GORDON,
The Red Shoes.
GEORGI GOSPODINOV, *Natural Novel.*
JUAN GOYTISOLO, *Count Julian.*
Exiled from Almost Everywhere.
Juan the Landless.
Makbara.
Marks of Identity.
PATRICK GRAINVILLE, *The Cave of Heaven.*
HENRY GREEN, *Back.*
Blindness.
Concluding.
Doting.
Nothing.
JIŘÍ GRUŠA, *The Questionnaire.*
GABRIEL GUDDING,
Rhode Island Notebook.
MELA HARTWIG, *Am I a Redundant Human Being?*
JOHN HAWKES, *The Passion Artist.*
Whistlejacket.
ALEKSANDAR HEMON, ED.,
Best European Fiction.
AIDAN HIGGINS, *A Bestiary.*
Balcony of Europe.
Bornholm Night-Ferry.
Darkling Plain: Texts for the Air.
Flotsam and Jetsam.
Langrishe, Go Down.
Scenes from a Receding Past.
Windy Arbours.
KEIZO HINO, *Isle of Dreams.*
KAZUSHI HOSAKA, *Plainsong.*
ALDOUS HUXLEY, *Antic Hay.*
Crome Yellow.
Point Counter Point.
Those Barren Leaves.
Time Must Have a Stop.
NAOYUKI II, *The Shadow of a Blue Cat.*
MIKHAIL IOSSEL AND JEFF PARKER, EDS.,
Amerika: Russian Writers View the United States.
GERT JONKE, *The Distant Sound.*
Geometric Regional Novel.
Homage to Czerny.
The System of Vienna.

JACQUES JOUET, *Mountain R.*
Savage.
Upstaged.
CHARLES JULIET, *Conversations with Samuel Beckett and Bram van Velde.*
MIEKO KANAI, *The Word Book.*
YORAM KANIUK, *Life on Sandpaper.*
HUGH KENNER, *The Counterfeiters.*
Flaubert, Joyce and Beckett: The Stoic Comedians.
Joyce's Voices.
DANILO KIŠ, *Garden, Ashes.*
A Tomb for Boris Davidovich.
ANITA KONKKA, *A Fool's Paradise.*
GEORGE KONRÁD, *The City Builder.*
TADEUSZ KONWICKI, *A Minor Apocalypse.*
The Polish Complex.
MENIS KOUMANDAREAS, *Koula.*
ELAINE KRAF, *The Princess of 72nd Street.*
JIM KRUSOE, *Iceland.*
EWA KURYLUK, *Century 21.*
EMILIO LASCANO TEGUI, *On Elegance While Sleeping.*
ERIC LAURRENT, *Do Not Touch.*
HERVÉ LE TELLIER, *The Sextine Chapel.*
A Thousand Pearls (for a Thousand Pennies)
VIOLETTE LEDUC, *La Bâtarde.*
EDOUARD LEVÉ, *Suicide.*
SUZANNE JILL LEVINE, *The Subversive Scribe: Translating Latin American Fiction.*
DEBORAH LEVY, *Billy and Girl.*
Pillow Talk in Europe and Other Places.
JOSÉ LEZAMA LIMA, *Paradiso.*
ROSA LIKSOM, *Dark Paradise.*
OSMAN LINS, *Avalovara.*
The Queen of the Prisons of Greece.
ALF MAC LOCHLAINN,
The Corpus in the Library.
Out of Focus.
RON LOEWINSOHN, *Magnetic Field(s).*
MINA LOY, *Stories and Essays of Mina Loy.*
BRIAN LYNCH, *The Winner of Sorrow.*
D. KEITH MANO, *Take Five.*
MICHELINE AHARONIAN MARCOM,
The Mirror in the Well.
BEN MARCUS,
The Age of Wire and String.
WALLACE MARKFIELD,
Teitlebaum's Window.
To an Early Grave.
DAVID MARKSON, *Reader's Block.*
Springer's Progress.
Wittgenstein's Mistress.
CAROLE MASO, *AVA.*
LADISLAV MATEJKA AND KRYSTYNA POMORSKA, EDS.,
Readings in Russian Poetics: Formalist and Structuralist Views.
HARRY MATHEWS,
The Case of the Persevering Maltese: Collected Essays.
Cigarettes.
The Conversions.
The Human Country: New and Collected Stories.
The Journalist.

SELECTED DALKEY ARCHIVE PAPERBACKS

My Life in CIA.
Singular Pleasures.
The Sinking of the Odradek
  Stadium.
Tlooth.
20 Lines a Day.
JOSEPH MCELROY,
  Night Soul and Other Stories.
THOMAS MCGONIGLE,
  Going to Patchogue.
ROBERT L. MCLAUGHLIN, ED., *Innovations:*
  An Anthology of
  Modern & Contemporary Fiction.
ABDELWAHAB MEDDEB, *Talismano.*
HERMAN MELVILLE, *The Confidence-Man.*
AMANDA MICHALOPOULOU, *I'd Like.*
STEVEN MILLHAUSER,
  The Barnum Museum.
  In the Penny Arcade.
RALPH J. MILLS, JR.,
  Essays on Poetry.
MOMUS, *The Book of Jokes.*
CHRISTINE MONTALBETTI, *Western.*
OLIVE MOORE, *Spleen.*
NICHOLAS MOSLEY, *Accident.*
  Assassins.
  Catastrophe Practice.
  Children of Darkness and Light.
  Experience and Religion.
  God's Hazard.
  The Hesperides Tree.
  Hopeful Monsters.
  Imago Bird.
  Impossible Object.
  Inventing God.
  Judith.
  Look at the Dark.
  Natalie Natalia.
  Paradoxes of Peace.
  Serpent.
  Time at War.
  The Uses of Slime Mould:
    Essays of Four Decades.
WARREN MOTTE,
  Fables of the Novel: French Fiction
    since 1990.
  Fiction Now: The French Novel in
    the 21st Century.
  Oulipo: A Primer of Potential
    Literature.
YVES NAVARRE, *Our Share of Time.*
  Sweet Tooth.
DOROTHY NELSON, *In Night's City.*
  Tar and Feathers.
ESHKOL NEVO, *Homesick.*
WILFRIDO D. NOLLEDO, *But for the Lovers.*
FLANN O'BRIEN,
  At Swim-Two-Birds.
  At War.
  The Best of Myles.
  The Dalkey Archive.
  Further Cuttings.
  The Hard Life.
  The Poor Mouth.
  The Third Policeman.
CLAUDE OLLIER, *The Mise-en-Scène.*
  Wert and the Life Without End.
PATRIK OUŘEDNÍK, *Europeana.*
  The Opportune Moment, 1855.
BORIS PAHOR, *Necropolis.*

FERNANDO DEL PASO,
  News from the Empire.
  Palinuro of Mexico.
ROBERT PINGET, *The Inquisitory.*
  Mahu or The Material.
  Trio.
MANUEL PUIG,
  Betrayed by Rita Hayworth.
  The Buenos Aires Affair.
  Heartbreak Tango.
RAYMOND QUENEAU, *The Last Days.*
  Odile.
  Pierrot Mon Ami.
  Saint Glinglin.
ANN QUIN, *Berg.*
  Passages.
  Three.
  Tripticks.
ISHMAEL REED,
  The Free-Lance Pallbearers.
  The Last Days of Louisiana Red.
  Ishmael Reed: The Plays.
  Juice!
  Reckless Eyeballing.
  The Terrible Threes.
  The Terrible Twos.
  Yellow Back Radio Broke-Down.
JOÃO UBALDO RIBEIRO, *House of the*
  Fortunate Buddhas.
JEAN RICARDOU, *Place Names.*
RAINER MARIA RILKE, *The Notebooks of*
  Malte Laurids Brigge.
JULIÁN RÍOS, *The House of Ulysses.*
  Larva: A Midsummer Night's Babel.
  Poundemonium.
  Procession of Shadows.
AUGUSTO ROA BASTOS, *I the Supreme.*
DANIÈL ROBBERECHTS,
  Arriving in Avignon.
JEAN ROLIN, *The Explosion of the*
  Radiator Hose.
OLIVIER ROLIN, *Hotel Crystal.*
ALIX CLEO ROUBAUD, *Alix's Journal.*
JACQUES ROUBAUD, *The Form of a*
  City Changes Faster, Alas, Than
  the Human Heart.
  The Great Fire of London.
  Hortense in Exile.
  Hortense Is Abducted.
  The Loop.
  The Plurality of Worlds of Lewis.
  The Princess Hoppy.
  Some Thing Black.
LEON S. ROUDIEZ, *French Fiction Revisited.*
RAYMOND ROUSSEL, *Impressions of Africa.*
VEDRANA RUDAN, *Night.*
STIG SÆTERBAKKEN, *Siamese.*
LYDIE SALVAYRE, *The Company of Ghosts.*
  Everyday Life.
  The Lecture.
  Portrait of the Writer as a
    Domesticated Animal.
  The Power of Flies.
LUIS RAFAEL SÁNCHEZ,
  Macho Camacho's Beat.
SEVERO SARDUY, *Cobra & Maitreya.*
NATHALIE SARRAUTE,
  Do You Hear Them?
  Martereau.
  The Planetarium.

FOR A FULL LIST OF PUBLICATIONS, VISIT:
www.dalkeyarchive.com

SELECTED DALKEY ARCHIVE PAPERBACKS

ARNO SCHMIDT, *Collected Novellas.*
  Collected Stories.
  Nobodaddy's Children.
  Two Novels.
ASAF SCHURR, *Motti.*
CHRISTINE SCHUTT, *Nightwork.*
GAIL SCOTT, *My Paris.*
DAMION SEARLS, *What We Were Doing*
  and Where We Were Going.
JUNE AKERS SEESE,
  Is This What Other Women Feel Too?
  What Waiting Really Means.
BERNARD SHARE, *Inish.*
  Transit.
AURELIE SHEEHAN,
  Jack Kerouac Is Pregnant.
VIKTOR SHKLOVSKY, *Bowstring.*
  Knight's Move.
  A Sentimental Journey:
  Memoirs 1917–1922.
  Energy of Delusion: A Book on Plot.
  Literature and Cinematography.
  Theory of Prose.
  Third Factory.
  Zoo, or Letters Not about Love.
CLAUDE SIMON, *The Invitation.*
PIERRE SINIAC, *The Collaborators.*
JOSEF ŠKVORECKÝ, *The Engineer of*
  Human Souls.
GILBERT SORRENTINO,
  Aberration of Starlight.
  Blue Pastoral.
  Crystal Vision.
  Imaginative Qualities of Actual
  Things.
  Mulligan Stew.
  Pack of Lies.
  Red the Fiend.
  The Sky Changes.
  Something Said.
  Splendide-Hôtel.
  Steelwork.
  Under the Shadow.
W. M. SPACKMAN,
  The Complete Fiction.
ANDRZEJ STASIUK, *Fado.*
GERTRUDE STEIN,
  Lucy Church Amiably.
  The Making of Americans.
  A Novel of Thank You.
LARS SVENDSEN, *A Philosophy of Evil.*
PIOTR SZEWC, *Annihilation.*
GONÇALO M. TAVARES, *Jerusalem.*
  Learning to Pray in the Age of
  Technology.
LUCIAN DAN TEODOROVICI,
  Our Circus Presents . . .
STEFAN THEMERSON, *Hobson's Island.*
  The Mystery of the Sardine.
  Tom Harris.
JOHN TOOMEY, *Sleepwalker.*
JEAN-PHILIPPE TOUSSAINT,
  The Bathroom.
  Camera.
  Monsieur.
  Running Away.
  Self-Portrait Abroad.
  Television.
DUMITRU TSEPENEAG,
  Hotel Europa.

  The Necessary Marriage.
  Pigeon Post.
  Vain Art of the Fugue.
ESTHER TUSQUETS, *Stranded.*
DUBRAVKA UGRESIC,
  Lend Me Your Character.
  Thank You for Not Reading.
MATI UNT, *Brecht at Night.*
  Diary of a Blood Donor.
  Things in the Night.
ÁLVARO URIBE AND OLIVIA SEARS, EDS.,
  Best of Contemporary Mexican
  Fiction.
ELOY URROZ, *Friction.*
  The Obstacles.
LUISA VALENZUELA, *Dark Desires and*
  the Others.
  He Who Searches.
MARJA-LIISA VARTIO,
  The Parson's Widow.
PAUL VERHAEGHEN, *Omega Minor.*
BORIS VIAN, *Heartsnatcher.*
LLORENÇ VILLALONGA, *The Dolls' Room.*
ORNELA VORPSI, *The Country Where No*
  One Ever Dies.
AUSTRYN WAINHOUSE, *Hedyphagetica.*
PAUL WEST,
  Words for a Deaf Daughter & Gala.
CURTIS WHITE,
  America's Magic Mountain.
  The Idea of Home.
  Memories of My Father Watching TV.
  Monstrous Possibility: An Invitation
  to Literary Politics.
  Requiem.
DIANE WILLIAMS, *Excitability:*
  Selected Stories.
  Romancer Erector.
DOUGLAS WOOLF, *Wall to Wall.*
  Ya! & John-Juan.
JAY WRIGHT, *Polynomials and Pollen.*
  The Presentable Art of Reading
  Absence.
PHILIP WYLIE, *Generation of Vipers.*
MARGUERITE YOUNG, *Angel in the Forest.*
  Miss MacIntosh, My Darling.
REYOUNG, *Unbabbling.*
VLADO ŽABOT, *The Succubus.*
ZORAN ŽIVKOVIĆ, *Hidden Camera.*
LOUIS ZUKOFSKY, *Collected Fiction.*
SCOTT ZWIREN, *God Head.*